D0707720

Vestiges of Flames

Vestiges of Flames

a novel

Lyn McConchie

Lethe Press
Maple Shade, NJ

Published by Lethe Press
118 Heritage Avenue • Maple Shade, NJ 08052-3018
www.lethepressbooks.com • lethepress@aol.com
Print ISBN: 9781590214831

Book design by Peachboy Distillery & Designs

Library of Congress Cataloging-in-Publication Data

McConchie, Lyn, 1946-
  Vestiges of flames : a novel / Lyn McConchie.
    pages ; cm
  ISBN 978-1-59021-483-1 (pbk. : alk. paper)
  I. Title.
  PR9639.3.M343V47 2015
  823'.914--dc23
                                        2015003869

Vestiges of Flames

This book is dedicated to Glenda Palmer and Alison Grace who married in December of 2014, may their lives be long and their happiness together continue as long as their lives.

Chapter One

Jo watched her mother die. Clinging to her hand until the last breath sighed out and was gone. Afterwards they told her to go home. There was nothing more she could do and the hospital was filling too fast for anyone to have the time to offer comfort or even information. She hadn't known, shut in her mother's ward, as she had been, just how bad it had become outside. The ward had been a formerly disused one at the rear of the cluster of buildings. The double doors, which cut it off from the other wards, were soundproofed. Unsuspecting, Jo walked out into the corridor — and into chaos with a full orchestra.

The noise was incredible. People sat, lay, walked, and all the time they cried out; in their own pain, for a doctor to aid their loved ones, or against a God who had permitted this to happen to them. The girl could only stand aghast, gaping at the assembly as her eyes and ears took in the fact of their presence. Her look sharpened as she suddenly recognised the illness that had killed her mother was here reflected, over and over in an endless series of cascading mirrors. She switched her gaze from person to person, seeing in most of them the coming death. She'd known vaguely, from what she'd overheard from the nurses, that the infection had mutated and spread. Now she began to understand just how far and how savagely it had bitten into the capital city's population.

And where else had it attacked? She'd heard snatches of talk from the nurses about that as well. Now they came back. Quick whispers which had hinted of horrors, of death that stalked the world, a pandemic spread by modern travel. By fast travel and a bug that lay in hiding for one week — two, even three, before striking down those it infected. Most attacked did not survive. Some who might have lived could not be brought to a hospital in time. Doctors and nurses died on their feet from the same disease as they struggled to save the stricken.

Jo went home, finding a taxi that would take her. Even in an epidemic a driver must have money to buy food, to pay his rent. That night she lay sleepless, dry-eyed and grieving. The house was well stocked with food, and she would not starve, or not for some weeks, but her father was still in America. Would he even survive, let alone be able to return? What would she do if she were left alone? In the silence of her bed, she found a watery giggle, she *was* alone, and that "left" was merely semantics. He mother would never return, and to be realistic, it was unlikely that she'd ever see her father again either.

Through the dark hours she could hear the city sounds, ambulances raced by. Police sirens sounded. Fire-engines whoop whooped their way to fires as usual. Tomorrow would be better. A cure would be found, something that would save all those she'd seen waiting in the hospital. She watched through tinted windows and the light curtains once dawn came. There were few people on the streets. Some staggered and occasionally fell. She could see them where they lay and none came to help them rise.

Through it all she was somehow incredulous. She, Josephine Taylor, known to her acquaintances as Jo, to her family as Josie, and the only child of a thin middle-class line, had never suffered. She'd never felt hunger, or much fear, or great pain. And all about her lay the suburbs of New Zealand's capital city; a city, in 2035 that was ruled by law and blue-clad guardians. If someone fell down there was always someone to aid, there always would be. It was a belief so entrenched that finding it no longer happened left her dazed and sick. If others were left where they lay it might even happen to her. So she cowered in her home, thinking only to fill every container with water as if brushed by an earthquake.

It gave her something to do during the hours of daylight. Now and again she halted to peer through windows. A man clung reeling to her gate. He groaned in pain, his hand within his shirt as thin serum-diluted blood tricked down to stain his elegant trousers. She would have gone to him but new fear overrode old habits. He fell down after a while and lay across the entrance. For perhaps an hour he moved feebly now and then. After that he was still. It dawned on her to turn on their radio. There was always a small solar and generator-powered radio with the earthquake kit. The television seemed to be silent but on the tiny radio there was a voice so that she sobbed once and fell silent to listen.

The voice was slightly familiar. She'd heard it on a light classical and golden oldies music programme to which she listened sometimes. Now she held her breath to hear him again. Out there not everything had changed. Things must be under control, or if not, then there were still those who tried. The voice was calm, quiet, and oddly compassionate so that she could hardly believe the message as it came to her. He was talking as a man might to himself. Explaining the whys and wherefores of an undeserved punishment, which had befallen him. It was his initial words that caught her.

"...nothing better to do than talk to you out there. No one who's caught this has lived more than twelve hours. Not unless they're partly or wholly immune. You can tell by how fast it eats into you if you're one of the immune. I'm not and my wife died last night. I don't have anyone left but all you out there.' He seemed almost casual but she could hear the pain under his words.

"I thought you should know what's happening. You'll die, but at least you won't die ignorant. While we still had researchers they had just enough time to look at the bug. I didn't understand it all myself. But briefly, it's our old friend Staphylococcus A. Back in 1994 it had a brief fling terrifying people here and in England as a flesh-eating bug that killed in days if it wasn't stopped by a doctor."

His voice went a little bitter. "Of course being idiots we assumed that the doctors knew everything. They said it wasn't widespread in that form. That it was quite unusual. That mostly it just gave us sore throats and that about ten percent of the population carried the germ at one time or another. It was quite common and we weren't to worry. When it came back in 1997 as resistant to antibiotics they said the same. They found some other medication that worked and told us to forget about it. They didn't mention it when the bug came back in Africa."

His voice dropped and became confiding. The girl found herself straining to hear, as if he told a precious secret to her alone.

"It was a lot harder to get rid of that time. It's a clever little germ, you know. That time it killed a lot of people — dozens at least; maybe hundreds, but they kept it quiet. For the good of the population so no one would start a panic — they said. It came back a few years after that in the twenty-teens. It tied in with a civil war there and they put all the casualties down to the war. We're all so used to hearing that half the population in some African country has been wiped out in a war that we never questioned it."

His voice rose savagely so that she jerked back from the radio. "The bloody authorities! It's the year 2035, they said, not 1935. It never occurred to them that it might get to civilised countries. Right up until last night they were still saying not to worry. That America would work out a cure. We'd all be okay. Well, we bloody aren't okay. If we're so damned all right why are we still dying? Why are the doctors and nurses mostly dead? Why did my wife die when they said they didn't have a doctor or even a fucking ambulance to send for her? Why? I'll tell you why. They lied! They said it was okay, that America would help us.'

A mad laugh crackled from the radio. 'Help *us*? Last night a friend of mine got through to a friend in America. They're dying there too, even faster than we are. He told us the truth even if the authorities have been keeping quiet. It's the same in every country. Everyone's dying. All over, every country, they're dead or dying and it's the end of the world while the authorities sit telling us not to worry. Everything will be fine by and by." His voice wavered into song. "Pie in the sky by and by, by and by." His voice cracked and went silent for a few moments. When he resumed it was to speak quietly and soberly once again.

"Some of you listening to me *will* survive. Before the bug got to most of them the scientists estimated that it works like this. About ten percent of the population carries Staph. A. Of those carriers the ones who'd had a recent infection, a throat flare-up or something like that, will be completely immune. The longer ago the bout the worse you'll be hit. The very worst would still survive — *if* they could be given intensive care. None of them will be. Those in the medium range may live if immunes are available to care for them. Most of them won't have immunes in the family.

His voice came flat and slow. "But the estimate is that one percent of the population will survive the infection. That's about half a million here. But thirty years back when I was younger I reported on civil wars. I can tell you. That may be how many are alive after the bug is done. But after that there are other things to create a secondary die-off. You out there, you'd better fear your fellow man for a start. I won't be here to fear, but some of you out there may be. My estimate, and believe me, it's closer than any ivory tower merchant, is that maybe ten percent of that one per cent will still be around a year from now. There have already been cases of people turning on scientists, authorities, medical staff, all because they can't save them or their families."

He halted and seemed to be panting. Then came a soft groan. "I won't be talking to you much longer. But now you know the truth. Maybe five thousand of you will still be alive in a year. Find books on survival, on self-sufficiency, about weapons, and how to care for and breed animals: anything at all of that kind. Maybe enough of you will make a new start, a better life."

Again came the moan, then a soft sad laugh, a sound of honest amusement. "The radio management always complained when I did things my way. Sometimes I read you poetry as well as playing the old songs. Well, there's no one here to stop me now. So that's my choice. For all of you out there who may live through this, a couple of verses by the seventeenth century Welsh poet Thomas Ross:

The fire falls into coals and ash,
But if some other traveller came,
To stir the coals they yet might find

13

Some flickering vestiges of flames.
But looking at the flickering light,
That lives again as flames flare higher,
It could be asked by one who sees,
If this is the same — or another fire?"

His laugh came, almost carefree. "And for all you out there who aren't going to make it. As well as for you who want to fight fate and circumstances regardless, I'll play you a golden oldie. After this one I'll be gone but I'll leave the digital system on permanent re-loop for you. No one should have to die alone in the silence. However for those of you who can remember that far back, here's a song sung by Jon Bon Jovi. 'Blaze of Glory.' Goodbye to you all."

The song soared up and beneath the passionate guitar she heard the flat harsh bark of a shot. She heard the song out as tears filled her eyes. She wept then for her mother, for the father she sensed she'd never see again, for the man in the studio, and for herself most of all. Then she went to bed and fell into a sleep like death. She woke again in the early hours and lay holding her breath at the sound she heard.

It was a long soft sighing, as if city itself moaned. In it, was the wail of a people's sorrow, unable to understand why this had happened to them? There were the howls of dogs, bereft of their owners and grieving that loss. It was threaded through by the soft call of sirens, keening the deaths of those who sounded them. Once civilisation had been a fire; it had burned, blazed higher and higher, lighting a path for all to see. Now it died, smothered by a bug that had learned too much. Human existence was a bonfire dying into coals and ash. She turned on her back, listening as the slow tired tears ran again.

In the morning she'd look through the bathroom cabinet. There might be something there that would help her follow painlessly those who'd gone ahead. She was a girl, city-born and bred. She had as much chance of surviving as the lap dogs howling out there. With her mind made up she slept again.

Morning came and she woke, her head ached, her eyes burned and she felt hollow inside. And with the waking her decision swept back and she climbed out of bed. The cabinet was a soft peach colour against the pale walls. Her mother had been so proud of the old house she'd redecorated. The door stuck a little and she wrenched at it. Within were the usual headache remedies, sticking plasters, and other minor medications. Nothing to do her any — well, no, not good, that wasn't the word? She giggled stupidly. Nothing to do her any harm? That was it. But good or harm there was nothing. She shut the door hard hearing something fall over within the cabinet. She opened it again and picked up the fallen item, medicated lozenges, for the sore throat she'd had a week ago. In a spasm of fury she hurled them across the room.

"Fucking useless bloody things. Jesus! Nothing's any good, Mum, mum, oh God, mum." She tore items from the cabinet, throwing them wildly about the bathroom, screaming, crying, gasping and using every crudity she had ever heard. Some were so childish she found herself laughing, then crying wildly again as she remembered her mother's death, that she would likely never see her father again. At length she calmed a little, wandering in a semi-daze into the kitchen.

The set of carving knives caught her eye. They glittered, was it only three days ago her mother had cleaned and polished them? She could cut her wrists, but she found her hand pulling back. There would be pain and blood. She remembered a classmate. He'd cut his wrists, years back, when he'd been disappointed in love. He hadn't done it right. He's passed out, the blood had coagulated and the bleeding had stopped. He'd lived but they'd had to repair the tendons, and if she made that sort of mess of it who'd repair hers? It was bad enough to be alone and healthy in a dead city, it would be far worse to be without hands and vulnerable to everything.

She went to the window and stared out. The man at the gate was moving. Her eyes swiveled away then back. It was impossible. He'd died; he'd been dead for a day. She looked again as the body moved and briefly something showed through the hedge. Jo pressed her face against the glass. A dog? It moved to where she could see it more clearly. She recognised the Hanson's dog, a small tan and white mostly-terrier from two doors down. Then she saw that it was tearing at the man's back, exposed by his shirt as he fell. She ran for the bathroom and vomited until there was nothing left to bring up.

The animal must have been starving for days, and — was that what *she* had to look forward to if she ventured out? The next time she peered through the window the small beast was gone. The body had shifted further. Almost hidden by the long hedge. She could see the feet jerking and now and again a snarl sounded; other hungry dogs had found the banquet and they feasted avidly.

For something to do she checked the house. With utilities automated the water still ran, electricity still powered the house. But power and water would be there only so long as no major problems arose. Still, while there was power she'd be clean. She showered compulsively until the hot water ran out, dried off and ate, before settling to counting her supplies. They lived only five minutes drive from a large supermarket. They'd never had to keep full cupboards but her mother had been a pessimist, and even after several days there was at least another week's food remaining in tins and packets. And as well as that, the fridge and its freezer were full.

She considered, her thoughts slow and clumsy, as if she must strain them through cloth before they reached her. She was tired again. It would all be easier tomorrow. Tomorrow her father might come home; her mother could be back from hospital. She wandered into the lounge. An array of bottles stood on a polished corner table. Her father had always said a drink made him relax. He could think much better he'd said, when he had a drink in his hand. A glass seemed to have found its way into her trembling fingers. She reached for the nearest bottle.

The contents were clear, like water. She knew what that was — of course she did. It was just that right now she couldn't think of the name. Not that it mattered. She wanted to drink the stuff, not call it to heel. She drained the large glass, refilled it, drank again, and placed it back on the table. Up the stairs to bed. She felt so exhausted, so dizzy. But it would all be okay again in the morning. She slipped into a stupor, which lasted until the bed began to rise and fall about her. At every swing her stomach was more nauseated until she rolled to the bed edge and vomited once. The stink made it worse so that she continued to retch.

Her head hurt, her mouth was dry. It tasted awful. Her stomach still heaved. She was unable to see why on earth her father would believe a drink helped anyone to think. The only thing she was thinking was that he must be mad and she'd never try this again. She got herself a glass of water and lay back sipping. Her head still pounded so she added a couple of the fast-acting dissolvable heavy-duty analgesics from the cabinet. Outside dogs barked and snarled, squabbling over their meal. She shut her ears to the sound. Her mind was starting to work again. It must have been the shock of her mother's death that had made her so crazy.

She looked over the house in her mind. Picturing it room by room. She couldn't stay here. She had only vague ideas of what happened in civil wars but her intuition told her to escape the city. Here there would be starving dogs by the thousand. There'd be little for them to eat apart from other small animals — and humans. In the countryside there'd be fewer dogs and more for them to kill. There'd be more human survivors in cities as well. Somehow she didn't feel she wanted to meet most of them. To some at least she'd be prey just as she'd be to starving dogs.

Out in the country she'd meet fewer people. She'd need weapons, food, water, books, everything the man on the radio had said. In the house she had almost none of that. It meant she'd have to go out. Her heart quailed. If she stayed here for a few days longer she could keep watch. See if there *were* others out there. She felt too full of adrenaline to stay in bed. She dressed and explored the house, putting aside things that might be useful when she left. She looked over the food remaining in the peach and green cupboards.

If she ate things she didn't really like and was careful, there was enough for another three weeks — or enough to take with her so that she didn't have to make any stop she thought dangerous. She entered her father's bedroom. There on a shelf were his personal books. Only one would be of use, a plump hardcover about native plants and their uses as food or medicine. She carried it out to place on the kitchen table along with her mother's sewing kit. Then she slipped quietly through the house. The door to the inner garage was shut, she opened it and stood a moment considering.

It was a double-sized area. On one side was her mother's small electric citi-car. On the other her father's larger vehicle. It would be better to take his car. There was far more room for supplies, it had two spare wheels, one on either side in the large boot, and there was all the equipment to change them and make minor repairs. She paced down the tidy workbench selecting items. She had to remember that most of his gear was electric. It would be useless eventually. For that day and the next she weighed and discarded.

She felt galvanised, full of energy. She soaked up some of the need to be moving by cleaning the house. By hand and using only a cake of lavender soap and the hot water which continued to flow. Her mother had been house-proud. If Jo must abandon her home she would still leave it as spotless as her mother would have wished.

She washed all her clothes, the bedding, towels, and other items. Each night she showered until the hot water ran out, and went to bed scrubbed until her skin was pink. At other times she also watched at the window, reading or simply standing fidgeting behind the curtains and tinted windows until some sound caught her attention. It was this that drove home the radioman's words. Twice she saw a man pulled down by dog packs. Once a girl raced by, two men in laughing yelling pursuit.

It was the latter that decided her to risk an expedition in her immediate vicinity. At dawn the following day, she stole out of the back door and across the yard. Around the sides and back of their property, almost twenty years ago and with the neighbours' agreement, her father had built a high fence. Only from the upper floor could she see the streets beyond but they'd looked clear. She opened the gate silently peering past the edge. Nothing moved. She slipped through and into the neighbour's yard.

The Karawai's had gone on holiday to Fiji and her mother had been left a key in case of emergency. If this wasn't an emergency she didn't know what would be. She unlocked the back door, stepping inside as a guilty feeling suffused her. It still felt as if she was an invader. Nice people didn't walk in and out of other people's houses without invitation. She hardened her heart. If the Karawai's hadn't come home by now they were probably no longer in any position to invite anyone. It was *her* survival that mattered now.

She made herself walk into every room. She searched through the drawers finding a number of useful items including to her surprise, a shotgun and shells. Dimly she recalled that Mr. Karawai went duck-shooting in season. The gun was locked to a bar within the cabinet, but there was a key on the ring they left with Jo's mother. She made herself take the weapon then gather up all the shells she could find. With the gun she'd have more of a chance. There weren't many shells; maybe she'd find an un-looted shop with more ammunition somewhere. There were a couple of books on shooting. She took them as well as a small box containing cleaning gear for the shotgun.

She slipped home without seeing anyone and ate while she nerved herself further. There'd been no extra food there beyond a handful of tins. People going on holiday for weeks don't leave full cupboards. The neighbours behind the house should be home. She felt faint at the idea of confronting what might be left of them. Again she told herself that it was a matter of survival. The dead wouldn't begrudge her food that they no longer needed. She had one day before the time she'd set herself to be gone.

Dawn again and she walked down her back yard and opened the narrow door in the back fence. A heap of rags fluttered by the clothes-line in the light breeze. Eyes averted she skirted that. She had no desire to look more closely. She'd known her neighbour as a pleasant-faced elderly woman with several grandchildren, all of whom seemed to loose their toys regularly over the fence, which was why her father had added the door after several years.

At least there should be no one left in the house. She found she was wrong. Her hands thrust open a bedroom door just as her nose registered the stench of decaying flesh. Staring up at her from a low chair a younger woman sprawled. Beside her in the cot a baby lay bloated and green. One of the old woman's daughters and her child, come home to die.

Jo slammed the door and leaned against it feeling sick. Not even for her survival could she have opened it again. Anyway, she was sure there'd be little of use in there. She forced herself into the kitchen. Here were riches. Unsure when any of her family might visit the old woman had stocked her cupboards heavily. The girl piled food into carry bags, dumping them by the back door. Then she continued her search. Each door she opened a crack and sniffed first. Nothing. She plundered with discretion. It was useless to take more than the car could carry or she could use. She checked all cupboards though. It was very unlikely but a second gun would be useful.

There was no gun, but in the attached garage a fishing rod and gear that had belonged to the deceased husband caught her eye. She added that and the tall waders. She liked fish, and it would surely be easier to catch those to eat than for her to shoot an animal. There was a book on fishing and she took that as well thinking that she'd have a library if this kept up. She cautiously returned home to stow her booty in the car. Added to what she already had in there it filled the boot and she decided to remove the back seat. That way she could reach anything without having to open a car door. It took her hours and a set of bruised knuckles but she managed at last.

She glanced at her watch. Thank heavens for the new long-life batteries. She'd bought a new one at the airport when she and her mother had gone to see her father off less than a month ago. The battery would be good for ten years and could be recharged on a solar panel. If she checked shops too no doubt she'd find other of that type.

She grinned bitterly at a random thought. Just after her father had left her mother had taken in a family heirloom to be repaired. The jeweller had demanded a huge amount once the work was completed. They'd been waiting until her father was home. Her gentle diffident mother had not been able to face the man down although they both knew the amount was exorbitant. Now the girl need pay nothing. She could visit the shop, take back the pendant, and take batteries and a charger for them as well.

Then as if her mind had hidden the thought and now allowed it to go free, she remembered her mother. Somewhere in the hospital to the east the body might still be lying. How could she leave without doing something about it? She slumped into a chair, her mind recalling that day's events. What had the doctor said as he sent her home? His voice came back to her.

"No need to make arrangements..." as she'd questioned him. She'd been asking about a death certificate for the funeral home.

"This illness is severely contagious. We're required to cremate the bodies of the dead at once. I can post the certificate and that will be all you need for any legalities or the insurance." He patted her shoulder then. "She didn't suffer. I gave her sufficient hydrapheine to be sure of that." She knew it for truth.

The needle had slid in and the pitiful moaning had stopped soon after. The restless tossing stilled. At the end her mother had opened her eyes, known her for a brief few seconds, smiled and whispered her name, the fingers of the hand Jo held tightening briefly before falling away. Then she'd slid into the final unconsciousness, her rasp of breathing slower and slower until it stopped minutes later.

Besides, Jo counted the days. Even if she went back and her mother was still there, would she be able to recognise what days and disease had left? Better to believe that there'd been time for them to give her mother's body to the fires. She would find her mother's treasured heirloom pendant; she'd wear it in her mother's memory. That would have made her mother happy.

She reached for paper. For her father she would write down everything that had happened. She had no hope for his return, but if by some miracle he did make it back to this house, he should know what had become of his wife and daughter. She talked into the computer late into the night until a thin stack of paper lay in a neat sheaf beside the machine. She gave another order and produced a second copy. The small machine would run on batteries once main power failed. It could also run on a generator handle and solar power — having a small panel that could be attached for that purpose.

Jo weighed the item in a hand. Yes, it wouldn't take up much room and she was familiar with it. She'd take it with her; keep a record of the days. Probably no one would ever read it but she liked the idea that one day, when she was very old, the record would be there. Not that she'd be likely to live long. However she'd act as if she'd make old bones and hope belief would create reality. She wrote her father's name on a sheet of paper, placing it atop the stack. Then she retired, not bothering to put the computer away. In the morning it could go straight into the car.

She slept late and had a long shower, staying under the hot water again until she was wrinkling and the water went cold. Then she dressed sensibly in jeans, and boots. She added a jersey in autumn-toned wool, which her mother had knitted for her the previous winter. Lifting the small cased computer she took it to the garage, placed it and its accessories on the front seat of the car, opened the garage doors and returned to shut the house door. For a long minute she looked up at the building. In this house she'd been born, lived all her life.

She touched the wood of the door gently. How long would the house stand without human care? Would she ever return to see it again? She felt as if she was abandoning something that trusted her. Moved by a gust of emotion she reached for the knife on her belt. Quickly she cut free a lock of hair and kneeling, she buried it under the edge of the house. She stood and patted the wooden siding.

"Stay safe."

She'd shut off the house's water and power as well as those of her neighbours'. It was time to stop looking back. She opened the main gates cautiously before returning to the car. On the passenger seat by the computer, lay the loaded shotgun. She seated herself, started the engine, and drove out into the quiet street. First she'd visit the jeweller's shop, then a service station. They'd have maps of all the roads. Once she was past the suburbs she'd stop to eat and decide where next. The car sounds faded into distance leaving the old house to itself. It was a month after her twenty-first birthday, May of twenty-thirty-five. As yet Jo Taylor had no conception of death, despite past days.

As a homeless traveller she would learn to survive — or die, but she would not return. Nor would she know the house would not out-last her first weeks away from it. She had done all she could, but there were other places for fires to begin. From far forward on her road she would look back and wonder. But she'd never return and never know for sure. She did not wish to. It would always stand as home in her memory. That was enough.

Chapter Two

The powerful Lantana handled comfortably. It was the new model, barely a year old and with — as her father had put it — optional extras. It ran on petrol or diesel, had four wheel drive, and even a light winch which could be mounted on either back or front bumper bars. It carried two spare wheels and a built-in case in the boot had a good range of tools for the vehicle. It was a handy, useful car, more powerful than it looked. And once her father had got through with it, it could do quite a lot more than the maker's specifications.

The girl grinned briefly to herself. It had another unobtrusive ability as well. Her father was a communications specialist. The vehicle was virtually thief-proof and had some interesting refinements that he had added in that line as well.

She left the tunnel, circled the basin reserve, and then headed into the city centre. Ah, there was the jeweller' shop. The streets were still empty but she had to force herself to pry open the door with the car's tyre lever. She imagined the silent alarm light blinking on and off at the police station. She waited, listening, but no one came. With growing confidence she marched in to sort through the repairs shelf. There! That was the lovely gold and greenstone pendant that had been her mother's pride. She snatched it up.

A chain? Once it had hung from a plaited flax string but that seemed to be missing. Jo searched until she found a steel chain. It was gold-plated, but the case's labeling told her what lay under the gold. It should be really safe on that. She slid the pendant onto the chain's loop, dropping the precious weight down the front of her jersey. Then she left. Not far away was a service station she could check.

There were road maps in plenty and she sorted the plug-ins hastily. She'd use them to Palmerston North. Once there she could find the new building that had been finished only that Christmas. It was a special repository for topographical maps and certain other documents. She knew all about it. One of her university acquaintances had spent time in the new building, helping them move in. A summer job.

To her surprised interest when she investigated, the pumps were still working. She filled the tanks, petrol and diesel both and added fuel cans to her carload. From now on she'd save those. She would fill the car tanks any time she could until nothing worked any more. The garage had few canned goods, but what there was she took, adding minor medications; dispirin, Band-Aids, medicine for coughs and colds, and dumping all the available bars of chocolate around the stacks of other food and gear.

She drove away and as she circled for the main road out, she passed a sports shop. She swung the car to the side of the road and halted abruptly. They probably wouldn't have guns. Not in central Wellington? But they could have shells or other items. She parked the car across the door and pried yet another entrance open.

She had no use for the hockey sticks, tennis gear, or rugby jerseys and boots. But she took a magnificent case of hunting knives, along with a booklet explaining the use of each. Towards the back she found shells, a second gun-cleaning kit, and a book on tanning hides. She scanned it rapidly then added all the containers of tanning solution she could find and another case of fish hooks and lines.

She surveyed the car. The spare front seat was still empty apart from the shotgun and computer, however most of the car remaining was now crammed full. Best leave it at that. She hopped almost gaily into the seat, locking the doors. So far survival hadn't been difficult. For a city girl she thought she was doing fine. The car purred along the main roads north. By now it was mid-afternoon but it would be light for a while yet. At this time of the year, and in fine weather, it could be light until seven or eight. She remembered to be grateful that it had been fine most of the last week.

She turned on the radio as she headed north. The station she listened to was still playing as the man had promised. Not the more modern stuff, just the good older songs — a lot of Meatloaf's work from the 90's, some country, light classics, and now and again a song from a New Zealand group. She found tears blurring the road. All that was gone, there'd be no more.

Nothing she'd known would ever be the same. Even if she made it, if she survived despite the odds, she'd never sit over a glass of cold orange juice talking to her mother in the morning. She'd never discuss politics with her father. There was no longer a busy University where she studied, no friends to laugh with, cry with, and learn with. There was no one, and nothing familiar left. She stopped the car, laid her head on the steering wheel and howled like a lost toddler. Sometime later she was cried out. Red-eyed and sniffing, she lifted her head. She would have to stop this. Bawling every time she realised what she'd lost would get her nowhere.

She sat up, started the car and drove on in silence having turned off the radio. She passed Plimmerton, and began ascending the long hill to the coast. At the top she halted the vehicle. One thing she had found in the sports shop: binoculars. She'd taken two of the best pairs. Now she studied the road ahead. There seemed to be no obstructions that she could see. The bug had mostly taken hours to kill even at its swiftest. Those stricken had usually made for home or hospital to die. They had used their cars to drive; why abandon them on the road?

But it was best to he cautious. Some could have been alone and pushed on for help until too late. She allowed the car to drift slowly down the hill. Not until the bottom did she speed up a little. Paraparaumu was passed, then Waikanae and the smaller townships north. She halted in Levin.

Here there had been fires, there was some appearance of looting, with smashed shop windows and ruined doors. Not a place to remain. Then, too, she was tiring. Let her find a place to sleep outside of the main town. Jo halted briefly at a pharmacy that appeared unlooted; there she loaded up on recognisable medications, particularly antibiotics, antiseptics and the stronger painkillers, adding several books on drugs that she found on a shelf at the back. She moved swiftly, furtively, peering around as she worked.

After that she drove on a few miles into the countryside until she spied a tiny group of houses. Five of them, all close enough together to be walked between in a few strides. She halted the car, picking up the shotgun. Then she blew the horn a couple of times. No one would hear that from any distance but if someone was still alive in the houses they would hear her. She waited.

Only birdsong answered until she left the car. Then there came a thunderous growl and a black form launched itself at her from behind a bush. In her panic she staggered backwards, losing her balance. As her hip struck the car she involuntarily pulled the trigger. The dog fell, scrabbling weakly at the ground. He whined, then jerked once and was still. Jo, an animal lover, burst into tears again despite her resolutions. The poor beast had only been protecting his home. She felt like a murderer. Her guilt was far less once she had been through the house. A partly-eaten body in the back porch showed that her assailant had been less scrupulous in his beliefs.

She slept in one of the houses that night, but only after dragging the dog's body away. After a little thought she'd left it by that of the human. A quick search of the houses before she left next morning, netted her a second gun, to her delight. It was a rifle, old but well-cared for. And most useful of all, it had a fine telescopic sight attached. Further search found another shotgun tucked away in a bedroom cupboard. She giggled as she added them to her carload. She was starting to look like a small war on the move.

After that she sat a while reading the gun manual she'd found. She'd been luckier with the dog than she knew Jo realised as she read. The safety catch. She knew vaguely about them. But the one on the shotgun had been off. She could have jolted the gun and fired it accidentally at any time. She'd have to be more careful.

But then too, if it hadn't been off the dog would have savaged her before she understood why the gun wouldn't fire. She drove along the unpaved road behind the houses and practiced with each weapon. Flicking the safety catches on and off until she could do it with each of them.

By nine a.m. she was on the road again, driving cautiously. One never knew what might be around the bend. And if anyone else should be driving south they'd surely stick to the most direct route. She'd swung off to the north-west as she left the house. She would take the less direct route since it should be safer for a girl driving alone. She passed Foxton — dead and silent — then swung east at Himatangi. Soon she was into the outskirts of Palmerston North. There she stopped again to consider.

The radio man had said that only one per cent of people would be alive and relatively healthy. Palmerston North had had a large population. Even with one per cent there could be too many possible predators. Of course they'd had time to start killing themselves off, but there could be enough left to endanger her. Come to that, even one person who was a predator was one too many if he took her by surprise. Nevertheless, she wanted to find those maps. She'd have to risk it. She loaded all three guns and placed them handy. The car doors were all locked. Then, keeping to the centre of each street, she advanced. Fortunately the service station maps had been right. The road she was already on led to the maps' building.

Once there, she was nervous about leaving the car. Anyone trying to break in would find it a task. But they might prefer to wait for her to return. The idea pulled at her nerves until she drove around the building. At the rear there was a vehicle entrance with double gates. Her fingers flicked down a dashboard flap and played skillfully on a tiny keyboard until with a whoop of pleasure, she saw the gates swing open. She drove in and turned to watch as they shut behind her again and their locks clicked into place.

Jo marched to the back door. The door too was secured but a couple of hard wrenches with the tyre-lever and it gave way. The silent alarm would be ringing at the Police Station but even if there were anyone left there they'd have more worries than a possible burglar. Now for the maps. All of the rooms were listed on a front hallway directory. She had to break open some doors still but she found the maps, took a plug-in copy of each, (and, after careful thought, several sets of composite plastic ones as well.) She made a quick check through the building. No bodies, no sign of any disturbance, water and electricity still working. She'd spend the night here, perhaps several nights, while she looked over the maps. Downstairs in the underground garage she found the official cars. All would start and had fuel but none were better than her Lantana.

She ate, slept, and studied map after map over the next three days. None of the places she saw appealed to her as a suitable home. She had to remember that vehicles wouldn't last forever; one day they'd stop working. It would be no good then to have to walk for weeks to get to other people. On the other hand, she didn't want to be close to danger. She'd never had to consider this sort of thing before. Now she had to, she found herself at a continual loss.

Could she find others who'd join with her? But how would she know if they were safe to approach? She continued to scan the maps. Looking down at them, she grinned bitterly. The Government, fearing she knew not what, had arranged for all computers with this sort of information to wipe their hard drives and backup drives clean, if they didn't receive a regular signal. Only in a repository like this, where the documents were on plastic composite or on separate computer plug-ins, were such items still in existence.

Four days later she was still unable to decide. Out of inertia and depression, she remained in the building. She ate, slept, and read everything she found, down to some science fiction magazines found in someone's office. Somewhere, she thought, there would be something to help her make up her mind.

Finally she had enough. There had been no sign of others. Perhaps this city was deserted, all the inhabitants' dead or departed. At last she took one of the small electric citi-cars out to browse about the deserted streets and shops. On the far side of the square she found another sports shop. This one had been thoroughly looted. It made her jumpy again. But she needed to top up her food and drink supply. She strolled next door to the supermarket and filled a sack she found in the back. She was dragging it to the car when a voice spoke.

"Well, well, and what have we here? What a nice little chicken."

For a moment she froze. She'd put the shotgun down to use both hands on the sack. It was too late. Big hands closed on her and she was heaved away from it.

"Naughty, naughty. Mustn't shoot the nice man."

She squirmed around in his hold — and screamed in utter horror. When the bug hit, it had attacked him, probably through a scratch or scrape on his cheek. It looked as though it hadn't done more than ravage his face, but that was sufficient. From between the patches of a tangled beard, great areas of raw-looking flesh gaped. One of his eyes had gone, and the scars spread down his neck like a vicious burn.

Once he might have been a nice-looking family man, a good husband and father. Now he was a madman, as anyone would know who looked into the empty eyes. He called and another man stepped out to join them.

"Where'd she come from?"

"Dunno. Not far, not in that little citi-car. That kind won't go further'n forty-fifty kilometres without another charge."

The second man turned to her. "Where'd you come from?"

She thought fast. If she could get away she would still have her car. If they knew about it she'd never get away, they'd wreck it, plunder it...she must say something quickly.

"Himatangi. I came to see if anyone's still alive. Out there they're all dead." He should believe that. The citi-car should have just made it to here on a single charge.

He grunted, as the other nodded. They'd believed the lie. Thank any God listening. Now, if she could only escape. She must appear docile, perhaps a bit stupid.

"Are you all that's alive, Mister?"

"Uh, yeah! Just me'n Joe here." That was the second man. He

reminded her of a ferret she'd seen in the zoo.

"Uh, we've got another girl with us though. Come back and you can meet her."

As if she had a choice. "Thank you, I'd like to do that."

They took an arm each and walked her along the pavement. Joe had a limp but it didn't seem to be slowing him. She managed a smile.

"What's your friend's name? The one who found me?"

"Uh, him? He's Rewi. Used to be a member of the Provincial Rugby team. Lost all his family to the bug. He's gone in the head. You wouldn't want to make him mad." He looked at her threateningly. "You wouldn't do that, would you?"

"No." It was all she could say. They walked on until they came to the Police Station. They ascended the steps as Joe giggled.

"Real home from home, this."

She guessed he'd been a petty criminal or worse originally. He obviously found it amusing to be camping in the place where he'd often been brought. On a wall covered with small lights and map references she could see lights blinking wildly. She kept her eyes from it. Clearly neither man had understood the significance. Nor did she want to call attention to the refuge they had not realised she had. They conducted her through to the rear where several neat cells stood. The door of one was swung open.

"Meet our other girl." Jo received a hard push so that she fell forward. "Just get in there with her. We'll get back to you, darling."

A door slammed and she was there with her fellow woman. She sat on the long bench and stared at the empty eyes, the tangled hair, and the badly bruised face. The woman's clothes were filthy and she smelled. But when she spoke, the voice was low and clear, an educated voice.

"Who are you? Where did they find you?"

Jo deliberated. Could the men be out there listening? She'd keep her mouth shut on some things, just in case. Besides, there was nothing to say that this girl could be trusted, educated or not.

"Everyone in Himatangi's dead. I took the council's citi-car and came in to see if it was the same here. That pair found me in the supermarket looking for food. I had a shotgun but they took it."

"What's your name?"

"Jo. Jo Taylor. What's yours, and how long have you been here?"

"Ngaire Weber. I think I've been here a week." She cocked her head at a sound. Jo realised suddenly why the eyes were empty.

"You're blind?"

"That's how they caught me. I had to come out to find food. I lived in the annex for the blind at Massey University here. Everyone else was dead or gone. I got the bug just a bit. It made me feverish for several days. At first a friend stayed with me and brought me water. After a couple of days she didn't come back, but I was already getting better. They didn't do the cooking for us in the annex. That was just for sleeping, and with study and recreation rooms. I ate everything I could find there. Then I had to come out to try and find a shop."

"Did you hear any dogs?"

"Dogs? No, not really. A bunch of them howling in the distance once. Why?"

Jo told her.

"Ugh! I've heard shooting in the distance a few times. I just thought Joe and Rewi were shooting up the place for fun." The blind eyes turned in Jo's direction. "You do know why they've brought you here? I can't get away. But you could if you get a chance."

Jo looked with sick pity at the bruises, the torn clothing and grime. "If I get the chance, I could try to get you away as well?"

There was a soft sigh. "Don't bother. What good's a blind woman nowadays? Soon there won't be any computers, anything I can use or do to help. I'd just be a burden on anyone I was with. Joe and Rewi aren't so bad. They do feed me and they don't really hit me that often."

Jo shivered. Fancy being glad that you were fed and only hit now and again. She knew what Ngaire would have to do for the food too. She couldn't do that. She couldn't! But if she stayed she'd be given no choice. There'd been no indication that the men were listening to them, and she was coming to trust this battered woman.

"How could I get away?"

"When they caught me, they celebrated. They brought in lots of different kinds of alcohol. They made me drink until I was so drunk it didn't matter what they did. I think I passed out. You could suggest they have a real celebration again. Say you're so glad you'd found someone alive. Joe may even believe it, he thinks he's God's gift to women. Pretend to drink but don't. Maybe they'll give you a chance once they're drunk enough."

Jo nodded. "I'll risk it if there's a chance. What about you?"

"If you get away they may hit me once or twice. But I'll survive. Now lie down and try to relax a while. They didn't go out to look for you. They were after more food and that'll be where they've gone again now, if they look for something to drink as well, they may be gone for hours."

Jo lay back on the hard bench. The stress of capture had left her feeling exhausted. She drifted into an uneasy sleep until screams and shouts woke her.

"What on earth is that?"

Ngaire had moved to the barred part of the door, listening with her ear to the bars. "It's a child's voice. A girl. I'd guess they found someone else looking for food."

"From your annex?"

"No, they only took women over eighteen for the University studies. Other blind children are usually at a boarding school up North."

The commotion came closer. Ngaire stepped back. "See if you can see anything."

"Nothing, nothi...yes. You were right. They've got some child. She only looks about ten or so." An awful thought struck her. "Ngaire, they can't be going to... not a *child*!"

"Rewi probably won't. But Joe won't care. If she's female that's good enough. In fact, if it was a boy I doubt he'd care either. Just so long as whoever it is, is too small to fight him off successfully."

By now Jo could see as the child was dragged closer. In an undertone, she relayed the scene to the other woman. "She's fighting them all the way. I think she must have bitten Joe. His arm is bleeding. She's kicking as well and they're having a real job hanging on to her. She must be stronger than she looks."

"They probably don't want to damage the merchandise too badly," Ngaire said dryly.

"Maybe, otherwise they'd just knock her out. She's making enough noise to wake..." she shut off that sentence.

Ngaire's voice was drier still. "Not too likely. But if she has any friends around, she might bring them in. A child of that age may not have managed without someone." She moved back to one side of the door. "Be ready, we can always hope."

The child was dragged to the door of the cell and tossed inside. She landed with a grunt. Both men stood looking through the bars as she snarled back at them. Joe snorted.

"Regular stroppy little bitch. We keep catching women like this and we'll have ourselves a proper harem, just like one of them Arabs."

He smirked at the captives. His and Rewi's backs were turned to the main door. It was Ngaire's blindness-honed hearing that caught the sounds. To cover those she began to shout. "She's a little girl, you pigs. Are you going to rape her every night the way you rape me? You'll kill her. Maybe it'd be better if one of us just strangled her now and saved her all that." As she continued to shout, she put her hands around the child's neck. In an undertone she hissed, "Pretend. Pretend!"

Quick-wittedly, the child played up. Joe shouted back, first in anger, then in anxiety. "Goddamn you. I want her alive." He reached to swing open the door again. From behind him there was a loud click. He and Rewi spun. Ngaire had scooped the child to one side of the sheltering wall. There was a massive blast as a shotgun discharged both barrels almost at once. Then there was silence apart from the choking moans of one of the men.

"Ani, are you okay?"

"Yes." The child darted out past the men. Jo moved slowly to the door, hissing to Ngaire as she did so, "Keep your hands in sight."

Slowly they exited, to stare at the figure in the doorway. The girl, Ani, clung to her. Jo scanned the shape. She lifted her empty hands up into clear view.

"Thanks for that. They had us all prisoners in there."

The woman shrugged. "Wasn't after you. It was Ani I was hunting."

It didn't look likely they were related. Ani was clearly at least half Maori, but the girl who stood there was European. Her eyes were a deep blue and her short curly hair was a medium to light brown. She stood with a comfortable stance, shotgun under one arm, another with the barrel sawn off, slung across her back, a belt full of shells supporting a hunting knife encircling her slender waist. She had a deep green scarf holding her hair out of her eyes and a wild barbaric look.

"Is Ani a relative?" Jo ventured the question

The girl threw back her head and laughed. "No, I found her. Finders keepers, I reckon." Her voice was uneducated but pleasant.

One of the men moved slightly and she glanced down. Then before they understood the girl's intent, she had produced a knife and leaned over, jerked Joe's head back by the hair and slashed swiftly, allowing the body to drop to the floor again. Blood pooled about the victim's neck as Jo swallowed, feeling sick.

"You can't *do* that sort of thing!"

"Who says?" The girl appeared genuinely curious.

"It's against the law."

"So's taking little kids to rape. So's locking up women or killing them. You see any one enforcing the laws around here but me?"

"No, but—"

"Look, lady. There aren't any laws any more. You make your own. I made mine. Mine says it's better I'm alive than them if it comes down to it."

"But he couldn't fight any more."

"Second law says don't leave any grudges behind you. They may turn up as an ambush some other time."

Jo stared helplessly. She was sure the girl was wrong but she didn't have the arguments to convince her. "Uh, I'm Jo Taylor. This is Ngaire Weber." She waited expectantly.

"This is Ani. She can't remember her other name so I gave her mine. I'm Shay Griffin."

She stooped to pick up the men's discarded weapons. There was a lithe catlike flow to her movements. Jo guessed her age to be around seventeen or perhaps a year older. She could never have been called beautiful or even pretty; her hawk-like face was too strong for that. But she was striking, the kind who went their own way regardless of others. It surprised Jo that Shay had even allowed Ani to join her. Perhaps the helplessness of the child had softened that rugged individuality. She wondered what 'Shay' was short for, or if it was even the girl's real name? Better not to ask; it wasn't her business after all. She took Ngaire's hand.

"Let's find a bathroom somewhere, I want a bath and..." she stopped, embarrassed.

"And I need one. I know." Ngaire followed.

By the door where she had moved, Jo could see Shay register Ngaire's blindness. She nodded once, as if making a decision.

"You can come to our place if you like. Power's off to part of the city but it's still working there. You can have a real bath." She grinned wickedly. "You want to see the bathroom we've got. Looks like a scene from one of those Roman orgies."

"You don't mind having us there?" Ngaire asked.

"Nope, be nice to have company for the night."

She led them out, slamming the door on the motionless bodies behind them. Out of sight, out of mind, appeared to be another of her laws. They pattered after her down the silent streets. Three females who had survived thus far — and one who was born to.

Chapter Three

The house was all that Shay had promised. Luxuriating in an enormous tiled spa pool, Jo and Ngaire soaped, rinsed, and scrubbed again. They finished with Shay's stock of shampoos, working industriously until Ngaire's hair was clean. Then they combed and plaited it.

"That looks fine. The ribbon goes with that dress Shay found for you." Jo hesitated. "You're pretty."

"Thanks, what do you think of our hostess?"

"I've never met anyone like her."

Ngaire looked thoughtful. "I have. I never told you but I was studying to be a sociologist. It's one of the professions that are easily handled by the blind. Well, that sort of thing, dealing with people and computer records. Funny thing is that people with problems will often talk to someone who's blind far more easily. We often get more out of voice tones, too."

"So what do you think of Shay?'

"I'd be prepared to bet that she was in some kind of state care. Shifted from place to place a lot. She may have been in one of the girl street gangs at some time. Believe me, they're as dangerous as any of the male gangs. She's intelligent, but most of her education will have come from reading rather than school. From what you can tell me of her and from what I heard, she's a law to herself. Kids who've spent time in the gangs reckon the law doesn't protect them so why should they uphold it? They may not verbalise it that clearly, but it's the way they feel. Now that she doesn't have the fear of what will happen if the police catch her doing something illegal, she sloughs the law off like an old skin."

She paused to consider. "The thing is, that in many ways she's far better adapted to survive than either of us. She'll do whatever is necessary to live without either guilt or regret. And she won't hesitate as we would."

Jo remembered the quick movement as the knife had slashed, the casualness of it. "No, she doesn't."

Ngaire shrugged, "I guess I'll have to find my annex again. I know the address if you can help me get there."

"Stay with me."

"What were you going to do before they found you?"

"That was it. That was why I was in Palmerston North." From the corner of her eye she saw that Shay and Ani were standing in the doorway. She nodded to them and continued, "I came here from Wellington. My mother was one of the very earliest ones to die. We took my father to the airport and ran into an acquaintance coming off a plane. I think that was how mum caught it.

My father was going to Michigan on business. Even if he lived, he'd never be able to get back. He'd need to find at least one internal flight to start with and I heard that in America they grounded all planes. I took everything we had that might be useful and drove Dad's car up here. There's a place over on Church Street they only finished last Christmas. It has complete sets of topographical maps of the country. All on that plastic composite and in boxes of plug-ins, not just on computer, so they were still useable."

"The big brick and green building?" Shay broke in.

"Uh huh. I was going to use the maps to choose a place for myself. Somewhere I could have a small farm. Maybe grow or breed something there I could trade."

She could almost see Shay's ears prick up at that. She continued to talk, laying out her ideas, hopes, and her belief in a possible future.

"It's much better right up north," Shay said.

Jo looked at her with interest. "Why?"

"It's warmer. I read once that it was why civilisations did so well in Egypt and around there. 'Cos it was warm they could raise more crops each year. With a surplus they had time to have hobbies."

Jo hid a slight smile. Civilisation as a hobby? But oddly though the idea might have been put, it was right, now that she considered it, and interesting that an uneducated girl could have thought of it. She nodded.

"What do you know about the area?"

She received a small grin. "Not much about most of it, but I lived on a farm near the head of the Hokianga Harbour. We used to walk there in a couple of hours sometimes." She looked thoughtful. "That'd be a great place to make for I reckon."

"Why?" Ngaire inquired.

"It's a women's commune. They're into self-sufficiency and they have this back to the Earth lifestyle. All of the place is fitted up to be as self-sufficient as possible and it isn't easy to find. It's well off main roads and they don't get many visitors so there's a fair chance that a lot of the trouble will have missed them."

"You mean they use it as a women's refuge?"

Ngaire was quick, Jo thought. She was already turning the idea over in her mind as Shay talked. It would be a hell of a trip with just the four of them, and how about getting through Auckland? The population there had been almost one and a half million. If the original figures still held, around fifteen thousand must have survived initially. Of course by now that could be a lot lower, say ten or twelve thousand. Ngaire was talking again and she began to listen.

"...all right for you three. What use would I be?"

She would have spoken, but Shay got in first. Her tone was scornful. "You aren't stupid, are you? Earlier you said you knitted the jersey you gave me to wash for you. Right now we can get all the jerseys we need out of the shops. But how long do you think that'll last? Then we'll have to do our own knitting — and what do we do when the store wool runs out? You said that you can crochet too."

Jo could recall having seen demonstrations of a spinning wheel. They would have to keep their own sheep, shear them, and spin the wool. They'd eventually have to weave it into cloth as well. She said all that, watching as Shay absorbed it. She waited. It would come better from one who Ngaire would believe had no motives in trying to keep her alive. Shay laughed.

"Then that's it. And Ngaire, you're blind which means you can hear better than we can. You'd make a useful guard at night. Particularly the kind of night where there's no moon and it's pitch black, You'd be able to walk around without a light. During the day you can learn to spin and knit all our jerseys for us in between crocheting blankets."

She bent down and picked up a huge fluffy towel. "Now come out of that bath before you look like a prune. Here!" She tossed the towel over so that it landed by the woman. "We can talk more about it over a meal, but I'm for going north." The door clicked behind her. Ngaire climbed out of the bath, stooping for the towel.

"What do you think, Jo?"

"If you mean about you being very useful — then I agree with Shay. If you mean about going north, then she had a point there too."

"I think this place she was talking about *was* a refuge. It sounds as if there may have only been women there. But we'd need to take more than one vehicle. I wonder if Shay can drive?"

"I can't see her not being able to. I just wonder how she learned," Jo chuckled as she opened the door.

Behind her a voice came, loaded with equal amusement, "I've flashed more cars than you'll ever drive, lady. There's nothing I've found I can't drive and that includes most trucks too."

Jo turned. "I'm sorry."

"s'all right. Sure, I learned to drive that way. I've jiggered a few shops in my time too. And tapa'd a man here 'n there who wouldn't take no for the answer. But I've never dumped a friend with the law. You ask Ani if I haven't taken good care of her?"

Ani bobbed up in front of them. "She has," the child yelled at them both, red-faced with anger. 'She came to get me when those men took me, didn't she? She's my friend!"

Jo held up her hands in surrender, "Okay, don't hit me, I give up. Look, I wasn't being nasty. I just guessed you could drive but that you — um — hadn't learned officially. That's all." She'd heard some street slang from a friend a year back who was working with a gang, and Jo had understood what Shay had said. Shay continued to speak.

"You were right, I didn't learn to drive — um — officially," she mimicked Jo's words. "I sure as fuck learned a lot of other things unofficially as well. Some of them may keep us alive, if you don't mind sticking with a criminal."

Jo wrapped her towel around her, tucking it in securely. Then she marched over to where Shay stood defiantly.

'I don't mind sticking with *you*! You were right in what you said at the jail. We make our own bloody laws from now on. We guard each other's backs and we do whatever we have to. If you'll have me as a friend then I'd be proud." She thrust out a hand. Shay studied it a few seconds then took it gently.

"The Pagans hug," she muttered.

Jo hesitated, then hugged. Ani pushed in to share, and somehow Ngaire was gathered in with them. They broke blushing and giggling.

"These maps you were talking about," Shay started. "Can we go there and take a look at them?"

"Now?"

"After we eat maybe?"

Jo glanced at the windows. "It'll be dark by then. Let's wait until tomorrow. If we show lights in the building it may bring hunters."

A grunt. "Makes sense. Let's eat."

They ate and talked, exploring each other's backgrounds, beliefs, and how they had come to this place. Later in her bed, Jo lay thinking. Ngaire was easy. She'd come here to study two years ago after living in a boarding school for the blind for six years prior. She had no hope of ever returning home, her family was almost certainly dead, and they had lived in the South Island. Nor did she sound over-fond of them. Jo had gained the impression that they'd counted Ngaire as not worth much because she was blind.

Ani was a mystery to even Shay. She'd found her wandering down one of the roads into the city. At first, the child hadn't even remembered her name. Later, she'd said it was Ani but was still unable to remember more. It was obvious to the three women that the things the child had seen had been wiped by a merciful amnesia.

Shay had talked about her after the child had been put to bed. "I don't think she lived in town. I reckon they brought someone in that was sick and died here. She probably wandered away from the hospital after there was no one around to keep her there. If she was there during the worst of it, watched her family and a lot of others die, I'm not surprised she doesn't want to remember anything. I don't try to make her. She's happy, healthy, and quite bright. She reads and writes. She knows about gardening, too. That's why I think her family may have came in from the country."

Then it had been Jo's turn. She'd described her journey, all that had happened, and how she had been captured. She ended with something she'd been thinking about throughout the discussion. "If we go north, we really need at least two vehicles. If you can handle a truck, Shay, then we can take Dad's car and a truck. But we'd do even better if we could find others to join us. People we could trust."

"Women only?" Shay asked.

"Well..." Ngaire was doubtful.

Jo shook her head. "Mostly women to start with maybe. Until there's enough of us that men like those two will think twice before starting anything and if they do we can handle it. But there's good men too. If we find any we think are okay we'd have a bit of muscle that would be useful. Besides, men think differently. Right now we can use any advantage and other ways of looking at things is one. We have to get as many good shotguns as we can. Shay can teach us to use them."

Shay nodded. "There's a gunsmith's place down near the hospital. Hang on a minute." She vanished, to return with a shotgun in one hand. She displayed it. "Look, I cut down the barrel on this one. A mate of mine showed me how to do the job." She grinned briefly. "He was into stuff where that's useful. It's a pump-action. Holds ten. One of the real new models. You wear it on a sling under your arm and behind."

"But it's upside down?" Jo said blankly.

Shay's smile widened "Gun doesn't care which way up it is to fire. This way it isn't obvious and with the short barrel you have a hell of a spread at a distance. You saw those two blokes after I shot them, didn't you? Someone told me that in the old days they called those sorts of guns 'alley-sweepers'. Those two guys would have known why, huh?"

"Yes." Jo didn't want to recall that. It made her sick. But there were a lot of things likely to do that now. Life wasn't nice any more...or peaceful, safe, protected. She'd have to get used to it. She turned to Shay, making it clear politely that it was her turn to share something of herself.

Now in her bed, half-asleep and warm, Jo pondered. When Shay was nine her parents had died or left her, the girl didn't know which. She'd been shuffled from foster home to foster home, several of them abusive. Her salvation had been the ability to read before that began. She had always been able to retire into another world. She had a good mind and a retentive memory. But the constant interruptions in her education had left her with little of the formal kind.

At twelve she'd escaped with a major chip on her shoulder, gone north and found the commune. There she'd lived for almost two years, afraid to go far in case she was seen and taken again. But eventually restlessness had caught up with her. She'd been taken by the police again near Taupo as she headed south. Once back in the system she'd survived more foster homes, more abuse, until she'd managed to flee again.

Somewhere along the line she'd had a good criminal education in both minor and major abilities. Shay knew guns and knives. She could flash — steal a locked — car, jigger her way into a secured shop without setting off the alarm, and she had developed a solid dislike for being coerced in any way. She was prone to resent it with violence and Jo wondered if there were bodies behind her from before the pandemic began.

Not that it mattered now. As the country was, the girl's abilities were survival-oriented. She saw movement or buildings as would a fighter. She knew how to travel safely and how not to be ambushed. She'd be invaluable to them just so long as she saw them as her friends. She had the kind of narrow tribal-loyalty street-kids often learned. First there was you. After that came your friends, and any family — maybe. The rest of humanity was just there. They had no claim on you and you owed them nothing. Shay wouldn't kill for the fun of it, but she wouldn't hesitate either if she believed it necessary. She could walk away after that. In her eyes if they brought it on themselves, why should she feel guilty?

Nor would she cause trouble with any men who joined them. It was clear from some of her talk she'd walked on the fringes of the criminal element for some time. She'd learned how to be just a good mate to dangerous men and to be accepted that way. Much of the time she appeared more like a young man than a girl in her attitude. In the loose clothing, with her hawk-like features she seemed sexless, although, Jo remembered, once she had stripped to bathe with them she had a good though wirily slender and surprisingly muscular figure.

The next day Jo guided them back to the maps building. She'd hidden a front door card and key in a building next door. Now as Ani raced up and down the polished corridors sliding and whooping, Shay and Jo considered the wealth of maps laid before them.

"If we take the main road we may run into trouble. It's never a good idea to be too obvious," Shay said.

"That's good sense, Do we go back to Wellington to pick out a good truck and guns?"

"What about picking up other people? There may be some suitable ones back that way?" Ngaire asked.

"What about looking around here? There may be more survivors."

"Don't forget Joe and Rewi," Ngaire said slowly.

"I'm not." Jo assured her. "But this is a city too. There must have been more who made it through the bug."

"So, how do we persuade them to come out?"

Shay leaned back from the map table and laughed. 'A good bait will bring out rats. Let's bait a trap and see what comes out to sniff.'

The other two were horrified once she explained, but Ani was delighted. At last she would be of use, accepted as a big girl, and able to help her friends. They made plans and two days later, Ani skipped gaily down the street singing and waving a tambourine they'd found her. Twice, men ran out but each time Shay appeared. She'd found an excellent method and if someone appeared she would not trust, she shot out of a side street on a motorbike. A quick pick-up and she and Ani were away. They then marked a map as to the home territory of these men. In this way they added two more children and another woman with a baby to their number.

The children were brother and sister. The woman was no relation to the baby she carried. It had belonged to her neighbour. She'd heard it crying, gone in to find all in the house dead but the child and taken it. She could drive, as could the older boy of the two children. He was still suffering from a broken arm however and was terribly bruised. He said little, just enough for them to guess at the reasons. He and his sister took to Shay quickly, still faster to the short-barrelled shotguns she made them. From occasional remarks, the older women understood he'd been injured attempting to fight off a man. He'd failed, and both of them had paid.

He was fifteen, his sister, Pam, was two years younger. The woman who joined them was nearly thirty but quiet, almost submissive, the sort who had never had to think for herself, always before there had been a man to make her decisions. Now she listened to them, agreeing with whoever spoke in turn. She was a hard worker and pleasant, if not too bright. She'd make no trouble, so she stayed. With seven of them, not counting the baby, they could take more vehicles, weapons and supplies. In a week, they'd found a truck that Shay could handle easily.

They added the motorcycle and Jo's car to the convoy. The boy, Billy, could manage the bike. He'd ride ahead as a scout. Shay found another bike and insisted on adding that too. If anything happened to the first bike they should have a replacement ready. And the bikes used less fuel.

Hari and the baby would ride in the truck cab. Billy had his bike. Shay and Jo drove, while Ani, Ngaire, and the subdued Pam rode in the car. There'd been a minor argument over that.

"Hari can drive." Ngaire protested. "Why don't we take another car or truck?"

Shay's voice was flat. 'I don't trust her, no...' as they would have broken in. "I don't think she'd do anything against us on purpose. But in an emergency she'll do exactly the wrong thing. That's why I'm not giving her a gun either. I've seen the way she handles one. She's the kind who panics, follows the target around and then tries to shoot it through one of you. If I'm going to be shot, I'd rather it was on purpose by an enemy. You know what they used to say, 'friendly fire — isn't.'"

Ngaire agreed after that. So did Jo once she'd thought about it. And anyhow, Hari would have her hands full with the baby. They couldn't have her stopping everyone whenever it needed a drink or change. In the cab with Shay, she'd have room to do all that on the move.

They set out very early and were well clear of the city in an hour. They'd chosen to take the coastal road as Jo had done on the way in. Now they trundled along at a comfortable fifty k.p.h., with Billy scouting ahead and enjoying the bright sunshine as the day warmed.

Behind them Jo had carefully locked the maps building. They'd stop there again on the way back. And when they did, she'd collect a complete set of the plastic composite maps for the entire North Island along with a set of plug-ins for the whole country. It was unlikely that others would have either set. Under a lot of circumstances those maps could be very helpful. Shay had fighting in mind, while Jo had more peaceful pursuits. But they'd be an advantage for either reason.

In fact, as she drove, she was considering taking several sets of the maps, maybe as many as twenty. There was hundreds of each map in both types in the massive filing system. If they made it up north and settled they were unlikely to ever return and while the plug-ins would eventually fail, the composite maps should last for several generations and be a real boon. From now on they had to think ahead. Every move would have to be made partly in a consideration of the years to come.

She'd started off alone. Now she had seven companions, if she counted the baby. She had people she could trust, friends with whom to start again. She began to sing softly as she drove. Ngaire joined in, then Pam and Ani. They moved steadily south to the tune of an old song by a man who'd died young in a plane crash before any of them were born.

By the end of the day they were into the Kapiti Coast and an hour from Wellington. They stopped often to check on possible signs of life, to eat, pick up items they saw in shops, or in one case, to collect wonderful bunches of flowers. Shay stayed on the alert. Twice large dogs appeared looking aggressive, one she shot, the other ran when she raised her gun. She scolded her friends.

"This isn't a walk in the park. Don't go running off alone. Stay aware of what's around you. The dogs are starving, sooner or later they'll hunt in packs if they aren't doing that already. And don't trust anyone who strolls towards you either. Women can be just as crazy as men. I can't watch everywhere at once."

"Sorry," Jo said. "It's just that I've never had to do this sort of thing before. I keep forgetting."

"Yeah. Well, if *I* don't remind you something else may do it a fuck of a lot more painfully."

Shay hoped they'd remember what she'd said but of course, with a bunch like this they'd forget again. She just hoped she'd move fast enough if that time came. It arrived when a woman stumbled out of a shop, giggling, eyes glazed with either madness or drugs. Her left hand stabbed the air with a syringe. Ngaire, nearest to the approaching figure heard the movement but unable to see the danger she merely called out.

"Who's that? Jo, who is it?"

Jo was paralysed. Shay had moved away watching Ani and the

47

others. In another moment the syringe would reach out to stab the blind woman. There was only Jo to prevent it. Thoughts flicked through her mind. Drugs, contaminated blood, poisons, there could be anything in or on the needle. Did she have the right to assume anything. But if she didn't, if she failed to act and Ngaire died....without conscious intent she had raised the gun. As the needle thrust forward, she fired.

The woman screamed, staggering back as blood gushed from her mangled throat and upper chest. The needle, struck by a couple of pellets exploded into shards. Shay arrived in what seemed like a feat of teleportation.

"What happened?"

Jo was too busy throwing up to talk for the moment. Ngaire was backed up against the shop front, her head weaving from side to side in an effort to understand what had occurred. The intruder was down on the pavement, her aimless movements dying into stillness. Shay scanned the scene, guessed most of the events and discarded caring about the remainder.

"She's done for. Let's get out of here. If there's more crazies that shot will bring them down on us. Go!" She was bundling everyone into the vehicles, Jo last. She paused as the still retching woman took her seat. "Nice job by the way. God knows what was in that fucking needle.'"

Jo nodded. She might have saved Ngaire from some horrible way of dying but she didn't feel good about killing to do it. There should have been another way. She said so between retching gasps.

Shay looked at her. "Yeah? So while you're analyzing the lady's troubles, she kills Ngaire an' comes after you. Forget it. There's times you have to act first and think later. Look at it this way. Ngaire and you are okay. Better some crazy's dead than you two."

She had a point Jo knew. But she was afraid it would be a long time before she could accept it that casually. She remained jumpy all day, watching for someone else to appear, to threaten them. She felt weepy and irritable. She knew it was the shock, but knowing didn't help. It did however help her bite her tongue so as not to inflict her mood on her friends.

They spent the night at a large house in more isolated grounds. The water and electricity still worked and they were able to luxuriate in long showers or baths. Billy vanished to the nearby shops with Shay, to return with a gift for the small quiet Pam.

"It's her birthday this week...I think," he added doubtfully. "I've sort of lost track of the days. Anyhow she's always wanted a pony. I know we can't take one with us now, but I thought if we gave her the gear we could find one up North."

'Up north.' It was becoming their goal, their symbol of a new life. Time and time again it was 'When we get up north.' 'Once we're Up North.' 'We'll do that once we're north.'

Ngaire ran her fingers over the glossy leather. "Mmm, smells lovely. What else have you got?"

"The whole hutu," Shay said. "We got the saddle, bridle, cleaning gear, a blanket they need, and a whole stack of other stuff. Billy found wrapping paper in one of the shops, and a pretty floral tape to parcel everything. I found cards, as well as a couple of books on taking care of your pony. We wrap it all separately, see if we can lay out a feast and give it to her from us all."

"Where is she?"

"In the bath. I sent her in next. Jo can wrap her stuff and do her card first. Then she can go and keep her away from the kitchen. Okay, Jo?"

"Sure. I'll give her the cleaning stuff. Pass the paper and that card." She pointed and began to write.

It was a success. Crimson with happiness, Pam came out of her shell to laugh and talk as any normal child. She clutched the saddle to her and when Jo came in to wish her a good night it was on the end of the bed.

Shay must have talked to Billy while they were out. She found time the following day before they left to speak quietly to Ngaire and Jo once she got them alone.

"He still isn't talking too much about it. But the pair of them were jumped by some man just after they lost their parents. Billy'd gone out to find food and Pam went outside to watch for him. Billy got back just as she was being attacked. He got the guy off, an' he turned on Billy. Pam hit the man over the head and laid him out. They both got away and never saw the guy again. I suspect she killed him and so does Billy, but he's never said so to her."

"So they were both..."

"No, they were real lucky, Billy got there in time to save Pam an' she hit the guy in time to save Billy, still, they're both pretty jumpy."

"We'll have to be more careful ourselves. All of us." Jo remembered the woman she'd killed.

Shay nodded, her face set. "No one goes anywhere away from the others alone from now on. We always travel in pairs at minimum. Have a gun ready. And we'll see if we can find any of those Personal Screamers. You know, the hand alarms you set off if you're attacked. Some shop will have them and batteries." She turned to the door. "Early start. Let's sleep."

The morning was fine again. The road was empty and they made good time without hurrying. In the distance several plumes of smoke showed where fire had attacked some of the suburbs. Jo averted her eyes. If any of those was where her home had been, she had no desire to know. They drove into the central city, parking outside one of the large supermarkets. Just down from it were the other shops Jo had originally plundered.

They stepped out, all but Hari and the baby, in an almost military formation, guns ready. The city now belonged to the strongest.

Chapter Four

They drove their vehicles along the city's main road to the empty heart. Leaves blew in the silence by the cenotaph. Pigeons still dropped down, flying upwards again with an echoing clatter of wings. No city had ever been so quiet.

They halted in the long crooked Lambton Quay. From where they had parked it was possible to see around the bend. Shay vanished into one of the huge clothing stores to emerge again with an armload of clothing for them. Jo shivered.

"Can we get out of here? It's like a cemetery."

"It *is* a cemetery," Shay told her. "I reckon some of them died looting. There's half a dozen bodies in that place and all have armloads of gear. They've been shot, I can't think why. It isn't as if there wasn't ten times what that many could use in twenty years."

Jo drove away with a feeling of relief once everything was loaded. The grimness was beginning to get to them all. They chose a hotel for the night, giggling their way up escalators that worked once Jo found the power switches. Ani had to be hauled in to eat. The child had rarely if ever ridden one of the moving staircases. She travelled up one and down the other with squeals of delight. Shay put the girl to bed at last. Ngaire marveled that the power still lived but Jo, at least in this thing, was more pragmatic.

"It's like the water systems. Automated, multi-backups. I'd bet big sections of the city won't have power by now but the system's on cut-outs too. Major faults any place and that section drops off the line until a real person sees to it. But the rest of the system keeps going. It'll all stop soon, but for now there can't have been any major problems in this part of the city." She shrugged. "Water's the same. Every place, even small townships, have their own water system and they're all lined up with fail-safes and back-ups. Less goes wrong with water. You'll probably be able to turn on a tap and get water in a lot of places for years to come."

They were up again early to hunt through the centre city shops with a careful discretion. But the eerie silence plagued them. Between the attack on Ngaire and the silence, they were becoming jumpier in a place that no longer felt natural to their kind. A city should have life, bustle with people, traffic, and city noise. There should be open doorways with merchandise lined up, cafes with bright umbrellas and eager baristas. Instead there was only the increasing stench of the dead and the gentle whistling of the wind as it whispered around forever silenced buildings. They spent another night in their hotel reluctantly.

"When do we start looking for others?"

"Let's pack the truck first," Jo said slowly as Shay looked at her.

"You mean be ready to leave at once in case anything goes wrong. You're learning. Okay. But we've been here two days and we have just about everything. Apart..." She broke off looking doubtful.

"Apart from what?"

"You lived here. Didn't you say that out the other side of the city there's a military place?"

Jo nodded. She could guess now what Shay had in mind. She stared along the roadway, considering. "There's just one problem. Places like that had real security. Steel and concrete doors on special locks. We probably wouldn't be able to get in."

"Maybe not. Then again, it isn't as if there's likely to be any one there to come running if an alarm goes off. And how much time would it take to check it out?"

"A day, that's all. You're right. It would be stupid to miss out if there's a chance."

"If there's still someone there alive who can get us in. I reckon we go and see first thing tomorrow," Shay said.

They were on the road by seven. Billy riding scout ahead on

the brand-new, more powerful, and better motorcycle he'd found, and with other motorcycles in the vehicles. They wheeled into the wide entrance of the army depot and halted to confer.

"Probably only alarms here," Jo said. "That could be useful. It might bring anyone still alive running to see who's arrived." She pulled out past Shay's truck and drove through the shut but unlocked gates. A siren began to sound somewhere deep in the complex. They ignored it, driving on.

The centre of the place was almost like a village square. Buildings stood around a large lawn with flowerbeds. A flagpole still flew the New Zealand flag. In the light wind it flapped and fluttered bravely. Jo climbed out to stand staring at it. She thought of all the things it had once stood for, the hopes and dreams of a country. Now everything was gone. She sighed, tears in her eyes. Would anything ever be the same again?

Shay nudged her. "Never mind standing there working on your memoirs. Make yourself a target too often and they stop earlier than you'd like. How do we bring out anyone who's here? Ani again?"

"Any better ideas?"

"One. We check through the place to see if there's any signs. Someone here may not be found if they don't want to be. But they won't be able to hide the place they've been living so easily."

"No one should take too many risks."

"Park the vehicles alongside each other facing opposite ways. Hari and the baby stay with Pam in the truck. Ngaire and Ani sit in your car. They each watch or listen at their front and the clear side. If they see or hear anything they don't understand or see anyone at all, they blow the horn. You, me, and Billy do the run through. Watch each other's backs."

They sorted themselves out as Shay suggested. Then the three slipped off around the first buildings. An hour later they were behind a large barracks, talking quietly.

"There's been someone in this one all right. Several someone's if you ask me."

Shay grinned. "I didn't but I reckon you're right. Five I think

53

from the beds. That's if they haven't been double-bunking."

"Adults?"

"Maybe two, maybe four if they're doubling up. Question is: are they likely to be friendly? If any of them are soldiers, we could be a bit out-classed."

"I know. They could under-estimate us though. I mean, two women and a...young man. We don't exactly look formidable."

"Why not have one of us break off?" Billy asked. He looked eager.

Shay glanced around. "Not a bad thought. You two go on. Do just as you have been and I'll trot along behind. Far enough back that they may miss me if they come out to watch you two."

She scrutinized the area as Jo and Billy moved off. Then she followed, well back. Her eyes looked everywhere, her ears sought for a sound. She had the sawn-off shotgun cocked, safety off. If she needed it, she could shoot without any time to waste. She padded slowly on, drifting around opposite sides of buildings. She just needed to know where they were. Ahead of them as she slid around a corner she saw figures approaching. She sped up, calling in an undertone to Jo ahead.

"Some of them coming. Don't move too quick."

She fell back again to cover. Ahead Jo and Billy had halted, They allowed the gun muzzles to point downwards held only in a left hand. Each displayed an open empty right hand. By now Jo could see that it was a man and a woman who were approaching. Both still looked weak and sick, the woman leaning heavily on the man. Jo stepped a pace forward, nodded politely to them.

"Hi, I'm Jo. This is Billy."

"Fred and Hine Eruwhata. You here to talk?"

"We'd like to. Just talk. If you really want us to leave, we will."

The man managed a faint grin. "That go for the one sneaking around back of us?"

Jo showed teeth. "Yes. She's just making sure you're all as friendly as we'd like to be." And, making a guess. "What about the ones covering you? Want to call them in?"

"Why not?'

Two people signalled. Shay closed in carefully. From behind an adjacent building came another four figures. One was an adult, in height anyhow, but the other three were clearly children. Shay counted. Well, basically that gave them six to six with her group on the downside. They had Ngaire. On the other hand, from the look of this lot, the two adults who'd first approached weren't exactly in fighting shape either. Her eyes went to the woman standing by Jo. If she wasn't pregnant, Shay would lose a good bet. Not that she showed it that obviously as yet, but there was something in the way that she moved and stood.

Shay moved up behind Jo, who was now talking comfortably to the pair. The others also approached, to stand behind their friends. There was a quick exchange of histories, names, then to Shay's disapproval, numbers. Still, now that all of the possible opposition was here, she was evaluating them as less able to fight despite the even numbers.

The Eruwhatas had been ill ever since the original outbreak. The bug had hit them hard so that they were still not fully recovered. The four with them were children from four different families. Each had been the only survivor. The tallest was a boy around Billy's age of fifteen. The other three were all girls, ranging up between nine or so to perhaps Pam's thirteen.

The kids looked healthy enough, but Shay didn't think the adults would make old bones. She'd reckon on some kind of major damage to the bloke, the woman, too, possibly. Neither moved as if they were strong, the occasional wince indicating they could be still in pain. She strolled forward to join them.

"Were you a soldier here?"

"Yes. That why you're all here. You came after weapons?"

Shay nodded. "You been outside this depot anytime since it happened?"

He shook his head. "Not me. We had our own medics. They died. Couple of the guys who weren't too sick to start with went out to see. They had radios. Called us back and said the whole place had gone mad. Said we should hole up and wait it out."

Shay looked about. 'I'd a' thought more of the army would of made it?'

Fred sighed. "Yeah, well, we might have but they vaccinated all army personnel a month ago. I reckon they'd heard about the bug starting overseas. They probably wanted the army in shape for martial law if they had to do that. Hine, me, and the kids here already had some sort of sore throats. They said they'd wait to vaccinate us. I dunno. Maybe the vaccination made the bug worse when it got here. Anyhow, everyone else died over the first week or so. Me 'n the wife were really sick. The kids looked after us. The others never came back and we wouldn't let young Bob over there go out after them.'

"But no one's tried to get in here yet?"

"Not yet. We figured that'd come though. It isn't me I'm so worried about. It's the kids. Good kids. They should have a chance and Hine is gonna have a baby."

Shay looked at him and he stared back quietly. So, he knew he and his wife were likely to die soon. But he wanted some kind of future for the children, his child and the others. She made up her mind slowly, and told him about the place up north where they planned to go and make a new start. Maybe even a new civilisation as generations passed. He listened. Finally as they came to the door of their barracks, he spoke quietly to her.

"Me and Hine aren't going to be around for ever. Maybe not even that long. You and your friends seem like decent people. You wouldn't have a blind woman and a baby along if you weren't. I can let you into the truck depot and stores. Even the hand weapon depot. If you take amphib. trucks you can go just about anywhere. The trucks are armoured, and the glass is bullet-proof. Four-wheel-drive and winches, everything you'd be likely to need."

"You'll come with us too?"

"Yeah. Just one thing, I want a promise from you all. Take care of the kids, and our baby if Hine lives long enough to have it. Okay?"

Shay nodded. Her gaze meeting his squarely as Jo turned back.

"We'd like you to join us. All of you. It isn't safe here. Sooner or later someone is going to remember this place is here. When they do they'd come hunting weapons."

Fred grunted agreement. "I can deal with that if we're all leaving. How many of us can drive?"

Shay was counting. She could drive, and Jo, Hari in a pinch, and Billy. "What about your people?"

"I can, and Bob although he hasn't got a license. That's it." He glanced at her. "There's another group. I know where they are, but they don't know about us. There's a man with a couple of women. We could talk to them? They don't have to know the plan and they might know where there's others."

A week passed slowly. They found the tiny group Fred knew: introduced as John, Marion, and Jessie. No surnames and they had a furtive look about them. Few of Jo's group liked one of the women, but the man and the other woman seemed okay. Shay had slipped off on her own concerns several times. At last Jo queried her, she shrugged.

"Just checking up on things. Picking up bits we may need sometime. I read in one of Fred's books that time spent on recon isn't ever wasted." She had her own backpack. One of the modern kind, of a material that would not cut or tear easily. It could be flapped down and locked. Now it bulged, with what Jo had no way of knowing.

They could take a convoy of nine trucks. That left them with Jo's car. She didn't want to leave it behind, but if it meant another truck and the supplies it could carry — Fred had fixed that problem.

"Car can be run up into the truck. I've driven them up that ramp before. An' you don't have to worry if something does happen to a driver, These babies are geared to be towed if you need to." He surveyed the trucks with pride. "When do you want to get going?"

"Shay's gone out again. She isn't saying anything but I think she may have found us a few more people. I'm just not sure why she hasn't said."

When Shay arrived with them that evening she found out. The two men with her introduced themselves with an air of faint belligerence. Jo hid a broad grin. Shay hadn't been too certain how everyone would take the two, but that sort of prejudice was well in the past. However, it had lingered longest with the most blatant, and this pair was that all right. They leaned on each other's shoulders, eyeing her through long false eyelashes.

They'd been introduced as Michaela — call me Mike if you'd prefer — and Rome — yes, just like the city, okay? They undulated their way across the floor to greet everyone, earrings dangling as they squealed in high-pitched voices. They were such a parody of the 'Queen' type that Jo wondered.

But this pair could drive. And besides, Shay was a wickedly shrewd judge of character. If she'd thought the two men wouldn't stand up to the work or would abuse children, she wouldn't have even brought them in. Jo watched them as they greeted the others, then suddenly smiled. Under that attitude their eyes gleamed with amusement. They were enjoying freaking out the straights, that was all. She guessed they'd chosen to do this to see how they were received at their most obvious. If they were accepted they'd know the attitudes of those with whom they'd be travelling.

She shook their hands in turn. "Shay says you can both drive?"

"Yes."

"Good, then we have a truck for you. Take turns in driving and riding shotgun. Suit you?"

"Fine by us."

They delayed another day to load one of the trucks with stock from the nearest pharmacy. They stuffed the truck, looting every medication and drug they could find. They included some of the simpler medical devices as well as bandages, slings, and adhesive wound dressings.

Jo found that it was for her to make the broader plans. Shay came into the discussion only when possible danger was considered and it was a system that bothered Shay as being unstable. If sudden danger threatened everyone was too used to doing whatever occurred to them at the time. But she said nothing. The situation would iron out eventually once they realised they needed a proper leader. Any attempt now would have them seeing her as wanting to give the orders. As it was, Ngaire also gave sensible advice, and the children were eager to help.

Only the trio who had come in from a suburb next to the base was difficult. But all three could drive. Jo didn't want to lose them. Still, if they made too much trouble they'd have to go. She intended to have them drive in the centre of the convoy. That way at least she would know where they were. All three complained about the work. Jessie was a real whiner but it was the man Shay had her eye on.

She'd summed him up the day he arrived. He was the kind of man who thought no woman really knew what she was doing. It took a man to lead and women should obey. He'd looked over their groups and apart from women and children, the only man was already ill and no challenge. John would see it as his right to run things — his way. That was okay by her for now. Let the three of them drive the trucks up North, while she kept an eye on him.

She also noted his covert amusement as Jo gave her courteous orders. He was seeing himself in that position. There wouldn't be any polite consultation then, nor any long discussions in which even the children could speak. They were ready to go when she noticed something else. Pam was quieter than usual. Whenever the man appeared, the child slid hastily in another direction. Shay scowled to herself. If he'd been trying anything on that child he'd be sorry.

At last they loaded every truck. Drivers were assigned and people sat in passenger seats with guns at the ready. Jo led off and one by one the others wheeled in line, following her out of the gates, down the main road and back into the central city. They may have been seen, if there were still those alive on the route. No one challenged. Ten army trucks implies an ability to take care of trouble. At a sedate 50Km, the convoy purred out of the city, down the motorway towards the north. They'd left at first light. They drove steadily, broke briefly early afternoon to eat, and then moved on.

By evening they reached Palmerston North again. Jo let herself into the maps building, opening the rear entrance so the trucks could drive into the underground garage. Then yawning and stretching, everyone emerged. Shay was keeping her eye on John without letting him see that. One minute he was there, the next he wasn't. Nor was Pam. She drifted silently along corridors until she heard voices.

"No! No, I won't, I don't *want* to. Let me go! Let me *go!'*

She slipped to her knees and peered around the door frame. The guy had his pants open and Pam's hair gripped in one hand.

"Yes, you will, an' make it good. Get smart and you'll hurt so bad you'll wish you'd hadn't."

His grin was loose-lipped with anticipated pleasure. He was bored with Jess and Marion. The one was too easy, the other too passive. He liked fresh meat and it was even better if it was fighting. If the cops had only known. He'd had more than one bitch this way, made them do what he wanted. He'd never been caught before and he wouldn't be now. He hauled the kid closer. Last bloody whore had bitten his arm. The bite had infected and he'd been treated, that was why he'd survived. It was ironic.

Anyway, the law could only lock him up and with all the law gone he could do whatever he fucking well liked. Just now he wanted to be blown, and he was gonna be or the kid would regret it. Once they got north to wherever they were going he'd start taking over this lot just as soon as he had the chance. Running things would give him access to any of the women.

Shay stood up again as the child writhed whimpering in the man's grip. She stepped through the doorway. Damn, the man's body was partly covered by the squirming girl. He hadn't seen her as yet. She stepped back into cover again, pulling off her top. Her gun she tucked into the waistband of her jeans at the small of her back. Bare-breasted she walked into the room. Shay pouted deliberately, and thrust out her breasts.

"Geeze, what would you want with a kid? Bet I could do a lot more for you than she can." Her tone was coarse.

His eyes widened as he focused and he grinned at her, he wouldn't mind this one. From what he'd seen she wouldn't be the passive kind anyway. His grip loosened and Pam was gone.

Shay smiled into his eyes, watched as his smirk grew, then sudden terror pulled his features askew as her hand slid behind her and the gun came up.

"No, *no!*'

"That's what Pam said. You didn't listen. Too bad."

He leaped for her in a twisting motion. The gun boomed, the pattern of shot catching his shoulder, slamming him backwards. The shot was a off-centre, but it would do. Shay considered the shuddering body clinically. He'd die, just not quite yet. Running footsteps sounded as two joined her in the doorway. Shay glanced at them.

"He had Pam. He was trying to make her blow him. Any objections?" Behind them Pam had returned, holding Jo's hand and shivering. On the floor the man looked up.

"Little bitch cock-teaser. I shouldn'a fucked you back at the base."

Shay smiled chillingly down at him. 'I thought you might have tried something then. That was your trial, you just confessed." She shot again, the close-range shell blowing away half his head. "Someone drag this fuckin' dog shit out of here and dump it. It stinks up the air for the rest of us." The two men in the doorway moved in.

Mike and Rome had risen early and not bothered with makeup. Faces hardened by a tiring day's driving, they looked far more male than their first impression. The anger in their eyes helped. Wordlessly they took the heels and hauled. The body left a trail of blood and brains. Pam stared down and vomited violently. Jo held her.

"Did you have to kill him in front of her?" she asked.

Shay glanced up. "Yes. She had to know what happens to anyone who tries to hurt her like that. I knew he'd scared her some way."

She crouched on her heels, gentle fingers turning the child's face towards her. A window slammed, footsteps returned and halted. It was Rome who spoke.

"We dropped him out of the east window into the alley. Dogs will clean him up."

Pam was sneaking quick looks at them all.

"Come on, Pammie, tell me what happened?"

"He... he said I was pretty. He said I should come with him and he'd show me something."

"Back at the base?"

"Yes. I did 'n' then he grabbed me. He put his hands...' She choked. 'He was like the other man who tried to hurt me 'n' Billie. I fought until my dress tore and I ran."

"So after that you stayed away from him. You should have told Jo or me."

"He said if I told, I'd have an accident. He said little girls had accidents all the time."

"What happened just now?"

"I was looking for the bathroom. Billy said it was down this corridor. I came down here 'n' he jumped out at me. He made me come into that room an' then he...he wanted...he...e...e..." She dissolved into inarticulate sobs.

Shay stood, hard-eyed. "Well, he won't 'want' again. Anyone got anything to say about what I did?"

Mike's angry growl came a split second ahead of his lover's. "They'd better not have. By God I'd have tapa'd him myself if I'd been here first. Picking on little kids. We don't need any bloody perverts like that with us."

"Fuckin' right," came the endorsement from beside him.

A shrill voice made itself heard, "Well, I don't like it. What's there to say Johnny wasn't tricked into it? I mean, Shay's standing there showing us everything she's got. Maybe she asked and he said no. Then she just made it all up to get back at him. Johnny didn't need to fuck any kids. He's got me and Marion."

Mike turned. "You calling us all liars? We heard what Pam said.' He looked puzzled. 'Although why *are* you..."

Shay was slipping back into her top. "He had Pam held against him. I had to take him off guard. If I'd marched in there waving a gun, calling him what he was, then he'd have hung onto her and she could have been hurt. So I walked in bare, he eased up on the grip trying to figure which of us he'd rather have, Pam got away and I had a nice clear shot."

She turned to Jessie. "If you don't think that was justice, you're free to piss off. Take your personal gear and get out. You got tonight to make up your mind. Either you're in the driver's seat first thing or you're gone."

Jessie stared first at Shay before turning to face Jo. "Is she running this lot now?"

"Just when she's right." With that, she led Pam off to where savoury smells came from the building kitchen. The others, all but Jessie, fell in and followed.

After they'd completed an early dinner, Ngaire moved with the still nervous child to another room. She'd been far enough into her degree to know that Pam needed to talk out much of her horror. Already Ngaire was becoming counsellor to the growing group. Her blindness helped, they saw her as someone who had suffered too. In a way, knowing that she could not see their faces they felt more able to confide personal terrors. She'd heard from Billy twice about the original assault on him and his sister. Now Pam found a comforter as she confided further.

"Why did he want me to do that?"

"Because he was greedy."

"Greedy?" The child was puzzled. Ngaire reflected that Pam often seemed younger emotionally than her years. She thought that could possibly be caused by the trauma of the original attack. But now she replied as if to a younger girl.

"It's like when you have a whole box of chocolates. You can eat them all yourself, or share. Isn't it more fun to share with a friend?" Pam nodded slowly. "Then if you don't have any chocolates and really want some there's something else you can do. If you don't have any chocolates, you can steal them. Or take them from someone by force. That's greed. Wanting something you aren't offered. Do you understand?"

Pam's face lit with intelligence. "I think I do. An' it's easier to take something from someone who's smaller than you?"

"Exactly. Just remember that anyone you don't know could be like that. Even someone you know a little bit, or quite well. Trust people, but never let them do anything you know is wrong." She reached out and hugged the child gently. "But you can always come to me if there's a problem." She listened as the footsteps pattered away more confidently.

Shay too was busy listening, but unknown to those she had stalked. She sat on a last turn of stairs, one hand resting lightly on a gun. From the garage below the building came the sounds of muttering, two women arguing, and the clunk of a shutting truck door.

"I don't care. I'm not staying with them. They'll have to leave one of the trucks behind. What do I care? I don't need that Shay cow telling me what I can or can't do."

An indistinct objection from the other. Then the thump of a pack hitting the ground. "*No*, I said. You stay with them if you want. I'm getting out. Of course I didn't love that pig, but having him around was handy. I can pick up another man. None of this lot'll do me any good. A sick man, bunch'a kids, and two queers. They'll leave the truck and I can have it once they're gone. What?" A smug laugh. "Course I can get back in. There's a whole sets of spare keys and cards in the receptionist's desk out front. I picked up everything I'll need to get back in before I came down here."

Other footsteps rang on the concrete as Shay ran silently down the stairs. She saw the vanishing figure of one, the other who waited. She spoke as if surprised.

"You're really going then?"

"Yeah."

"Well, I just wanted to say, no hard feelings. Here." She thrust a bottle of brandy towards Jessie. "Have a drink of the good stuff and remember us. I'm sorry you won't be coming. Are you leaving now or will you stay the night?"

"Now." The word was a sullen grunt.

"Your choice. Don't drink all that at once. They say too much isn't good for you." There was a patronising note in her voice, which flicked the other woman on the raw. Her face flushed a dull red as she reached out to grasp the bottle.

"Thanks for nothing." She turned on her heel abruptly, snatched up the pack and marched for the door. She threw a demand over her shoulder. "Let me out of here.'"

"Whatever you say."

Shay noted the direction. She'd seen the glances at the truck. She'd also counted keys and cards as a check on what she'd heard. Jessie certainly could get back in once they'd headed North. Shay smiled unpleasantly. Madam out there had an agenda, but so did Shay. It fell under her second law. She took the lift to the top floor and once there she knew which window to use. Sure enough, she could see her quarry below and going to ground a block away. Shay descended to eat with the others, then announced her intention of making a final sweep of the area.

"Will you be gone long?" Jo was worried. "And did Jessie really leave?"

"She left all right. I checked that she only took her own stuff. I don't know how long I'll be. Maybe only an hour, maybe longer, but don't worry."

"Take care."

Shay padded out of the garage entrance, having met Mike and Rome checking the trucks as she slipped away through the side door. They looked at each other as she disappeared. Neither spoke, and after a moment they returned upstairs and said nothing. The girl paced down the street, a dark flicker like the other late evening shadows.

Shay found the building she had seen Jessie enter. She inspected it carefully from cover. It was a shop selling furnishing and bedding. She smiled grimly. Beds to lie back on, sheets, blankets, and all the comforts of home. She checked the side. Ah hah. She thought she'd seen a fire escape from their building. She ghosted up it and in through a window she jiggered skillfully. Then she sat on the upper stairs to listen and watch.

Below in the storage area Jessie whined on aloud to herself. She saw recent events as grossly unfair. They'd forced her to leave. Damn, she'd miss Johnny, the sex wasn't bad and he'd done all the heavy work. She had only to stand back and talk admiringly about how strong he was. She didn't reckon he was really gonna hurt the kid. She'd been about the same age when she started an' it hadn't hurt her. Their precious Pam wasn't any better than Jessie was. Then that snot of a Shay had as good as said Jessie couldn't hold her booze. She took a hearty drink. Good expensive brandy too. She'd always liked brandy.

Shay was aware of that. She remembered everything she heard — or overheard. In the past it had often been useful. She watched as the woman drank again. The complaints became louder as the brandy hit the spot. Jessie'd show them. So they were going north, were they? And perhaps she could find other men here who'd see that they didn't. That fancy pants lot would make good pickings for a few men who'd share. She tilted the bottle again. Pheeoo, but this was the good stuff. She was feeling wonderful. Like being wrapped in pink fluffy clouds. She gradually slumped back on the bed.

Shay waited. An hour later there had been no further movement from the still figure. She padded down the stairs. Never leave an enemy behind without making absolutely sure of them if you could. She'd known someone once who'd been in the paras. That's what he'd always said. She reckoned these days it was even better advice. Jessie moved a little but the laced brandy held her from waking.

Shay reached into her pocket and produced a handful of white pills. She dumped half that into the sagging mouth, Jessie swallowed when the brandy bottle was tipped to wash them down. She swallowed the other half of the pills, the remainder of the brandy, until Shay knew it was sufficient to do the job. She tossed a blanket over the sprawled woman and her pack.

"Goodbye, Jessie. You won't be arranging for anyone to follow us now."

She was sleeping peacefully when Jo called. Before ten the convoy was on its way north. Behind them the last of the summer's flies were already homing eagerly towards a furnishing and bedding shop. Humanity had always done very well by *them*.

Chapter Five

With two drivers gone and only one replacement, there had been a quick conference. It had been Fred who was able to manage a solution.

"I told you these trucks can be towed. There's gear here that means we can make the spare into an articulation for another one."

"What about the weight?" Jo asked. "Won't that be too much for one engine?"

"Nope. She'll go through fuel like water but the engine will cope, just so long as we keep the speed down."

He'd dug out the bars needed and hooked everything up. Rome, to their surprise, admitted to a heavy traffic license. He was given the articulated result and drove it efficiently. They did have to keep their speed down — to around 50Km even on the open road. But to Jo's mind, that was better than having to leave one of the trucks behind. Fred, when questioned, had said that all the trucks were equipped that way. After the morning, Jo took over Billy's truck as an articulated section to her own. That way they could use him as a scout.

That first day had been quiet, just the trucks rolling slowly through quiet countryside, passing small towns and clumps of houses. Now and again they had to detour tangles of cars partway across the road. In some the bodies of their owners still lay. The trucks were powerful though and their winches made quick work of any obstructions. The group had chosen to swing further to the West, passing Feilding, Bulls and up the coast. The roads were almost as wide and the townships smaller. Thus there were fewer road-blocks to sort out. Jo pushed them, not in speed but in hours. They continued without stopping other than quick dashes into bushes, until it was near dusk.

Then Rome signalled. "Truck's getting hot."

They halted. Jo and Shay, who had walked up the line to join her, peered at the temperature gauge.

Shay glanced in at it, then at Jo. "He's right. We should park."

"Where?"

Shay turned, calling, "Mike, can you run my bike out? Billy 'n I'll head out to look up the road aways." There came a distant assent and the clang of a ramp. She turned back. "We'll check up the next five K or so. The truck will make that much further without problems, I reckon and after this we'd better keep scouts out on the bikes. Be safer."

Mike wheeled the bike up and she slid astride, pressing the starter. With a yell, Billy was off after her. The hum of the two bikes faded up the road. Hari was taking the opportunity to cuddle the baby. Marion, the last of the trio, stood alone. Jo watched her out of the corner of her eye.

She heard the bikes return. Shay spun to a halt in front with a broad grin. Billy spun in beside her, whooping.

"Perfect place just up around the bend. It isn't more than a couple of K. All the beds we need, food, drink, bathrooms and all."

Ani was squealing in excitement but Jo was more cautious. "Are you sure it isn't occupied? You weren't gone long."

"It's occupied, one of those country pubs. They said to come in. We're their first customers in the month." She looked up, "I'd say they were maro, but crazy in the nicest way. They've convinced themselves that the tourists are just having a bad year. But they aren't dangerous. They're a couple of mid-lifers who can't quite handle what happened."

"Okay, then we'll take up the offer." She climbed into her seat to start the engine again. They moved on around the bend to come into sight of the old building. Outside two people stood, waving happily. Jo parked in front of the hotel, dropped from her seat and walked to meet them. They looked harmless to her as well, she thought.

The women took her hand eagerly. "It's so wonderful to have tourists through again. How many of you are there? Will you be wanting a cooked breakfast in the morning? Are you staying just the night? Is there anything special I could arrange? I'm Mary Jorgansen and this is my husband Alec."

Jo broke in before she lost track of the spate. "There's seventeen of us counting a baby. We'd love a cooked breakfast for us all. I'm sorry but we're on our way North so we'll only stay tonight. Would there be a cot available for the baby?"

The woman beamed. "There certainly would. Please come in and register. I'll give you a list of our charges." She led Jo into the office, placed the register before her then asked, "Cash or charge?"

"Cash. I'll pay you as soon as we're settled in if that's all right?"

"Oh, perfectly, my dear." She bustled out and Jo fled to find Shay. She was fighting an urge to giggle at the unreality of it all.

"You'll have to make a run up the line on one of the bikes."

"Why?"

"Because your nice, slightly mad landlady expects to be paid cash tonight. From the map there's a township just another two or three K up the road. Raid a couple of shops or the bank or something. If you can't find any money, and there isn't much about nowadays, then look for a cheque book. Since it'll never be cashed, it won't matter."

"Well, okay. But I'll take Rome on the other bike. He can ride and use a gun."

"Fine." She trotted back to sort out rooms and baths for the children. In an hour, she heard the bikes return, then Shay's light footsteps,

"Well?"

"No problem. Rome's putting the bikes away. Here." She thrust a small canvas sack into Jo's hands. "The bank wasn't locked up since the manager's dead on the floor. I got a stack of money out of the vault, all in mixed bills." She grinned. "I took a bunch of coins too. Just in case we run across any vending machines that still have stock. The kids would love to work them."

"Clever."

Shay's look was smug. "I thought so."

"Go and grab your bath while there's hot water left. Tea'll be ready in an hour. The old lady offered to cook for us if we pay extra. Seems her husband isn't a bad shot and we're having mutton."

Her friend whistled. "I wonder how they reconcile that with everything else they want to believe?"

"I don't know. It isn't any of our business anyhow. There's no way they'd come with us, so we'll never see them again. Will you stop yattering and get your bath. I'm not waiting to eat for any longer than I have to."

Shay chuckled as she vanished in the direction of the bathroom.

They found that the food was excellent. As a gesture, Jo checked the price list, ordering cooked breakfasts for all. Then she paid the presented bill. Afterwards, she chatted as she helped with the dishes. She'd wondered how this pair managed, although from what they said, they'd been so pleased to see Jo's group because of the money. They travelled into the next township once a week, solemnly "shopped", leaving money at the stores before returning home. That was why they had looked so pleased then about the cash payment. She guessed they have to shop again after providing food for her group.

Quietly Jo slipped away to the office. Once there, she took out the canvas sack and emptied it into the till. She arranged the bills in their proper compartments. Shay had come back with enough to buy food at a two-people rate for years. If no one else came by less happy to cater to the old people's fantasy or if a dog pack didn't get them, then this would give them a while longer before reality intruded.

She stood looking up at the stars a moment as she left the office. How many others were out there like this couple? People who couldn't live with what had occurred. Ones and twos who'd drifted into a fantasy they found preferable to the reality that was too bitter to accept. This had to be the secondary effect that the man on the radio had talked about.

A city the size of Wellington should have had thousands surviving initially. They'd found only a handful, with two of those already self-destructing. Fred and Hine too might not live beyond another couple of years. Out of those they'd found, then, almost half were dead or dying shortly and in the smaller places where only one or two people might have survived in the entire township, they'd have left — or gone mad, committed suicide.

For the first time in weeks she remembered her father. Was he even alive? Was he somewhere in Michigan looking up at the same stars, worrying about her? The comfortable suburban middle-level life she'd lived seemed incredibly far away. It was growing chilly outside just standing here. She headed back.

Shay in her own way, too, had been kind. She waited until the trucks were lined up to leave. Then she considered the delicious food, the genuine kindness they'd received and decided to return it. She padded around the back of the hotel to find the old man.

"I'm a medic." The term was vague enough but still convincing. From her pocket she pulled a small bottle. "I'd like to leave you something. You're very isolated here and you may need them if a doctor can't get here quickly." She handed the bottle over. "If you take one it will stop really severe pain for six to eight hours. But do be careful. Three at once would be fatal to either you or your wife."

There would have been some fifty tablets inside the plastic container. His eyes lifted to hers and for a second a shrewd intelligence showed before being veiled again behind the gentle smile.

"Thank you, dear. Very kind of you to think of us like that. I promise we won't use them unless they're really necessary." He patted her arm. "I'll split them up too. That way we'll always have a few somewhere."

They could accept a portion of reality at need, they just preferred not to acknowledge it. A horn blew. She smiled quickly then ran to rejoin her friends.

It seemed like a reasonable deal to her, she thought as she drove away. They'd fed her, been polite and kind. In return, she'd given them a painless easy death when or if they required it. She'd checked various shops while in Wellington. Only the larger chemists carried that strength of pain-killer, and mostly of them were locked away securely. Not that locks mattered now, a tyre-lever was a good key. Once they arrived in Auckland, she'd raid every suitable shop. Already she'd found a use for them twice. At that rate there'd be a lot more times they'd come in handy.

Ahead of them Jo was recalling the woman they'd left behind in Palmerston North. Poor Jessie. Jo just hoped the woman was managing, but it had been her decision. She sighed. Some people were fools but you couldn't cure the world of that. She drove on, admiring the day.

If one looked for them, there were growing signs even here that things were changing. In some places, fences had fallen, helped either by desperate animals or perhaps by still more frantic people. Now and again they passed a house burned to the ground. Around those standing, the lawns were already knee-high. Weeds were taking over once-tidy gardens. Branches littered one section of road. A storm had ripped them from a nearby row of trees and there had been none to clear them again. As they travelled, they halted several times at seaside townships. There may have been people hiding, but they saw and heard no one.

Over the time driving north Mike and Rome had changed day by day. Jo watched the transformation with a quiet smile. She had become certain that their first appearance as Michaela and friend, loaded with false eyelashes and makeup had been a try on. They never bothered with that sort of thing nowadays. Their voices were clearly male, not harsh but deeper in register. The fluttery mannerisms had been dropped. On one halt Ani went exploring slipping away alone before anyone realised she was gone. Rome and Mike were closest when she screamed. Both dived for the sound, shotguns already lifting.

"Ani, *drop!*"

The child obeyed as Rome shot over her crouching form. Mike leaped forward to met the charge of the dog, caught it by one shoulder and whirled it, throwing it sideways away from the child. Rome's shotgun boomed again. The others of the group were all there within minutes, asking questions as Mike comforted Ani. Shay arrived glaring at the bodies of two of the largest dogs she'd ever seen.

"What was all that about?"

Rome looked up. "Dog attack. The bitch has been injured, looks as if she took on a cow or something big and got a leg smashed. She was crazy with pain and starvation. Ani must have walked right into them. She screamed, Mike and I shot the dogs."

He left it at that but later Shay got the story from Ani and came in search of the two men. She said little but from what she did say they understood the depth of her gratitude. Gradually everyone began to mesh as a group, each learning what they could do best. In her own quiet way, it was Ngaire who often solved disputes. In return, the children took her as their charge. They fetched and carried, watched her footing, and scavenged shops for bright skeins of wool. A jersey knitted by her had become a status symbol. In turn she did as Shay had once suggested, taking the moonless hours of the night as her turn on watch. She taught several of her companions to knit or crochet as well. More wool was looted until Jo complained, laughing, that they would soon have more than any flock.

Seeing their acceptance within the group both Mike and Rome had ceased to don the make-up and eyelashes. They appeared instead as two quiet-spoken men in their thirties. Competent, pleasant enough in looks, and, when clad in jeans and jerseys, no different in appearance from any other men of their age.

"Is Rome your real name?" Jo was curious as they halted once to eat and rest.

He grinned at her. "Nope. I was called Gavin. Who wouldn't want to change that?"

"I don't think it's that bad."

"Well, maybe not. But I didn't like it. I spent time in Rome when I was in my early twenties. I met Mike there. We teamed up, and I changed my name to Rome legally before we came back to New Zealand. Mike and I have been together ever since. That's almost twelve years, not a bad record."

Jo nodded. "Not bad for any couple."

They passed through town after town. Mostly the small convoy ground quietly along the outer roads, skirting city centres. Then it was Hamilton, a deserted haunted place bearing the marks of several unchecked fires. Again and again they had to spend time clearing a path. Even skirting the centre of towns they sometimes found roads that were heavily blocked. Two more of the trucks were over-heating with the slow pace and overloading. They stopped for Fred to do what he could. But from the maps they were almost in sight of the metropolis. Quick repairs would hold the vehicles for a while longer. None of them wished to rest. An excitement was beginning to possess them — north, the longed for goal.

Again they drove slowly but steadily all day. With Hari rode two of the girls, caring for the baby, so no stops were necessary. By night they had rocked and ground their way to a point where countryside was beginning to give way to suburbs. Ahead loomed the skyscrapers of Auckland, hard outlines against a sunset sky.

They stayed over-night at what had once been a guest house and motel. It had been an attractive small boarding house, a single-storied building, with twenty, ground-level, single-room cabins attached in a double rows. This time no kindly welcome awaited, only the stench of rotting bodies when Jan opened a wrong door. She backed out shaking, her face green with nausea. Silently Mike brought mattresses from another room at a distance. He laid them along the door, wedging them in firmly. Rome found air-freshener. That also helped, so that their small group were able to choose rooms all at some distance without distress.

Morning came. Jo called a conference as they sat over breakfast. How long electricity would last she had no way of knowing, but the power still flowed in this suburb at least. She had found ham, eggs, steak, and butter, all safely preserved in a fridge-freezer.

"Now, we have to make a major decision. Do we go straight through Auckland, find this place of Shay's and settle in, unpack, get comfortable, then come back? Or do we try to pick up extra people and gear on the way through to save time?"

Fred spoke firmly. "No. Best to find a base and operate from that. If that can be fortified, then all the better."

Jo blinked "Are you expecting someone?"

He stared at her, exasperated. "Use the sense you were given, girl. We have powerful, expensive vehicles, lots of women, and, if we find this place of Shay's, possibly a real town starting up again. I can think of the kind who'd love to take that over."

Shay chimed in, "So can I. We had one with us for a day or two, didn't we?" Involuntarily they turned to look at Marion, who blushed unhappily. She'd neither liked not trusted Johnny, but with everyone she knew dead around her, she'd gone with him, done whatever he demanded after he'd found her sitting helplessly in her house. Her husband had always told her what to do, and her father before him. With both of them dead she'd been paralyzed with indecision. Johnny had known what to do. He ordered and she obeyed. Shay was continuing.

"From what I remember of it, the place *could* be fortified if we get heavy machinery from the council depot near there. Mike and Rome know how to drive that kind of stuff. I reckon I could manage most of it myself if I had to. If we threw up reinforced concrete walls around all the buildings, and maybe dig a moat and divert the stream around it, put in a big set of gates.

"It'd take weeks to do the work, but some of that machinery can be programmed once you've decided what you want it to do. Rome knows how. That way we could leave the kids, Hari and maybe Hine there safe. A place like that could be easily defended by a few women and the kids once the gates were shut. Particularly if we comb local towns for a few more people to join us first. What do you all reckon?"

Jo listened. It seemed to make sense to them all. Auckland could wait a few weeks. It wasn't as if anyone there was likely to trail them north, or even to find them if they tried. The next day, they swept majestically through in convoy. From somewhere Shay had unearthed a loudspeaker and rigged it to the roof of her truck. As she passed she spoke into the face-piece clipped to her helmet.

"We're coming back in a week or two. If you'd be interested in joining us, start making your way north. When you see trucks like these come out, stand in the open with empty hands. We can talk... We're coming back in a week or two. If you'd be interested in joining us — " The loudspeaker sent the words booming clearly through the streets. It had been Hine's idea. A way of readying possible applicants, as she'd put it. It risked nothing, committed them to nothing but it could save a lot of time if or when they came back this way seeking recruits.

They passed northern suburbs once they were on the other side of the harbour. In another hour, they had broken through into country again. Houses thinned out, fields appeared. But to Jo's surprise, sheep and cattle seemed to have also thinned out although they saw increasing numbers of rabbits. The group halted so all could stretch their legs. She wandered around her truck with Mike, commenting on the phenomenon.

"I saw that too. I had a very nasty idea about it. You and Shay both mentioned loose dogs. What if for some reason most of the dogs ended up on this side of the city? Cities are great places for rats and mice to live. Cats would make out on them there and they could catch birds, but the dogs would have to go somewhere."

"Why would they all head North?"

"Because of the fires."

Jo looked at him, bewildered. "Fires, what fires?"

"You didn't see, I guess. But I went up to the top of that building next to the motel last thing before we left. Shay's got a few pairs of great binoculars. From there, with them, we could see that a couple of big areas on the southern side were all burned out. Neither of them was on the path we took coming through the city, but you could see them in the distance. If the breeze blew north from them, them any dog with sense would move to get away from it. Judging by what we could see, the fires could have started not long after the main wave of the bug hit."

"Hell!" Jo said, angry at fate.

"Yeah."

"That'll make it a lot more dangerous. We'll have to stick together, pairs or three at the least and plenty of firepower."

"That won't be all. We can use dogs of our own. They'll bark, warn us about people trying to get in. We can use them to hunt. If we find a pack, we should see if we can pick up a few small puppies, old enough to eat meat but only just."

"You know about dogs?"

"Some, so does Rome. We used to have a couple. They both died of old age last year. We hadn't gotten around to getting any more when the bug hit."

"Then you two are chief dog handlers. Try to drive it into everyone's heads how dangerous they could be." She glanced at her watch. "We're off again." He nodded as she ran for her own vehicle.

They halted the night, huddling together in an abandoned motel. First light and they were on the road again. Now they were into the country Shay remembered. She took the lead again, guiding them to the head of the Hokianga Harbour and then down a seemingly endless, circling, maze of narrow side-roads. Finally they left even these for a dirt path that swept around the curve of a stream. Shay halted her truck and signalled them to join her as she studied a gate ahead.

"That's the entrance. There's no sign of any car having been through recently. Some of the women had pushbikes. No tyre marks either."

"What do you think?"

"I think either they're all dead in there or they've decided to hole up as long as they can before coming out. We have to get in, find out which it is. Some of the local women knew about this place. Some may even have come in on foot if they survived. If there is anyone there they may remember me. I'll go ahead, to talk if there's someone there; if not, I'll come back."

Before Jo could suggest some kind of cover, Shay was gone, loping casually up the track. She gazed after Shay in affectionate amusement. By now she knew that if the girl believed there to be any real danger she would not have risked herself. Shay was fond of her skin. She intended to keep it intact as far as possible. But she also enjoyed making like a hero at times. Without comment, Mike passed her a pair of the binoculars. She watched as the girl trotted up the slight slope. The place would be very defensible, if it was surrounded by a good high wall and had decent gates.

Shay could be close-mouthed about her past. Now and again she let something slip. They'd made it a habit in the group not to ask too much about people's pasts. If anyone wanted to share that was fine. But for some it was too painful to talk about as yet. For others, well likely there were a few things they might not want known. Shay had told her something of this place. It was a refuge for women in two senses. Some came here to escape violent men, others' to escape the modern world. Here too it was the custom to ask few questions.

Jo gazed around, sweeping the lenses to and fro. The area flattened out here but with a shallow plateau rising in the centre of the flat land. It was on that someone had built the original farmhouse. This gave it a good elevation above the area. It would also have caught the wind but for the mountains curving in a semi-circle on the prevailing side. Yet they weren't so close that a sniper could shoot down among the buildings. She eyed those carefully. Shay had said that originally there had been only one house, a large one, but still one only. The son of the original owner had brought in two, cheap, re-locatable houses and placed them to form three sides of a square.

According to Shay he had died somewhere, somehow, and the women's group had then purchased the property. They had brought in a fourth house. That filled in the gap, giving them a completely enclosed sheltered courtyard in the centre. It was where they had held many of the meetings. It also made the houses difficult to search either quickly or easily if a husband came looking. Since it was often used as a women's refuge, this was of considerable aid to them. Numbers in Shay's time had fluctuated heavily. There was a core of perhaps five women who stayed permanently. Others came and went, with numbers occasionally as high as twenty.

That was adults. Counting children at any time could double the number. But spread across all the buildings, there were fourteen bedrooms. Most were double or even triple in size. It allowed any inhabitant their privacy. One of the women taken in had been a qualified plumber. Shay had been amused when she told Jo about that, it was the plumber who had seen to it that the power and water systems were in two forms. Water could be used from the mains or drawn by hand or powered pump from the stream. Electricity could come from the main grid, solar, wind, power or, in an emergency from a water generator. By the time Shay left, the group had almost achieved complete self-sufficiency in that they could provide most necessities.

Jo scanned further. It was beautiful country, a two hour walk, Shay had claimed, would take the walker to the harbour. There to fish, to swim, or just to enjoy the sea. Jo searched her memory of the maps. The lake couldn't be much more of a walk. Originally the lake had been shallow and muddy but a quake several years earlier had deepened it. A local farmer had paid for fish to stock the water. Shay could have chosen very wisely in convincing them to come here. Now all they had to worry about was the possible occupants in residence or roving dog packs outside.

Mike nudged her. "Shay's coming back."

They crowded around the gate waiting, knowing that from Shay's wide grin it was probably good news.

"We're in." Shay called as she got closer. "Two of them remembered me. I told them all about our lot. They like the idea but say they'll have to talk to all of us first. We're welcome to stay a few days and consider if we do want to stay. We should talk." Jo led her to one side. With her came Ngaire, Mike and Rome, Billy, Hine, and Fred.

"They're making conditions," Shay informed them quietly

"What?" Jo questioned." And aren't they being a bit casual about letting us in?"

Shay hesitated. "How many of you are real keen Christians?" There was a pause as they stared first at her then at each other.

Mike spoke first. "Rome and I used to go to the Church of John the Beloved Disciple. Not that we were dead keen, just — a lot of friends went there."

Billy and the two from the army base were already shaking their heads silently.

Ngaire spoke softly. "I used to be a Catholic but I never liked the way they treated women. I hadn't been for years. I guess you could say I'm nothing now."

Shay waited for Jo to speak. She cleared her throat. "Nothing really. My mother was one thing. Dad another. I ended up being neither."

"Then we likely don't have a problem. I didn't want to say anything before we made it here, no sense in asking for trouble. The original lot that started the women's commune here didn't much like the Christian religion. They said it was patriarchal and treated women as second-class. They were Pagans and that's what they practiced. A few Maori customs got added in along with bits of feminism." Shay looked around them. "In a way we've been doing the same with our lot. Agreement by consensus. I think they need us, and we'll be welcome, *if* we don't try to bring too-different ways. If we don't mind becoming Pagans or simply keeping our mouths shut about some of their customs, we'll be welcome."

Rome pounced on something. "Why do you think they need us?"

"I managed to get a good look around by walking the long way to the usual door. There are bullet holes around some of the doors and windows. A barn's been burned down recently. One of the women was wearing a bandage. I had the feeling they've been attacked, so wouldn't a whole bunch of us with guns and trucks be a real help around the place — if we fit in?"

Her eyes were fixed on Jo, who took a deep breath. "Yes. We would. I think we could fit in, too. How many are there now?"

"There's the two who remember me. Then there's a real old lady. I think she is or was somebody's mother. There are four more women who've come in since and there's five kids. One of the women has her husband with her. They allowed him in because both of them are quite old, around late fifties. They think he's less likely to cause trouble. They may have something there too."

She was clearly remembering Johnny and there was a soft mutter of agreement. "That's thirteen. Place is nowhere near full, and it could be easily expanded anyhow. Well, do we go up and talk?"

Jo was decisive. "Yes. Let's move, before it's too dark to see what we're doing."

She drove up the slope, parked her truck at an angle that she hoped inconvenienced no one. Then, as she sat there, the other trucks wheeled into line beside hers. She climbed down to follow Shay to the door. Within the opening, smiling, stood a plump middle-aged women. Jo was taken in a warm hug.

"Enter in the name of the Goddess and be welcome."

One by one they filed in, each receiving a kindly greeting, even Mike and Rome once a quick perceptive look had summed them up. The door shut and the newcomers were considered by twenty-six eyes.

"Sit, eat and drink in Her name." That was the woman who'd welcomed them. Jo guessed that she was normally the spokeswoman. "Once you're seated we can talk."

Obediently they sat, shared chilled milk and fresh bread with home-made butter and jam. If this was the usual standard of fare, Jo reflected, they'd have to carry her out kicking and screaming before she'd leave. She smiled to herself and settled to listen.

Chapter Six

It was the plump woman who had welcomed them who began the discussion. "Do any of you object to our religion?"

Jo could answer that, "No. I checked with those of us I could speak to and none of them object. In fact, I think most of us would quite happily join. If anyone doesn't agree, speak up now."

She scanned all the faces about her. Marion still looked sullen although for her that seemed to be a natural expression. She said nothing however and no other protest or objection was raised.

The other woman nodded. "I'll introduce us all then, I am Dana Cybele. I should explain. Those who join us may take chosen names to show their choice. My names commemorate two Goddesses, aspects of the Mother." She smiled across at Shay, "Just as your friend when she was with us chose her names."

That explained that. Jo had guessed that Shay had been self-named in some way. Later she would hope to be told about that, but this was not the time. Dana was introducing everyone in turn. Then, starting with Jo, each of their own group stood to say briefly who they were.

Dana gestured to the woman beside her to take up the story. This one had announced herself to be Neith. She was tall, with cropped hair, and powerful arms. Jo guessed her to be one of those who, like Shay, led if there was danger.

"We've had some problems. You know we hold to certain beliefs here. One of them is that none of us lead directly. Our choices are mostly made by consensus. Up in Kaitaia there is another group that's organised. Real traditional types. They'd like to have this place and they've had a couple of tries at shaking us out of it. Both times it was touch and go, There are more of them, but we had the cover here and we know every inch of ground. So far, we've managed to keep them out. Some of us would rather be dead than let them in anyhow." She sat down abruptly.

Shay stood. "How many of them are there?"

"Well — we don't know how many stayed home, but each time the ones who've attacked us have been about twenty to twenty-five."

Shay whistled, "Then you've done well holding them off. I think we shouldn't waste time with them." Her eyes collected nods and looks from her circle. "If we turn the tables and attack them one dark night, we'll have the advantage of surprise. Let us take a few days to sort things out. We can hide the trucks once all our gear is under cover. If they attack before then we can see to it. If not then it'll be our turn."

Neith reached over to grasp her arm in approval. Jo felt a strange anger. How dare that woman touch Shay. She looked away, bewildered at the surge of emotion. Now they were all looking at her. It was her job to make plans, to sort out arrangements. She began to do so very briskly.

It took several days and a barn raising. The new barn was placed on the site of the one burned in the last attack. But it was half as large again with two small back doors, one on the left one to the right at opposite ends. Into it went all the trucks with hay stacked before them but only one bale thick, in case they had to charge out. But by the time that was done, all was still quiet.

The two groups were integrating effectively and weapons had been shared. Neith and Shay were always off together, studying the lay of the land or talking; battle, ambush, and war.

"Shay, can you come talk a moment. I want to look at what to do with..." Shay waved in a way that said just a minute. She went on talking to Neith. Jo seethed. Damn it. Neith was always with Shay these days.

"Shay!"

"With you in a minute."

83

It was always the same lately. Jo found herself hating the very sight of them together without wanting to accept why. It made her short-tempered and almost belligerent. Shay was *her* friend while Neith was just an outsider. She tried to find things that she could do with Shay alone but Neith always seemed to have got there first.

"Shay, can you check the trucks over. I'll come and do it with you."

"S'okay. Neith and I already did it yesterday."

"What about the winches, we may need them for the building?"

"Done that too."

"You and Neith?"

"Yeah, she thought we should be prepared."

Jo nodded and walked away before she said something she might regret.

Billy and Bob, the boy from the army base, had been chosen to scout. Each morning they vanished on the bikes to spy around the roads. Both were armed with one of Shay's cut-down shotguns. Billy also carried a rifle with a scope and case. If they saw the attackers approaching they were to hold them up. Then, one would ride to bring warning. Shay amended that after a discussion with Neith a week later.

"We're ready to start putting up walls around here now. But once they see us doing that, it'll tell them more than we'd like them to know. From now on, you scout. If you see them, one watches whoever it is, but don't make any move against them unless you have to. The other one rides for me or Neith." She grinned at the disappointed looks. "Don't look like that. We need to know so we can ambush them. You'll be in on that?"

Her grin widened at the fervent assent. "I don't want you to be stupid. But if you scouted right up to their camp — where ever it is — it could be useful in case they don't attack, because if they don't, we'll have to."

"Uh-huh." The taciturn Bob.

Billy scowled thoughtfully. "You know, Shay. The wild dogs are getting dangerous. A big bunch had a go at me 'n Bob the other morning. I think a pack is working its way over in this direction. Maybe we should make sure that these men aren't over this way to see us, and clean out some of the dogs first."

"I'll talk to Neith about that. But it makes sense. Now go scout and be careful. We can't spare either of you and," she broke off, looking at them, "I'd better say this. If those men catch either of you, they'll try to make you tell."

"We know." Billy shivered. "I don't want any part of that. I plan to be real careful 'n so does Bob."

She saw them leave on the bikes, before walking back to find Jo. Her friend had been odd lately, sort of stand-offish and silent. Shay hoped she hadn't done or said anything to upset Jo. She was still wracking her memory to think of something when she found her.

"I've told the boys they're only to scout. No ambush, no risks. Mike and Rome say they have all the machinery here now to start on the walls. Everything is programmed, and we have all the material we should need. Do we start that, go to Auckland, or try to sort out this Kaitaia bunch first?"

"You're finally asking me?" "The tone was sarcastic.

"Of course I'm asking you. What do you think I just said?"

"Oh, I thought it might be a form. Just something you do to keep me happy." She didn't know why she was saying these things. It hurt her to see the puzzlement on Shay's face, then the growing anger.

"Look, what the fuck IS all this? You've been funny ever since we got here. Do you want us to leave or something?"

"Funny!" She mimicked Shay's voice viciously. "Funny means amusing, possibly witty. But then you have to be educated to know that."

Shay went white with anger. "And I'm not. What a pity." Her voice took on a savage edge. "What I was trying to say in my own uneducated fuckin' way, was that if there is something bothering you, it should come out into the open so I know. I'm sick of being bloody sniped at for nothing. If I've done something wrong, say so. Then we can clear this up now."

"Wrong? What could you *possibly* have done that was wrong? Little Miss Battle Maiden. Little Miss... "

There was the slam of a door. Jo sank to her knees, cradled her head in her arms. What was *wrong* with her? How could she have been so unpleasant? Shay had been her friend for weeks. She'd stood by her, done anything asked of her and listened to Jo's fears without ridicule. She brought them to this safe-haven, sharing a place that had been precious to her.

She knew some of their group had wondered about Shay. Why the self-sufficient tough-minded young woman stayed. Or why she had even joined them in the first place. Jo and Ngaire had talked about that over a couple of the quiet nights on guard just after they arrived. Ngaire had understood.

"Too many look at the outside, Shay has a heart. It may be well-hidden but it's there. That's why she saved Ani and took her along, and why she came to find her later on. Don't look at what Shay says. Look at her actions. The children all trust her, they follow her when she's around. Shay isn't obviously maternal, but there's a need in her to protect the weak, perhaps because she knows she's strong. It's an attribute that the best men have as well."

"We need to find some of them then. This place won't expand without men."

"I know, children need role models. Decent men provide that for both sexes." Ngaire chuckled in the darkness. "I don't think everyone here is cut out to be celibate either."

Jo remembered that conversation as she stood up wearily. There was work to be done; she couldn't stay in here moping all day. She wished she hadn't opened her mouth to Shay. Her stomach was churning and she felt sick, but she walked out to approve Dana's suggestion of an underground food store that would help to keep it cool as well. They retired to draw up plans on sheets of paper.

"If we have all this machinery we should use it while it still works and we have the fuel. What about an escape passage? We could put in an extra room made from those concrete blocks, onto a couple of the house corners?"

"You mean run the passage to the house, then build the extra rooms over the end?"

"Yes."

"We'd need to ventilate the tunnels."

"No. If we keep food supplies down there it shouldn't be necessary. As for the tunnels we just open both ends once a day. Make it a job for a couple of the children. A cross-draft will do the job. I'm not suggesting anyone live down there."

Jo smiled unwillingly. "Are you sure. I think if you had your way, half of this whole place would move underground."

"And why not so far as the supplies and gear are concerned? Earth doesn't burn, and if anyone gets inside the walls they'll have a much harder job finding things — or us. You did know we have a couple of our water tanks like that?"

"No?"

She listened to the explanation. It had been the plumber. She'd pointed out that it was always possible the stream could dry. It never had to date, but that was no guarantee. So she'd installed two huge concrete water tanks collecting all the rainwater. Then a pump, which could be easily screwed into a mounting just within the porch. It could be worked by power or by hand and would lift the cold clear water as needed.

"How deep down are these tanks?"

Dana laughed happily. "Deep. The tops are reinforced to hell and gone though. Don't worry. I know exactly where they are in relation to the house walls. I'll watch the machinery when it arrives. Have you decided yet what you're to do first?"

"Yes. One thing first, look Dana. We will need to ventilate the storerooms underground. If we ever need to retire there from an attack they'll need ventilation, and then too if someone is taking time hauling up something heavy."

Dana grunted. "Yes, all right, I hadn't thought that bit through. What else?"

"I think we need wipe out as many of the dogs as we can, so long as those men hold off another week. After that we make a run down to the city." Jo sighed. "There are so many things down there we could use if we could find them. We can't bring everything back, and we can't stock for a hundred years ahead. But I worry about our people. What will they have — what will their lives be like, in a hundred years? Will they have gone back to savagery?"

"They'll have more to begin with." Dana said consolingly. "Once we've dealt with the dogs and other problems, we should set up a school. Teach the children to read, to look up things in books — and computers while we have them. We may have to drop back in some ways, but not right to the beginning." She smiled, patting Jo's shoulder. "After all, we do have fire, the wheel, agriculture and domestic animals. We're well ahead of the game if we can just avoid making too many of the old mistakes."

"And we know a lot," Jo mused. "Our ancestors had to conceive new ideas, We already have the ideas. We just have to learn how to make them work again, especially if we can dump the ones that got us into this mess in the first place."

"Exactly. I think this time around we leave out planes perhaps." She laughed. "Now I have to be out helping Neith. She's extending the vegetable garden." She saw the involuntary flicker of emotion at the name. "You don't like her. Has she made...um, suggestions?"

"No." Jo's voice was curt, cutting off any discussion.

Dana persisted. "She's a good soul, Neith. She takes no for an answer, and she does more than her share of the work. I couldn't have kept us together when the bug hit if it hadn't been for her. Why does she bother you?"

"I'm not bothered," Jo snapped "Do we have to keep talking about her? 1 thought you had work to do."

Dana departed without another word, leaving Jo feeling guilty and angry at the feeling. That, too, was Neith's fault. Not content with destroying her friendship with Shay, she was now causing trouble with Dana. She stomped out to join the quiet Hari.

"Where are you going?"

"I thought I'd take the baby and gather nuts. There's a farm about a mile away with an orchard. Dana said I could have the carrier."

The item referred to was an adaptation of the electrically

powered citi-cars. It was no more than a large shallow bin on wheels, with two seats in front. It managed about fifteen kilometers an hour at top speed, but with its wide wheels, deep tread and gearing, it could climb quite steep slopes carrying heavy loads when fully charged.

"Mind if I come?"

"Of course not, Jo."

They pottered down the road, Hari holding the toddler while Jo drove. Once at the farm, the child was set down. She gurgled merrily, crawling across the turf to sit playing with a handful of nuts Hari provided.

"What are you going to call her? Have you thought of a name yet?"

Hari looked vague. "I dunno. I just call her baby." She brightened. "I could call her after my Aunt. She was Irish. Dana and them would like that."

"What was her name?"

"Maeve."

"That's a wonderful name. And you're right. Dana and the others would love it. We could have a proper naming ceremony next week."

Hari looked a little shy, but proud. "I'd like that. Would they all come?"

"I don't see why not. They'd bring presents and we'd have a feast." She laughed. "Pick all you can find. We might need it for Maeve's day."

She picked alone for an hour or so, carrying each basket as it filled to the carrier and emptying it there. Hari had moved away and the newly named Maeve had crawled after her. Jo was enjoying the warm sun, the mindless work. She stretched, hands in the small of her hack. Oof! All that bending to collect windfalls got to you after a while.

She gazed about. Once this place must have had problems with the site. Either that or it had been done to keep the prevailing wind from the house, because along the back of the building ran a high retaining wall. Originally a wall of open concrete blocks, the gaps were now choked with earth and wall plants. The wall ran for quite a distance as such walls went, with an inward curve at each end. Hari had walked around and down to where there had once been a vegetable garden. Berries ripened there and Maeve sat eating handfuls, her small face juice-stained.

Hari walked back to directly below Jo where she stood on the wall. "If I toss this lot up to you it will save us time hauling them around or wasting the carrier's charge."

She heaved the sacks of cabbages and other greens up one by one. The wall was around eight feet high, but Hari's powerful arms tossed the sacks up to land lightly just over the edge. From there Jo hauled them a couple of steps to where she had moved the carrier. She looked at the load that was stacked in the bins and called down.

"It won't take much more. The others will be expecting us back for lunch soon. Let's go home now and we can come back later this afternoon?"

"I'll just get a last lot of berries. Maeve likes them."

She hurried back to the bushes while Jo repacked their carrier and returned to the edge of the wall. Just as she saw Hari stand to bring the berry baskets, dogs raced into view. Jo screamed, pointing frantically. There was no doubting the intent. It was a deliberate attack to bring down meat.

For the first and last time in her life, Hari moved both fast and intelligently. Seeing she would be unable to reach safety in time, she made three fast steps towards the pack, scooping up the startled Maeve. She raced for the wall. For a second her eyes looked up into Jo's. Then the howling baby was tossed upwards. Jo caught her. She hesitated but the dogs were already rising to pull down Hari. She fled. Not to the carrier -- they could catch that in a few bounds — but to the trees. There, almost in one movement, she hoisted the shrieking toddler into the branches, leaping and scrambling frantically upwards after her.

She was just in time. Below the wall she could hear the main part of the pack snarling over their grisly meal. She clutched Maeve to her as she wept and shook. Some of the pack had raced the length of the wall and now snarled, leaping high about her tree. Jo clung shivering to their branch.

In a firm grip she held the frantic toddler who howled, struggling, calling for "Mumma, Mumma" in a piercing wail. Jo soothed her as best she could. How long it would be before they were missed? She had no idea. She was therefore surprised when the rescue party arrived only an hour later. They came fully armed. A volley of shots, yelping dogs and racing engines caught her attention. It would, she thought, have been noticed in the middle of a storm, so loud was the resulting row.

She leaned down to hand Maeve to an anxious Dana. "How did you know we were in trouble?

"The boys. They were scouting. You know Shay gave them a pair of binoculars each?. Billy said he saw something moving by the old farm. That it looked like the dog pack. They got closer and saw they had someone treed. Bob stayed to watch while Billy rode back. Then Shay started yelling that Hari had taken the baby to collect stuff there. She knew because Hari got the carrier from her and Neith a hit earlier. Where *is* Hari? Was she trapped in the house?"

Jo's look answered that.

"Oh, Dear Goddess. How did it happen?"

"They caught her down there. I was up here with the carrier. She'd heave her sacks up while I packed it. Saved us going up, down, and around the wall all the time."

She gave a sudden dry sob. "You should have seen her, Dana. She knew she didn't have a hope of getting away in time, not if she ran to pick up the baby. But she did. Then she threw her up to me. I just made it to a tree with her but by then I think Hari was dead. She never even screamed."

Jo began to cry quietly, tears pouring down her face. "Hari had just decided the baby's name. She was going to call her Maeve after her Irish aunt. She knew that the name would please you too. She was so happy when I said we could have a naming day and a feast. Then she...the dogs..."

Her voice disappeared into her weeping while Dana held her close.

"Maeve wasn't even her baby," Jo wailed before her crying became desperate. Dana shook her head, speaking very gently. "Maeve *was* her baby. Hari chose it that way. She chose to love and care for her. She chose again when she saved her and not herself. We'll call her Maeve as Hari wanted. But she'll also be called Hari to remember her mother's sacrifice. We'll have a feast to farewell her mother and welcome Maeve's name. It is the way of the Goddess. Life and death are both hers."

She hugged Jo hard. "Stop crying. Hari made her own choices freely. Because of them she will be remembered." Dana grinned abruptly, "Probably long after either of us are forgotten. Now, let's see about tidying up things."

She left Jo, to walk down to where the mangled body sprawled. Unwillingly, but feeling she should do this, Jo followed. Dana stood looking down once they reached what was left of Hari. Her throat had been torn out, part of the breasts eaten, her face bore an expression of agony and terror, which sent Jo staggering to a nearby tree. There she leaned against the trunk and retched again and again. Dana came over.

"She would have died quickly, Jo. What we must do now is try to prevent it happening again."

Many of the now melded group had turned out to fight the dogs. Encircled, most of the pack had died. Only a handful had escaped and almost all of them were injured. Billy arrived in a small hail of stones as he skidded to a halt.

"Mike and Rome think the ones that escaped will go back to their den. They'll kill all the adults there but a couple of the females are in milk. They want to bring back pups if they can find any suitable. Bob's trailing the dogs. Mike's got a truck and wants to know if that'll be okay?"

Jo sniffed hard, lifting her head. "Tell Mike, go to it. If we'd had guard dogs, this wouldn't have happened. But he's not to go crazy. We still have to feed whatever he brings hack. We don't want to be over-run or eaten out of house and home."

"I'll tell him." He was gone in another shower of stones."

Dana stared down as chaos began to resolve. "I think Neith

and Shay are going with them,"

Jo's face went hard. "So? I'm going back to the house. Sort out someone to see to Maeve. Pam's always been good with her." Before Dana could speak again, she had gone, striding off across the grass, the set of her back saying clearly she wished to be alone.

Dana sighed. She was starting to grasp at least part of the problem. She wasn't sure how much of it she understood, but some of it anyway. The question was, was all this simple jealousy? Just a friend who feared the loss of another friend, or was it something more? Certainly she had never seen anything more than friendship between Shay and Jo, but both were very young to her eyes. It was possible neither of them understood their own emotions.

She tramped back slowly. Beside her, Fred and Hine drove the carrier, cradling the whimpering toddler who still cried for her mother. Hine was now more clearly pregnant, but she didn't look well. Jo had shared her concern about that with Dana, and Pam echoed it. The couple had both been very ill with the bug. They had survived without hospitalisation but like Jo, Dana was sure they had suffered some permanent damage. She prayed Hine would live to bear the child.

Before she'd found the way of the Goddess, Dana had been a geneticist in an amateur way. She'd worked with sheep, but people were pretty much the same. The wider the gene pool that they could build here, the safer the settlement would be generations down the track. They needed men too. But the problem there was with some of the older women. Originally one of the purposes of the place had been as a Rape Crisis Centre. Under Crisis Centre custom men were not permitted on the premises so abused women would feel safer. That would have to change.

Luckily there was very little family crossover. Most of those here had lost everyone else in their family. If they were stern over faulty genes or careless inbreeding, they should be safe. It would sound hard, but they must not allow the birth-damaged to survive, or if they did, they must not be permitted to breed where any fault could possibly be genetic. She'd talk to Neith and Shay about that. Both were pragmatists.

She plodded up the slope to the houses. The carrier was already being unpacked. She stood a moment to watch the children as they worked. Jo would make a good leader. She was still slightly too idealistic in the world they had to live in now, but Shay would balance that — if they could sort out their problems. Maybe she should discuss it with Neith. She might not have seen what was happening. Dana sighed again and went in to join the work.

A week drifted by as the older children took it in turns to scout the land. Another dog pack had moved closer with the old pack's territory newly available. Neith and Shay wasted no time is forming a raiding party. The new pack was ambushed and wiped out, all but a handful of puppies. Word of Hari's death had spread even to the children. Having the puppies made the distinction that Jo and Dana hoped for. Wild dogs were dangerous, but not all dogs were killers.

Some of the smaller children, over-hearing or told gory tales of Hari's death, had nightmares but the puppies were helping with that. The original pack too had yielded two litters. From these Mike and Rome had retained the largest and most healthy of them. This they now did with the offspring surviving from the second pack. Nine puppies played, barked, and ate as if encouraging a famine.

Shay eyed them, at first in amusement then in worry. They would run short of food if this continued. The idea was that the dogs helped humans hunt. This lot lay around eating. She took her indignation to Neith.

"They're a waste of space."

"Give them time or did you think dogs were born trained? Haven't you talked to Rome or Mike about it?"

"No, I thought dogs had instincts."

Neith hid a smile. "They do. But those instincts have to be trained. A sheepdog, even as a puppy, wants to run around a flock of sheep. But if it isn't taught just how to do that, all it will do is spook the flock, scatter them everywhere. A pup has to live with people for a while, start to accept them as its pack. Then it'll start to bark at strangers. That's the first use they'll be. You haven't

seen that because we haven't had any strangers arrive here yet."
She chuckled. "When you do, you'll see just how ferocious even a
puppy can sound."

Shay envisioned the fat lolloping puppies as trying to appear
ferocious, throwing back her head with a yell of laughter. Neith
joined in, neither noticing Jo as she arrived in the doorway. Jo
slipped away, her anger rising. Shay always seemed to be with
Neith when ever Jo wanted to talk to her. Going somewhere,
talking in corners, laughing together. Had they been laughing at
her? It felt as if they might have been.

Under her emotional upheaval she was aware that she was
being silly. It didn't matter. She hurt. Shay had been her friend
ever since they'd met. She'd been the one who stood with her,
backed up Jo's plans or decisions. It was unfair. Just because Neith
— come to that, what *was* Neith? An Amazon with all muscles and
no looks. No brains either in Jo's bitter estimation. She stomped
unobtrusively away from the building. There were other people
who liked her. She didn't need some uneducated kid.

Dana watched events in distress. Over the previous couple of
weeks she'd tried to patch matters. She could see the problem, but
none of the participants were looking at things squarely. Neith had
flatly refused to interfere.

"Look, Dana. I'm not doing anything. Shay comes to talk to me
because I make sense. And because that Jo won't talk to her any
more without a squabble. The kid's unhappy. She feels as if she's
done something wrong, but Jo won't say what or make up again.
I'm not going to make Shay more miserable by telling her to go
away. That way she'll start to think everyone hates her. Jo is just
going to have to work things out for herself. If she doesn't, then
she loses Shay. That's it!"

"But..."

"No buts. I said that's it and I meant that's it. Shay's a friend.
When Jo wants to act like one too, she'll be welcome. Until then
she can jam off. Okay?"

It wasn't, but then Neith too had a point. Dana retired
unhappily.

With both of the larger dog packs in the area gone, the humans turned their thoughts towards a return to Auckland. The presence of several of the older children might reassure those who approached them. If the rest were adults, they would have sufficient firepower to be safe. The discussion lasted late, but once it ended the trip participants had been decided, Shay, Neith, Mike, Rome, Billy and Pam were going. Dana took that list up with the participants the next day.

"Take Marion too. She thinks you don't trust her because she was with that man." She'd long since heard most of that tale — all but the finale Shay could have told, and didn't. "And you could do worse than to take one of the other girls near Pam's age too, before someone starts to whine about favouritism."

"Okay. We'll take Marion. You pick which girl comes with us from your original lot. We're taking only two trucks. That way we can have a driver in each, a gunner that's obvious, and a couple more in the back of each that aren't easily spotted. If anything does happens, then with luck whoever jumps us won't realise that we've got more fighters than they can see."

They left on an overcast morning. Jo was at the back of the group that came out to farewell them. The others were all making a fuss with everyone hugging and a couple of the smaller children teary-eyed. Jo felt abandoned and ignored. Her misery turned to a through-going sulk and she turned her back as she saw Shay looking for her. Let them go without her. She didn't need them. She didn't need any of them. She heard the trucks pull nut and off down the track. Then she retired to her room and cried. Shay wasn't her friend any more. She hadn't even asked if Jo would come with them.

In the truck Shay watched the road scowling. Jo hadn't even come to say good luck to her. They'd been friends. At least Shay thought they had been. Maybe it was all these new people. Jo had called her uneducated. She guessed that was it. With all these others around, Shay was just another dumb mug. She glared at the inoffensive scenery as they passed, gripping her shotgun angrily. Well, what the hell. She didn't need Jo. She had other friends here.

They spent the night in the same motel they had used on the way north. Neith and Shay insisted on guards, it was good practice. They clambered into the trucks the next morning feeling nervous. How many survivors had heard the broadcast message as the group came through last time. And how many of those had come north to wait for the trucks again.

With her mind on Jo, Shay almost missed the first figure. Then she saw movement from the right.

"Over there, someone waving," she yelped.

Mike slowed his vehicle while, driven by Rome, the second truck moved to cover them. Then Shay emerged, showing empty hands. The figure slowly approached.

Chapter Seven

Shay noticed the limp first, then that the one advancing was a man, maybe in his mid-twenties. From the looks of him he'd had a very rough time since he'd survived the bug. He was bedraggled, footsore and miserable. She hoped that didn't also mean that he was useless, unable to manage even with help.

"You're the army lot that went through a couple of weeks back?"

"We're that lot. Are you interested in joining us? We can offer three meals a day, hot water and a say in whatever happens."

His face twisted. "*Hot* water, I'd almost forgotten what that's like."

"Why, did the power go off where you are?"

"Look, that's why I'm out this far into the suburbs. I thought I should warn you. Where I was there's power. I lived right near central city. But some guy's taken over that bit. You joined him or ended up dead. He isn't much, but he's nasty."

Shay was joined by Mike, Neith and Rome who'd been listening. Rome brought food and a canteen. Their applicant ate, drank, and seemed to perk up with every mouthful. After that it was question time.

Rome summed up. "So this chap's acting like a warlord. You join him and have food and women or you don't and likely get a bullet. That's if you try to stay in any territory he wants. If you join, then try to leave, you get dead. Your friend joined up, and changed his mind once he found out what it was like. He got to you, told you all about this, then ran into what's-his-name, Tregan? They killed him for treason. You've been keeping an eye on Tregan ever since. How many fighters does he have?"

"A lot. I'm not saying they'd stay if they had a clear shot at getting away in one piece. But as things stand, they'll stick with him, It's safer. He keeps picking up another one here and there. Last I knew for sure there were maybe twenty would fight for him."

"Are there many other people who haven't joined up?"

"I guess so. We stay away from each other in case it's Tregan. but I've seen around eight or nine I reckon aren't with him."

"Is that all his name, Tregan?"

"No, I heard it's Philip, Philip Tregan, but Philip doesn't sound much like a hard man, so he uses just his surname."

"Excuse us."

Mike signalled them to draw aside, then he talked quietly. The young man sat happily working his way through the food they'd offered. He was all but moaning in bliss at the freshly baked bread.

Mike glanced back at him, smiling a little, "He's anchored a while. Now, what do we do? We don't want to run into this Tregan, not with twenty men backing him."

Neith snorted. "I'll tell you what you do. You pick up as many like him as you can." her head jerk indicated the man, "Then you take them home You leave the four of us, you and Rome if you're interested, and Shay and me. We scout Tregan's bunch. One day he's going to be alone. Just far away enough from cover for one of us to put a bullet into him. His bunch falls apart fighting over who gets to run things now. We pick up another bunch of the decent ones and the rest stay here. Kill each other off."

Shay chuckled. "Sounds good to me. I brought that rifle with the great scope. With that I could shoot his eyebrows off at a mile, easy. Gives us time to vanish, too."

"Rome, how do you feel about that?"

"Sounds good to me. Let Marion and Billy drive back with whoever we pick up." There was a murmur of agreement, Marion joining in looking pleased. "Okay. Let's tell our new friend what's happening. Not all of it though."

The man had finished eating and now sat eyeing them hopefully.

"You can join us. We're going to pick up a few more if they turn up. Tell us quietly if you know any of them aren't to be trusted. We'll keep you separate until we're ready to get out. Suit you?"

The man stood, extending his hand. "I'm Alex and I'll do my best. I swear."

"Right, Alex. Where should we start looking first?"

"Further in but not over the harbour. That's Tregan's area. Up along the bays would be most likely."

The trucks purred along empty streets. They went slowly with all nine pairs of eyes watching alertly. Gun barrels unobtrusively protruded an inch or two from the rear of each vehicle. In the cabs, too, the riders were ready. But nothing occurred that was more exciting than the appearance of others eager to join them. As Alex had said, they came in singles or couples. All nervously making certain the trucks were not part of Tregan's growing Central City Empire.

They broke off the search close to dusk. One of their new friends directed them to an old hotel where they slept, having posted guards from amongst the original eight first.

Neith took over as guard in the early hours while Shay retired to sleep. Neith's mind drifting into consideration of the various places one could stay. Motels weren't bad. They tended to be lines of cabins or attached rooms at ground level — useful for a fast departure. City hotels were more comfortable but dangerous. Most stood stories high and you couldn't leave in a hurry. The power in most parts of the cities had quit by now. Hundreds of steps might keep you fit but they were hell to use in an emergency. She liked the sound of the smaller country hotels and guest-houses Shay had used with her group on the way up. Like big houses but with extra bedrooms.

She sat up after an hour. She could hear someone moving. Footsteps pattered lightly down the stairs. She withdrew into shadow. It had been her idea to set guards, Rome's suggestion that they should mention this only to their own people. The figure slipped around the door and vanished into the dark. She'd recognised him. That was the young man who'd come in some hours after Alex reached them. He'd introduced himself as Terry Morgan. There'd been something likeable about him, too.

Neith cursed silently, there was no time to wake Shay and warn her what might be happening. She slipped out of her corner, falling in behind the figure as he padded slowly down the empty black streets. Neith drifted along behind him. She'd like to know where he was going and who he was meeting before she pounced. It was clear to her the fool had no idea he'd been followed. City people! Neith had been a deer and pig hunter and she was used to moving silently and unnoticed.

After several streets, her quarry suddenly dived into a shop. Neith closed in cautiously as a barely audible mutter of voices came to her ears. She listened as the one she'd trailed talked. Nice. Terry was giving these people the numbers of her group, the weapons they had, and being lyrical over the big powerful trucks before making it clear since he'd done all this he expected his share.

The man that she suspected was Tregan grunted and gave instructions. Terry was to get back fast and stick with this lot like glue. If he could find out where they were based, he was to leave with some believable excuse. If not he was to stay with them until he *could* find their base then he was to escape. He'd be given any of the women he wanted and a position beside Tregan if he succeeded.

Neith smothered a disbelieving snort. Terry Morgan was an idiot if he believed any of that. If he succeeded, he'd have proved himself dangerously competent. Tregan would have him murdered. If he failed, he'd be more likely to survive. Men setting up as warlords didn't like competition. Her teeth showed slightly in an evil smirk. Let the little weasel find out something to run back to his boss with. It wouldn't be the truth and it would anchor Tregan for their sniper rifle. She slipped back to the old hotel and vanished into the shadows. Minutes later the door creaked quietly open and a dark figure scurried back up the stairs. Terry the weasel had returned.

They cruised the streets, each day picking up a few more eager to join an established group. They were still keener when they found they would be allowed to have their say, that the group was at least partially democratic. At the end of a week, Terry Morgan was still with them. But they had also collected almost twenty more including Alex. Shay was disgusted.

"They've sat around out here moaning that Tregan is evil and should be stopped. There's as many out here as he has. Why didn't they stop moaning and start doing?"

Rome looked over at their new recruits. "Simple. Tregan has close to thirty fighters by now. Look at this lot, there's maybe ten fighters if that. The rest are old or kids. Some still aren't fully recovered from the bug. Some are fighting age but they've never raised their voice to the cat. Tregan probably wouldn't have had them if they *had* wanted to rush out and join him."

"Fat lot of use they'll be to us then." Shay sounded sour.

"You know better." Mike chided gently. "We'll teach them to use weapons. With a home and friends to fight for, they'll fight in a pinch. But we aren't Tregan. We'll fight to defend ourselves. We're not setting up an Empire."

Shay nodded politely, hiding her response. Her gaze met Neith's hard look. Maybe they weren't, but to be safe, they might have to do just that. It was much easier to be kind and generous from a position of power. She shut her mouth, wandering away to have a word with Billy and Pam.

"Just be kids. Over-excited with all these new friends. Not thinking what you're saying. You know what to let slip."

"Yeah. Don't worry, Shay. He'll never know it was on purpose."

She grinned hack companionably. "I know. I trust you both."

Later she watched from the corner of her eye as the weasel shifted. He seemed to slide from person to person, listening to conversations. Then he came to Pam and Billy as they talked, looking excited and happy.

"We aren't?"

"We are. Shay says so. We're going to dump this lot up at base in Helensville. Then we're coming back. Shay wants to go right through to the other side of the city."

"But what about this bad man?" That was Pam looking impossibly innocent and much younger than her age.

Billy threw out his chest. "We'll take care of him. He can't have more than a dozen men. Shay says we can just blast right through. If he makes trouble for us, we kill him." Their talk switched to other topics as the weasel drifted away again.

Shay moved over to where Neith stood with Rome and Mike. They shared a long interested look. "Think he took the bait?" she asked.

Neith smiled savagely. "He's nasty, not bright. We'll follow him. If he doesn't slip away tonight I'm a blue-arsed baboon."

Her humanity and lack of rear coloration was proven later when Terry convinced everyone they should return to the motel before departure. They'd let him work just hard enough at that to persuade him he'd done it himself. In the early hours he volunteered for a final scout about the area. Both Neith and Shay followed his path, returning to pass on the news.

Terry had almost bitten his tongue in trying to recount everything he had heard and as fast as possible to an impatient Tregan. It was clear Terry believed each word he shared. So convincing was he that they'd be surprised if it wasn't catching. That at least meant Tregan would be searching for their base a long distance away from it. And if they'd estimated his plans correctly, he would also sit tight, put out scouts to the north and await their return.

Terry had been clever about his disappearance as well, or so he believed. He'd fired a couple of shots. Far enough away that it would take time to find the place — if Shay's group looked. If they did they'd find blood, drag marks, and a dropped scarf Terry had worn. He could always reverse it. Claim he'd shot someone but taken a blow to the head and lain unfound in some corner where he'd reeled away to hide. Shay had found that amusing as she listened to him telling Tregan. Just let Terry try returning.

They packed everyone into the trucks. The scout bikes were run out with two of the new recruits riding ahead. Standing in the quiet street, the four waved them off. Terry hadn't come back so it must have been Tregan's plan to keep him for now. It was Neith's guess that Terry was claiming his reward. She wondered if he'd received what he was expecting. Somehow she doubted that.

"How far is the shop?"

Shay pointed. "About two Kay in that direction. I saw a whole bunch of road and off-motorbikes we can use. They're the new silenced models too. I say we tank them all up. Park spares here and there around the place, that way if we need a one fast, we may have one near us somewhere."

The day was spent in checking over the bikes as Shay suggested. They stashed several in shop corners over direct routes toward the inner city. After which they slept half of the night. The other half was spent riding quietly south. All the next day they slept again before rising to eat and travel south with increasing care. That night, they reached the core of Tregan's territory.

Now they were like rats, hiding all day, emerging only at night. They found that with no real opposition, Tregan's men had become casual, They still stood guard, but now they drank, talked or even brought their women with them. Several nights of spying and listening gave the four some excellent ammunition.

"He's waiting for us to come back." Shay sounded thoughtful.

"Uh-huh. Then he wipes out the trucks, goes on to where he thinks we have our base and cleans that up. Pity it won't work."

There was a soft snicker from them all.

"Only for him," Neith murmured. "Now, according to the guards last night, he's off to Queen Street tomorrow. I didn't get it all but I think from what I did hear, Terry pushed his claims for a reward too far. Tregan plans to string him up and invite everyone to watch. For some reason they use the area by the corner up there.

Rome spoke quietly. "You know the plan. Now we've found another gun shop we all have top-quality scopes. We split up into a half circle. Shay fires first at Tregan. Once we hear that we all start firing. Pick your targets, don't waste a shot. Try to get all the effective men, the ones who might pull this lot together again later on. You fire no more than ten shots. But they probably won't stay in the open for more than two or three."

Shay took over. "Once they've gone to cover, we run for it, back to where we put the other bikes. They're tanked up, spare petrol for each on the carrier, and with extra gear. We split again, head out of town. We meet up before dusk at Maungatapere. If you ride hard, you'll make it there by then. Anyone missing and we'll start back slowly to look for them. And I have something."

She dug in a pocket, producing a small tin. "I went to the vet's near the bike shop. They had these. I know about them." She proffered several on an outstretched palm. "Mercy pills. These ones are for horses. Take one, die in a couple of minutes painlessly. Put it somewhere that you can still reach with your hands tied. It'll be better than what you'd get from Tregan."

Rome nodded slowly. "Give me two. I'll put them different places." Mike took two, as did Neith. They hugged briefly, wordlessly, before starting the bikes. Kilometre by kilometre they edged into position over the dark hours.

Then it was sunrise. The guards were just coming into view dragging a writhing, twisting, yelling figure. Shay looked down coldly. It amused her, the biter bit. The traitor betrayed. Well, he'd asked for it, and from the looks of things Tregan planned to give it to him. There was a lot of shouting, a couple of shots fired, then the weasel was hauled up onto a rough gallows. She peered through the scope. That'd be her target. The big one making a speech. She stared at his face through the magnification, not a good man. You didn't have to be bright to see that. The hungry leer of anticipation as he waited to watch a man die was enough.

She made her shot with all the ability she possessed. She hung on the scope just long enough to see Tregan's head spray skull and brains, before shifting aim. A second shot took out a small man trying to yell some command or another. Other men were going down kicking as her friends fired. Abruptly the street was empty. As agreed, they made another head shot into every figure down that hadn't been hit squarely there already. Shay hooked the sling over her shoulder, trotted out to her bike and was away.

She had a brief glimpse of Rome before buildings hid him again.

That was one who was fine. She rode hard for the rendezvous. Changing bikes took only a minute before she was away again. Behind her as she glanced back she could see the other three following. They split again at the outskirts of the city, weaving and winding through country roads, fast riding until they met again that night, jubilant.

"How many?"

"I counted eight."

"I counted nine and I'd say some wounded got to cover."

"Some of those will die maybe?"

"They'll die or tie up friends looking after them. That's all to the good. If Tregan had as many fighters as we thought, he's lost around a third of them."

There was a mumble of agreement from Mike. "Tregan doesn't have anything any more. Not even a head." He turned to grin at the girl. "Geeze, Shay, but that was a lovely shot. When he went down, half of them just stood there flat-footed waiting for someone to tell them what to do."

"And the other half," Mike chimed in, "went flat thinking the shot had come from ground-level. It took them that much longer to get up again." He stretched and groaned. "Home tomorrow. It'll be good to see everyone again."

"How many did we send back? I lost count there towards the end." his partner asked.

"I counted twenty-three," Neith told them. "That shouldn't give our bunch any problems. Even without us there, they still had more and the proportions are pretty similar. The new lot was about half adults, half kids with more women than men. The women and kids will stick with us no matter what most of the men decide. They've mostly seen what happens if some guy is running the show. According to Alex that's why most of them wouldn't join Tregan. Men were the bosses in that bunch. Women were just the fun."

"So what about the ones left in Auckland?"

"Leave them for a month or two. After that we can make a run in force. See who might want to join up."

"Did anyone see what happened to our weasel?"

Shay began to giggle. "I did. I shot Tregan just as they were about to pull on the rope. Terry boy was out of the loop and gone before the body hit the ground. You could never trust him, but bugger me, I wouldn't mind breeding for that reaction time."

There was a howl of laughter at her words. The evening became merry as they teased, talked and finally slept. Next morning was fine again so they made good time. As they approached the houses, Shay with her quicker hearing signalled a halt.

"I don't know what that is, but something's wrong. Listen."

They sat on their bikes, engines turned off, as they strained to hear. It was dim, almost inaudible until a gust of wind brought it louder. It was a sound carried on the previous puff of air that had alerted Shay. Now they too could hear. Not much, just a confused sound with sharper noises now and again. Neith re-started her bike, moving forward down the road until she was closer, the other in line behind her. She halted as they all listened. Now the sounds were clearer and they could recognise them.

"Damn. We did mean to take a crack at that bunch further north before we left. Whose idea was it to go to the city first?" Neith was angry.

"Mine!" Rome informed her tartly. "Just as well. That lot will have found they're facing twice the numbers they expected."

Shay coughed theatrically. "And an attack from behind?"

Their gazes met in grim smiles. Mike scanned the countryside. "If we swing right around by the main road we could be at their backs in an hour. How's everyone for rifle ammo? If we use those first from well back, it may take them a while to see where the shots are coming from."

They rode down the highway. In the distance they could still hear the crackle of shots, the wind bringing it to them in gusts of sound. They circled, knowing their land. One of Jo's suggestions had been that they all took it in turns to scout. They had done so. Those who could ride the bikes did, and those who hadn't learned to ride as yet had been their passengers. Now that knowledge was paying off. They swung east again, homing in on the battle.

Short of the enemy, Shay halted them. "Fill up the bikes. If we have to run or chase them, either thing won't be helped by running out of gas. Fill your magazines too."

They unloaded the gas containers, petrol gurgling into the tanks, bullets clicking home in magazines. Old Fred had worked out brackets on the bikes to hold shotguns. In fact, the brackets swivelled and the guns could even be fired from these at need. Merely line the bike up, reach down, and there was an effect rather like firing a small cannon ahead of the rider. A cannon loaded with grapeshot.

They strung out again keeping each other in sight but moving to approach in a line across the enemy's rear. The firing continued. Everyone wished that they could let their friends know they were there, but the radios were built into the trucks. Next time, Shay reflected, they'd better take portable radios. Why the hell had no one thought of doing that before?

Ahead a small hill rounded upwards, another to the right. Shay leaned forward as the bike wheels bit in. Short of the summit she dropped from the seat, wheeling the bike a little further. She craned to look. Hmm. Much further and she'd skyline herself. She hooked the bike onto its footrest and moved forward on foot. With her stomach pressed to the ground, she peered over. Perfect. The enemy were mostly below her, with a sprinkling off to the right and left. Neith had taken the other hill. Mike and Rome had split again and were on the flat ground to either side of the hills.

She lined her rifle but before she could shoot, there came the bark of another gun. Damn! No, *no*! Oh... yes, wonderful. The idiots hadn't realised where that had come from. Rome must have run into an enemy stray and had to shoot. But the fools had taken it as someone in their own lot shooting too eagerly. She could hear the shouts for him not to waste bullets. She bit back a harsh laugh.

Then, sighting in her rifle, she began to shoot. One shot at a time, men who were apart from the others, men who were lying down so their deaths went un-noticed, at least right now. She shot whenever a ragged volley sounded from below. The sound of her own different shots vanished into that background. Although the enemy was beginning to notice, not exactly what was happening, just that something seemed to be killing men. They shifted more often, stirring uneasily.

She switched to figures at the back, still those apart or lying flat. She was in the best position. They were clear targets for her, small figures set up to be knocked over. She emptied the magazine and switched quickly to another filled one. From below came a warning yell as someone found a body in the wrong place. There was a burst of shouting. Then they were in retreat, swarming around the hills, racing for cover on foot. Some must have run into Mike and Rome. There was an outbreak of firing from those directions. She waited. No one with half a brain and in a hurry to escape ran uphill.

However the enemy appeared unexpectedly behind her. Back there in a clump of scrub they'd hidden four open land-rovers. Now they flung the cut scrub aside, frantic to get away. They still had not grasped the ambush; they only knew they were dying. Shay turned slowly, a quick movement would catch their eyes.

She began to shoot again coolly. The gun and scope she used was a specialist duo from Fred's army depot. It was superb, the magnification seeming to show each target as if it stood within metres of her. She kept shooting. First those who took a driver's seat, then she switched to the tires as the vehicles were moving. Men tumbled out, running anywhere to escape the searching fire, which always seemed to find them. Neith was shooting too, more exposed than Shay, who had slid under several low bushes that crowned her hill.

Below them the enemy were rallying, urged on by some bull-voiced idiot. She shot, missed, shot again, only to drop the man beside him. Shay swore. He'd have them charging back in a minute. Stand still, so I can shoot you, dammit! A rifle and scope of this kind was harder to use in some ways. It was intended for longer range or less active targets. On her own hill, Neith stood up. The shot was tricky, but if she could get him in her sights long enough... She held the shot until the target turned slightly. There. He was lined up exactly right. She forgot that while she was holding the sights others would see her. A form of buck fever had her. She'd make this kill if it... She never felt the bullet as her heart exploded in a bloody spray.

Shay had not seen Neith fall; she was too busy trying to line up the man herself. He paused to glance up at the hill and she shot again. A hit! That was enough. His men broke, running, hiding desperately as they slid through grass and scrub. Shay jumped for her bike. Now was the time to finish it. The more of them gone, the less of them there'd be to try this another time.

She hurled the bike downhill, Mike and Rome closing in from each side. Together they pursued those in frantic flight. Each time as they closed they halted to shoot. Finally there seemed to be no one left.

Mike noticed first. "What happened to Neith?"

"Maybe her bike wouldn't start?"

"And maybe not," Shay said grimly, whirling her machine as she raced back towards the hill.

They found her on her knees, cradling the limp and bloodied body. Rome squatted down beside them.

"Damn," he muttered, sitting back on his heels. "Right through the heart, no hope. She's gone. Here, I'll carry her. We can put her back of me to take home."

Shay was weeping as he lifted the body. Behind them, a man half-raised himself. Those were the bastards who'd done them. He'd get one before they saw him. He shot just as Mike saw the movement. His hand shot out, stiff-arming Shay sideways. She jerked as the bullet struck. A small cry of alarm was jolted from her. Then she was falling. Across the gathering blackness stitched the sound of a gun.

"Get him?"

"Dead centre! What about Shay?" She never heard the reply.

Chapter Eight

Shay was ill for many weeks. The bullet had passed through and medical books, drugs, and devoted nursing were available. But even so, the wound was one that would normally have required a surgeon and hospital. Having neither, they didn't meddle with it. Dana merely dressed the injury, filled Shay with antibiotics and anti-microbials, hoping for the best. They buried Neith beside Hari, wept as each in turn recounted something their friend had done, then left the graveside. Jo was in constant attendance on Shay. She blamed herself, sure that if she had not quarrelled with Shay, none of this would have happened.

During those weeks everyone worked. The survivors of the enemy group were hunted down. They discovered their base, and freed a number of women and children to join them if they wished. Most did. They even accepted a few of the men the women assured them were decent. Mike and Rome made a second run to Auckland with trucks and guns in force. From that they returned with fifteen additions to the group and news.

"With Philip dead, some other guy tried to take over. No one knows who did it, but they found him knifed. After that it all fell completely apart. With luck there won't be any more problems from that direction. Not unless they find another strong leader. Dog packs are getting worse though. One of the lot we found says that they saw three people killed when they got too far from cover. The brutes lair up on the city fringe, then move out during the day to hunt the countryside."

"I know. Neith said that once we had more weapons and people we should have a dog drive. Shoot all of them that we find."

Dana sighed. "There are so many things we should do at once. Do you realize we've got more than eighty people here now?"

"I know, and most of them are sleeping in makeshift barracks. We have to sort that out soon too. Otherwise we could have diseases starting up. There's the old farm a couple of K away, the one where Hari was killed. If we added more rooms to the main building, and added out-building, then made it defensible like this place, we could shift half of them over to live there."

Rome nodded, "Mike and I can work the heavy construction machinery. Most of it is programmed. Once you've got it here and fed the on-board computers the instructions and parameters, it just goes ahead. Shay, Mike, and I did all of that before Shay got hurt. All we need to do is organise the materials and people to feed it to them. We could do the walls around here first. Then do the farm, and I think..." he paused.

Mike continued for him. "We think we should build at least one more place halfway between them. We should have an underground way that links them all. We need to start making long-range plans and stop muddling through day by day. We're in this for the long haul."

Dana considered that. "Why the hurry?"

"Fuel. Those machines eat the stuff. There's a limit as to how far we can transport it from somewhere else to here. No more will be coming into the country either. And the longer we leave it, the more possible it is that it could get contaminated with water leaks or other things." He shrugged. "There's something else to remember. You forget it here with your own power.

Dana looked stunned. "You're right. I suppose all of the fuel is in underground tanks. Once the power shuts down, it won't pump up."

"Exactly. More and more of the Auckland suburbs are out now. The fuel tanks there are still working though, because most of them are on an emergency generator. Civil Defense regulations, remember? But sooner or later some bright spark will think of tearing them out to use in some place of their own. Or they'll start to break down anyway. We reckon a run with every tanker we can find and every driver we have. Once we start the work it continues so long as we can think of something we may need and the fuel holds out."

Dana was decisive. "Then start. Do the walls around here first, then the farm. Do you have plans?"

She leaned over to study the plans as they were laid out section after section. She opened her mouth and subsided again. Walls ten feet high seemed ridiculous, but if they were planning for the distant future, well perhaps. Two separate underground roads to run between all three forts — with the forts spaced in a triangle, each covering the other. Escape tunnels to the outer countryside from each. She glanced up.

"But everyone will know about those?" She placed a finger on the dotted line with the legend "escape route" beside it.

Mike produced a cunning grin. "They'll know about the ones in the other forts, sure. But Shay and I found a borer in the council depot. It's for putting in concrete drain-pipes. The big ones around one point eight meters. It's designed to start at one end of a point and bore to the other, laying pipe as it goes. If we can get everyone out of here, we can do it without them knowing. That's why we want to do the walls here first." He chuckled.

He and Rome had discussed all that with Shay before their trip to Auckland the first time. It had been her idea that they should have ways out that very few knew about. The borer would provide it, but they must have some noise to cover the sound of it working underground. The walls would do that. Then, if they could empty the main homes here for a day, they could break through and cover the entrance.

"What material does this gadget use?"

"That's the beauty of it. It sort of fuses the earth it travels through. It can also be programmed to add in a binder material, something they'd just come up with, a form of liquid plastic that's injected as the machine travels and that bonds with the fused earth. The borer can be programmed to make that lining as thick as necessary, within certain limits. We checked. They had a stock, quite a large one, of the plastic in their store. There's enough to do this place here two escape routes, plus the main tunnel between us all. After that, unless we can find more, there's only the fused earth."

"Why two?"

"To different places. Much safer in case the enemy is sitting on top of one quite by accident."

"Well, okay. Start the walls going up. Once the borer is ready to come up somewhere, I'll think of a reason why everyone has to be out for the day." She stood, holding a hand to her tired back.

Rome looked up, "How's Shay?"

"Only half conscious most of the time. I'm keeping her sedated. Once she's back with us properly, I"ll have to tell her about Neith."

"But..."

"She doesn't remember. She's asked for her a couple of times. Jo is with her. She thinks that the wound is healing slowly. The weakness is mostly blood loss, and the shock to the system. She's going to have an awful scar, but she may come out of this without permanent damage."

"I hope so," Mike said soberly. "We need her. She's got the combat mind. She sees possibilities us ones who've always had it soft don't spot. The borer and two escape routes were her idea."

"We'll hold good thoughts. Go and get on with your walls."

For a week the machines boomed and scurried. Underground the borer moved more silently along its programmed route. It emerged late one morning, as, on a multitude of small fat wheels it trundled across the compound and dived into the earth in another place. Once out of sight it began to dig and fuse its way underground once again, creating the second intended escape route. Above ground those in the know worked furiously to cover both holes. It had been decided to use the original plan of adding extra bunkhouses at opposite corners of the house square.

The escape hatch in each case was based on an ancient film Dana had once seen. Free-standing enclosed fires were bolted to a thin slab. At a pinch the bolts could be removed and the fire shifted to one side, the slab would then be raised to reveal the tunnel. It would take either several strong people to lift fire and slab, or one person if the two were removed separately. Inside the tunnel a couple of short strong bars were set. These could be used to lower the slab again, thus making the escape route difficult to find, either by accident or by enemies.

Another week and the walls were complete. Now the machine's attention was turned to the farmhouse on the lower ground, The borer emerged and was stored away quietly. It would be brought out again once the centre fort was in place,

For weeks Shay was no more than a puppet, accepting the care of her body but not present in some way. She would thank Jo, yet it was as if this were the remnants of a mental programme. She initiated no conversation, asked no questions. Only occasionally in dreams would she call for Neith, Awake she no longer asked for or about her. Jo hoped the memory had finally reached her, that she knew Neith was dead.

Once Shay moved on the pillow.

"What's all that noise?" The voice was faintly fretful.

"Mike and Rome. They've started the walls."

"Oh." And she lapsed into limp silence again.

Jo was becoming really concerned. It was so unlike the Shay she knew. That Shay was a fighter, one who'd never lie back and accept anything. This Shay seemed to have no interest in life.

Jo had never been seriously injured herself. She did not understand the lassitude of body such an injury imposes. The mind shuts down its own and the body's energy, conserving everything towards healing. A severely wounded patient will lie hour upon hour, merely staring at nothing in particular. Vague unconnected thought drifts, occasional ideas, but nothing short of a major emergency is important enough to encourage the use of energy that might better be used to recover. The mind and body both have their own defenses — and sometimes their own agenda as well.

Yet Shay was recovering. It was several weeks after the attack that she hauled herself upright. "I can feed myself." The tone was snappish but Jo was elated.

"Of course, here." She watched as the spoon moved up and down. "I'm so glad you're feeling better." She gathered herself. She must explain, be sure what Shay remembered.

"Do you remember what happened?"

Shay glanced at her. "Neith's dead," she said flatly. "One of them was playing possum and shot me."

"I'm so sorry about Neith."

"You never liked her."

There was enough truth in that to sting. Jo rose to move restlessly around the room. In that minute before she replied, she faced something she had refused to acknowledge before now.

"I was jealous, " she blurted. "I — you were my friend first. I felt as if Neith shut me out." Her voice dropped as she forced herself to continue. "Then you were — I thought you'd die. I'd have let Neith have you so long as you'd live. I mean I just wanted you to survive. I swore if you did I'd be happy for you whoever you were with." She turned away, waiting for the cutting remark. The scorn.

Shay's voice was gentler than she'd ever heard it, "Jo?"

"What." Her back remained turned.

"You aren't being very clear. Are you saying you want me as more than a friend?"

"Yes!" She spun to look at Shay, still waiting to be hurt. "Yes, so I'm a fool. You only wanted a friend. But, yes! I've never had a real lover." She laughed harshly. "First it was school, then university. Never any time except to study. I had a couple of one-night-stands with men and wondered why I didn't enjoy it. But I've never — I haven't..." She took a deep breath. "Look, it doesn't matter. We can be friends."

Shay leaned back on her pillows. "I don't want to be friends."

The words pierced Jo to the heart. So that was it. She exposed herself, laid it all on the line — only to be rejected as anything at all. She turned for the door, her eyes dull with pain. Shay's hand shot out to seize her as she passed.

"I don't want you to be only a friend when we can be lovers too." She giggled weakly. "Oh hell, that sounds like a really sickly love song. Jo, you idiot. I was Neith's friend because I liked her and she could teach me a lot about this place and how to be self-sufficient here. She did hint at more once, I told her I liked her a lot as a friend, but that was it. She accepted that. Then you started acting weird and angry with me. I tried to find out if I'd done something to upset you, but you wouldn't talk to me any more. I spent more time with Neith because I was lonely without you." She tugged at the hand she held. "Come here."

Slowly Jo allowed herself to be drawn to sit on the bed beside Shay. Her gaze slid down inch by inch until she was staring into Shay's eyes. There was no anger there, no lurking cynicism. Instead they were clear and open with a warmth that Shay rarely showed to anyone.

"You mean it?"

Hands came up to grasp her shoulders as she was drawn into a warm gentle embrace. "Oh, I mean it. But the lover bit will have to wait awhile. I'm too weak to do us justice."

Jo gasped. After all her confusion, after all the jealousy and pain, and Shay was just noting they'd have to wait awhile. She began to giggle. Through explosions of mirth she endeavored to explain. Once she understood, Shay joined in the laughter. Dana entered to discover them both exhausted with emotion, holding hands still. She smiled, made some casual comment and took herself off. It looked as if things were all right there. She thanked the Goddess for it. There was enough work for the two of them and now it appeared they'd be together to do it.

After that Shay mended faster. She had visitors, lots of them. Including Mike and Rome, who brought a gift. It came in a plastic carrier, which moved jerkily as it was placed on the bed.

"What on Earth?"

"You said once that you'd have liked a kitten but you moved too often. You aren't planning to move from here — are you?"

Shay was scrabbling at the fastenings. She flipped back the top and stared in. From the box a small smudged black face emerged. An indignant wail announced that the occupant had not appreciated her incarceration. Not at *all*!

"Oh, she's gorgeous, where did you get her? She's a Siamese, isn't she?"

"Purebred sealpoint. One of the last lot we got in Auckland bred them. She said she'd join us but only if she could bring her cats with her. She had two pairs, all four from different lines."

"We said okay," Rome carried the tale on. "One of the females already had a litter. We reserved the prettiest female for you." He grinned, "A girl for a girl. You do like her?"

Shay beamed up, the kitten wrapped in her arms, her fingers already drawing purrs from the small beast. "I love her. It's odd, but I've hardly seen a cat out here. I guess the dogs got them mostly. We'll have to make sure that these new ones don't get too far from the houses."

"There's less trouble with that lately." Mike spoke grimly. "The dogs got one of the children that came with the Auckland bunch. We took every gun we had, all the vehicles and had us a dog hunt. We kept telling them, we explained about Hari, but some of the adults just didn't listen. Well, they're listening now."

He snorted. The mother had taken her five-year-old daughter on a ramble, a casual little saunter out into the countryside, ignoring all warnings they'd tried to drum into her. The child had been killed as she strayed away from her mother who was picking fruit. The woman had reached a tree just as Jo had and then been forced to sit and watch as her daughter was eaten.

She'd returned home after the glutted pack had departed. Once she ensured the child's remains would have a respectable burial, the mother had vanished. Two hours later she'd been found hanging in one of the sheds by another child who was now badly shocked and still having nightmares. Jo was still muttering about people with no commonsense as the visitors left, leaving Shay with Jo and the sleepy kitten.

"Bloody selfish cow. Didn't listen to anything, let her kid die, then leaves some other poor kid to find her. Just as well she's dead. We can do without that sort."

Shay propped herself up on another pillow, fingers tickling the kitten. "Look at it her way, Jo. Sure she was stupid. But how did you learn dogs were dangerous? At someone else's expense, right? But if that hadn't happened, would it have occurred to you to steer clear of them."

"Probably not."

"That woman would have been city. Ten to one she didn't know anything at all about animals. Being told is one thing. You know it here," she tapped her forehead. "Seeing it, you know it here." She tapped her heart. "It's the second one that makes the impression. You could do worse than to sit everyone down and have the ones that know talk about some of the dangers around here. Get the ones who have seen or experienced things to share them — in real stomach-turning detail. It'll sink in better."

"I can tell them what happened to Hari. Not 'She was killed by dogs', but a real production."

"That's it."

Jo uncurled herself from the end of the bed. "You should rest now. What are you going to call this object?" Her fingers gently nudged the ball of fur.

"Dunno. I'll think of something." She reached out for Jo. "So I'll be weak a while. I can stand a good-night kiss." Lips met, a brush as soft as kitten fur. Jo shivered, then hugged carefully.

"Sleep well."

She left them both lying down, and darned if Shay didn't look just as smug as the kitten. Jo smiled as she vanished out of the door. She felt wonderful. She wanted to sing, to dance, to fly! Shay was right. Jo had been a complete fool over all this. If she'd just talked instead of going dumb on her friend. She remembered her first sight of Shay, standing so casually slung with weaponry. The calm way she'd cleaned up two men who'd imprisoned them. All at once she was starving. It occurred to her she hadn't been eating well lately. Nor had she seen much of Ani and Ngaire. She trotted off to find food, then friends.

Ngaire was where she often was these days, in the big communal room with a spinning wheel, bags of wool, and bobbins. Shay's original suggestion, that Ngaire learn to spin as well as knit had been taken up seriously. After intensive work she could now spin well. While in Auckland the first time, Shay had thought to find the Institute for the Blind in the centre city. There she had discovered stacks of knitting patterns in Braille, also books, magazines, all sorts of information Ngaire could use. There'd also been a number of small electronic items with solar power panels and hand-wound generators.

Shay had stuffed anything useful into packs, returning in triumph to hand over everything to her delighted friend. Now Ngaire spun during the day, when she still required more concentration for the work. It was then that the room was mostly empty. Once it began to fill after evening meal, she switched to knitting or crocheting. Already she had chosen to teach two of the children interested. They were learning to spin and already discussing natural dyes for the wool.

Jo found her there alone and sat to talk. She felt guilty there too. Ngaire was another friend she'd been neglecting.

"So Shay will be all right?"

"Looks like it, and Dana says that so long as we can stop her overdoing things too early, she should be fine."

Ngaire gave small chuckle. "That may not be so easy. You know Shay. I think she was born with "up and doing" tattooed on her forehead."

Jo laughed. "Too right. Now she's with us again I think she'll be bored in no time." It occurred to her at that point that the gift of the kitten might have had an ulterior motive. Maybe Mike and Rome had intended it to keep Shay amused — and quiet. She explained about that to Ngaire, and her friend's face became wistful.

"I'd love a kitten. We only had an old dog when I was a kid. And in the annex there was a cat but he belonged there, not to me,"

Jo chatted for a while longer before vanishing. Once out of the room, she went in search of the woman with the kittens. If Ngaire would like a kitten of her own, she should have a kitten.

The owner, Sandra, was pleased. "Yes, give her one of the boys. I know Ngaire, she'll look after him" She blew a breath out, sounding like a tired horse. "I worry about them. To keep animals purebred you need a decent number. A real gene-pool. There used to be thousands of Siamese in the country, but they were pets.

Most of them were neutered, and the others were valuable. Those ones would have been in cages. I guess not many would have lived long after their owners died."

"We could keep an eye open. Didn't you say a lot of owners had special feeders?"

Sandra perked up. "Ah huh. Food and water dispensers. Some of the fancy varieties could be filled to last months. The really good ones have a way of cleaning cages and changing the litter too." She considered. "There'd be an owners list in the headquarters of the Breed Association. That'd give names and addresses of all the people with un-neutered cats. Didn't Rome say they were thinking of another trip down there?"

Jo departed after discussion, richer by one squawking kitten promptly gifted to an ecstatic Ngaire.

She continued to care for Shay, while in a short convoy of trucks others hunted over more of the great city to the South. By now it had been months, but one after another they found loved Siamese. Some barely alive, others miserably lonely but in good health. That wasn't the only reason they went, of course. So much material, so little storage was Dana's lament. They brought back clothing, boots and shoes, tools, more weapons, and so many odds and ends Dana had to set up two of the older children as stores clerks.

But the cats were a joy. They repaid their new owners with real devotion — and a ferocious desire to hunt. It was a rare day at least one mouse or rat was not laid at an owner's feet. Some might have complained about the cost of feeding, the extra effort required, but for Dana's comments.

"It was the problem in any agricultural society, keeping the rodents out of the food supplies. They eat while we starve over winter. The cats will take care of that. We just keep their numbers sensible."

They did so. Some of the rescued beasts had been neutered. These were shared as pets. Others were bred, with records being kept.

The puppies, at first unsure of these additions, learned to respect them. Any Siamese, or any feline for that matter, is *not* intimidated by a puppy. The cats also learned not to go too far from safety. The dog packs were creeping back, to Jo's annoyance. Sometimes it seemed that all they did was kill big savage dogs. It felt as if every person in the entire country had owned one, and all of them had bred.

Time slipped by. Shay was taking her first weak steps again. The kitten, now named Tai, was stretching out into a teen-kitten. The walls had been in place for the third portion of their string of forts, for a week. All the underground tunnels were in place, new barns and houses built. Their people numbered almost a hundred when Shay was strong enough to walk alone. It had been nearly ten weeks since the shooting. Above Neith's grave planted flowers bloomed. Jo had kept herself firmly as a friend all this time. She was content to know they would be more once Shay was fully healed.

Billy had visited Shay most days. He acted as scout with the bike often, he and Bob making a fast-moving cautious team. Twice they had taken supplies, roving far to the north, finding people who had survived alone. Of these they had brought everyone back who would agree to live by the rules growing up in the settlement.

Dana insisted still that those who joined must respect Pagan beliefs and customs. Thus far this had been carried out. Perhaps it was that they had been the largest true group. Even with Neith gone, they numbered a dozen. Jo, Shay, Mike and Rome were converts by now, as were quite a number of others. Those who were not, at least said nothing against the customs of those who worshipped.

Autumn came and the weather cooled slowly. Shay stood looking down at a set of plans as Mike jabbed an insistent finger at them.

She grinned at the lean man. His affectations were gone. There was no time these days for that. In their place there was now a wiry, well-muscled male with tanned face, wearing comfortable well-worn jeans, Rome, larger, quieter, but more powerful, stood shoulder to shoulder with him.

"We have the perfect setup if we continue to enclose it all."

Jo nodded. Because of the way the land lay, the three forts were not so much in the line they were called but in a rough triangle. If they added a fourth and continued the wall, they could enclose a large amount of land. It would make it safer for small children or the elderly. Make them more one also, less likely to split off from each other into each set of homes. They could double the wall thickness by making the inner side a continuous series of storage bays. Those on watch or guard above would have the roof widths as well as the wall to walk upon. In fact...

"Look, if we dropped the roofs lower, we'd be able to fight or patrol under partial cover. They'd be a walkway say a metre or a metre and a half lower on the inside."

Dana glanced at her. "We could use the extra storage space. We also need more living room. I know the place already seems huge, but... " She beamed around them, "Cece tells me she's going to have a baby. Hine will have hers soon, and there's bound to be others. People are starting to feel secure enough. This is becoming their home and our town. We need room to expand, as much as we can manage."

Jo nodded. "I agree." She took Shay's hand, "But we're out of here. Shay's looking tired."

They headed for the door, amidst amused comments. Jo had been acting quite possessive of late. Back in Shay's room she gently persuaded her friend to change into a house robe and lie down. She brought food and they chatted comfortably as they ate. Finally Shay discarded her plates. She yawned and stretched luxuriously, twisting and bending each muscle.

"You know I still feel good. I guess I'm really mending." She put an arm around Jo's shoulder. "In fact I still have some energy left. What should we do with it?" The arm tightened a little more.

Jo found she was unable to look up, to meet her friend's eyes. A loving finger tilted her mouth up to be kissed. Slowly they slipped down on the bed, Now there was no shyness, only the trust of friends and the growing hunger of lovers.

Later Jo lay awake, still lovingly entwined. Outside stars

showed against a black sky and a chill autumn wind blew softly. But inside for her it was spring. She had never believed she would live to see either. Only time would tell where they went from here. She did not care. She knew that whatever the road, she would have Shay beside her. For this night and the nights to come, it would be enough. She smiled wryly to herself. A ruined country, a world destroyed. But it seemed that people were still people. They ate and drank, lived and died — and fell in love. Still smiling, she slept.

Chapter Nine

But everything was not to go their way over that first year. With the trickle of new refugees joining them other beliefs and prejudices arrived. Mike and Rome were the first to discover this.

"Take two bikes and patrol to the west. Check out the harbour." Mike glanced up at the early morning sky. "If this fine weather holds a couple of days a group will go over to fish there." To his surprise the man, a recent arrival named Jonathon, remained standing there, his face obstinate. "What is it?"

From the open shed behind him Rome walked up to join his friend as Mike asked that question.

"It's you," Jonathon snapped. "I don't take orders from bloody queers, okay? Between you and all these dykes a man would think he'd lost his balls."

Rome snorted, "I don't know what you've lost. But here you work and eat or don't work and don't eat. If you start trouble for nothing you leave. I won't stand around arguing lifestyles. Are you going or leaving?"

Jonathon straddled the bike thrust forward to him. "I'm going. We'll see about you and your orders when I get back."

The two watched as the bike zoomed through the gate, followed by another ridden by a second member of the group. They narrowly missed Billy who stamped across.

"What 'n the hell's wrong with those idiots?"

"We're queers with no right to give him orders," Mike informed him tersely.

Billy nodded thoughtfully. "I didn't like to say anything, but some of that new lot are trouble. I don't think they like anyone here a lot. They aren't saying much in front of you older ones but us kids have heard plenty. So far, I've heard them running down you two, Shay and Jo, Ngaire, and Ani."

Rome and Mike stared at him. "Ani?" Mike said at last, "For God's sake, she's only eleven. What's *she* ever done to upset them?"

"She's Maori," Billy said quietly.

For a moment both men gaped at him. It was Rome, large, placid, and quiet, who spoke first. He was decisive.

"That lot will have to leave if that's the way they think. What do we know about them anyway?"

"They came in around three weeks ago." Billy brightened as he spoke, "Pam will know. She's been helping Jo keep the records. Maybe some of them talked to Pam, too."

They found Billy's sister with Jo, as the women admired the view from the new tower above the house. Behind the clump of buildings the hills lifted into green tree-furred mountains. Not high, but a pleasant dark backdrop to the lower paler-grassed foothills. In the far distance, water glinted from harbour and lake. Fat woolly white clouds sailed past indicating a strong breeze higher up. But below the day was warm and the air still.

The tower rose twenty feet above the roofline. It had been recently added to the fort's inner corner by a newcomer who had turned out to be a skilled carpenter. He was now making sets of twin bunks from some of the wood planking that had been carefully stockpiled. The bunks would go into the two bunkhouses originally raised to cover the escape tunnel entrances.

Since its raising, the tower had become a favourite haunt of many of the older and younger villagers. The younger because they were often forbidden to be outside the walls and in the tower they had a pleasant sense of looking down on everything. The older children climbed the stairs to admire the landscape and to watch for incoming friends. So popular had it proved that it was now intended to build on several more towers, probably one on each main building to form a set of four. Jo was just grateful that there was no shortage of timber.

In fact, it was of the stockpiled planks that Pam and Jo were talking as the men arrived.

"Storage places outside the walls would be good. We could dump dangerous items out there or the bulkier things that take up so much room." Jo was pointing downwards to where a small gully wound behind the walls. "If we blocked off an arm of that, put an open foundation of concrete blocks in and ran drains down the sides we could put all the timber there and have more room in the compound here."

"That sounds like a workable idea," Mike broke in, "It'd be best if we hid anything like that though. But right now we've got something important to talk about. It's urgent." He stopped unsure of what to say next.

Rome took over. "There's a problem with some of the new people. What do you know about the group who came in three weeks ago? They're headed by a nurse and her brother. There was a dozen or so of them without anything much in gear or supplies."

Jo nodded. "I remember. The brother and sister are Jonathon and Mavis Gallan. They belong to some small sect. We let them in because a nurse is valuable and they promised to respect our beliefs. Are you saying they don't?"

Mike shrugged. "I dunno about beliefs, but they don't respect *us*. One of the brother's lot just called Rome and me a couple of queers. Said he doesn't take orders from my type. Billy says that they've been talking against you and Shay..."

Jo turned to look at Billy. "For the same reasons?"

"Yeah."

"That isn't the worst of it," Rome said quietly. "Billy says they've been speaking against Ngaire because she's blind, and Ani because she's Maori."

Jo went white. "If they've said anything like that to Ngaire or Ani, I'll toss them all out with my own hands."

Beside her Pam suddenly spoke. "That's silly. Ngaire does as much work as anyone. And the other thing is stupid, too. Half of us here have Maori in the family somewhere." She glanced over at her brother. "Our grandmother was. And Dana told me that her great-grandfather was Ngati Awa. Are they going to offend *everyone?*"

Rome nodded. "I don't think they care. They believe that only those who are white, straight, and healthy have rights. I reckon they're against Ani in particular because she really looks Maori."

He saw Jo was thinking and stopped further discussion with a quick chopping motion. They stood in the sunshine waiting. At last Jo nodded to herself.

"We don't know a lot about them. They belong to one of these splinter sects called "In His Holy Name". It wasn't a big group, maybe a couple of hundred, and all of them in a place a bit like this over towards Kaeo. The bug made a real mess of them, then the Kaitaia mob hit them and just about cleaned them out. This lot are all that was left. They hadn't bothered with any defenses so the attackers ran right over them."

Her voice became dry. "I gather they expected God to defend them and were quite surprised when He didn't. The Kaitaia lot took over the sect's property and drove them out. Or this lot escaped, I'm not clear on that. They started wandering about looking for another home."

She paused as Pam took up the story. "They've started talking to me a lot the last few days. I didn't want to start a fight so I never said anything." She looked down, twisting her foot against the planking. "They don't like the way we run things here. We don't have a clear leader and we let in too many people that they don't approve of. I think they'd like to take over. If they did they'd kick out all the ones they call perverts. Ngaire, too, and the ones like Ani who really look Maori. They'd have that man in charge. They say it isn't natural to have women running the place." She stopped speaking abruptly to stand, eyes down, in embarrassment.

Everyone started talking until Jo hushed them.

"So they're a bunch of homophobic racists. Ideas like that didn't help keep the peace in pre-bug days," she said grimly. "They could be lethal to our whole group now. I guess it's my fault, too. I was the one who persuaded Dana to let them in. Shay always says I'm too soft-hearted. It sounds as if this lot would scrap the more-or-less democracy we have and set up a dictatorship with their precious leader to give orders. As for throwing Ngaire out, she's taught half the place to knit or crochet. her group spin, weave and dye wool. Okay, so we don't really need to do those things yet. But in a generation, those she's taught and *what* she's taught will be vital."

She stopped almost panting in her rage and distress. "I'll talk to Dana, maybe she can talk to their leaders. She's older and maybe they'll listen to her. If they want to stay here though, they'll have to live with our beliefs and be more tolerant."

She marched in search of Dana. Several hours later, both women intercepted Jonathon as he returned from the detested scouting. His sister, having spent her days doing little but grumble until his return, had been waiting for him at the gates. Dana eyed brother and sister for a few minutes as they huddled together by the scout bike. She'd been doubtful about them from the beginning but Jo had persuaded her. Now Jo was seeing that being too kind to a few could be dangerous to the many. It might be a useful lesson.

Dana eyed the pair as they muttered together. The air of secrecy was almost palpable. It was the norm for that kind. Little people with little beliefs — and even less sense usually. They kept themselves to themselves, not because they really feared corruption, it was more because they loved the feeling of being a secret society — of having sacred mysteries unknown to those outside their group.

She grinned to herself. Many women's groups had begun the same way. But this group was a danger to the settlement. She understood Jonathon as he would never understand her. He really believed that all women were less clever, less stable, that his God had placed females on Earth to serve men. He believed that same-sex loving was utter filth, that the physically or mentally damaged should be mercifully eliminated and that any non-white was inferior.

Jo was watching Mavis. She'd seen enough of the group to know that the woman was the real brain behind them. Jonathon did most of the talking, it was Mavis who crafted the ammunition. It seemed odd in such a group, but then Mavis was fairly subtle about it. Jo thought Jonathon would never quite understand how much his sister ruled him. From their respective attitudes to one another Jo guessed the woman was not only older but had something of a hand in bringing up her younger brother.

Mavis was a thin, sallow-faced woman with her coarse black hair cut short. Her expression reminded Jo of a lemon, or at least of someone who had just bitten into one. The thin-lipped mouth was pursed in permanent disapproval of the world. Mavis wore clothes to cover her body. They hung in sagging folds from neck to bony wrists to below her knees. All one ever saw were the sour face and the grasping hands.

And yet, Jo thought, Mavis could have been quite pleasant to look at had she made any effort. But the sect believed vanity was a sin. Allowing the hair to grow long, even brushing it too much to bring a healthy shine, was wrong. Now Mavis huddled hissing to her brother. Jo felt like groaning. It had been a mistake to ever allow this bunch in. Dana had warned her they looked like trouble.

From the corner of her eye Mavis suddenly saw the waiting figures. She nudged Jonathon then turned to greet two of the women she loathed.

"Dana. Jo. Can we help you?"

It would do no good, Dana knew, but she would try. She spoke quietly to them of the settlement's customs and of tolerance. That rejected, she spoke firmly.

"I am not harsh, but you knew our terms when you joined us. You are causing trouble. Learn tolerance or at least be silent — or leave."

Mavis gulped, looking at Jo whom she knew to be soft-hearted. "You'd put us out to die?" she asked pathetically.

But Jo was realising how much damage this pair and their friends could cause. Her own voice was firm. "If we must."

Jonathon took a step forward, face flushing in rage, "You and who else. There's others here tired of perverts running this show."

He fell silent as Mavis nudged him hard. He'd learned over their years together that his sister had an excellent sense of timing. If she didn't want him to push a confrontation now, he wouldn't. He'd remember this pair though. Most of the people here were trash. With them gone he could run it as a proper church. Daily worship, women in their place — all except Mavis of course, as a sort of Church Mother, and himself as Leader. He'd be looked up to and obeyed by all. For that vision it was worth keeping silent before the heathen — for now.

Jo left with Dana. She was less worried since Jonathon and Mavis had agreed to be more tolerant or at least to keep silence. Dana was older and wiser. Their word meant nothing to those two. She'd have someone keep an eye and an ear on them. She didn't feel well either. That evening she had the next of several minor heart attacks. She'd been taking medication but even that wouldn't completely prevent an attack. It was something she had kept from everyone thus far but this attack was couldn't be hidden. Her friends were frantic. Dana recovered quickly but in her distress she forgot to detail watchers for Jonathon and Mavis and their group, nor did it occur to Jo to do so.

Jonathon, Mavis and their group were quiet for a month before they struck.

"Dana," It was Jo, "We have a demand for a general meeting."

"What's it about?"

"No idea, but Marion called it. You know, the woman I told you about. She joined us with the man who attacked Pam before we arrived here."

"I remember," Dana said grimly. "But I think she's been got at. I've noticed her talking to Mavis a lot lately. All right. Tell everyone to be in the courtyard at five when the bell rings."

"But there'll only be an hour of daylight left. I don't want to run the big floodlights for hours."

"Then they'll have to keep the meeting short, won't they?" Dana allowed her lips to quirk upwards as Jo understood. "Yes, exactly."

Jo trotted away to spread news of the meeting while Dana sat down to rest. She was tired all the time lately. She knew why. Her grandmother had died quite young from a heart attack. Dana's mother would have also died except that medical knowledge had saved her for a longer life. There was nothing that could be done for Dana, the stress of her life was gaining on her health, all she could do was hang on.

Jonathon was right in one way. They did need a clear leader here for some things. Consensus had worked until now but it wouldn't for much longer. Jo would make a good leader if only Dana could train some sensible scepticism into her. The girl believed people to be good and decent. It was Dana's idea that in civilisation a lot of that apparent decency was simply a fear of the law or being found out. She sighed.

At five almost all were gathered, sitting on cushions or shaped logs. Marion stood. Jo listened carefully to a speech that sounded very formal. Quite different from Jan's usual way of talking.

"I joined this group early when some of us were a long way away from here. I've watched events ever since. Some of us aren't happy about being given orders by a woman. Shay is a criminal, a murderer and an evil-doer. A man that I knew, she killed him in cold blood. It's wrong she should have the right to give orders to decent people. Perverts and killers shouldn't be here amongst us. They should be cast out."

Her sideways glance made it clear she was speaking against Rome and Mike as well though she did not name them. Jo waited to see if she was done then nodded to Shay who rose to reply.

"Marion says I'm a murderer an" a law-breaker. First, what law is she talking about? Country's laws were eaten by the bug. Settlement law? I killed the man Marion's talking about before we ever got here. If you're gonna try me on the country's law what about the rest of you?" She grinned widely. "I see arsonists, adulterers, looters and burglars, and people who've been real nasty to poor little dogs." She paused.

From the listening group came an encouraging yell, "You tell 'em, Shay!"

"I will." So," she spread her arms outward. "Whose law?" She met Marion's angry glare with a look of sweet innocence. "Has anyone been told just why I killed this... victim?"

Heads were shaken.

"Anyone think I killed him just for fun?"

There was a mutter of amusement but heads were shaken again. They knew Shay. She could be savage but she wasn't cruel.

"Well then, I'll tell you why. And there's witnesses to what happened that you can hear. After that you can vote on it. If most of you think I should be tried and you can decide whose law I broke, I'll accept it."

Speaking briefly but clearly she outlined the events of that evening. Pam stood un-prompted to add her side. Mike and Rome testified to Johnny's dying admission of guilt.

Dana rose to clap her hands for silence. Then she spoke briskly, "All right. You've heard. Shay killed a man who was attempting to rape a thirteen-year-old girl. What's more, he'd attacked her before and made threats to keep her quiet. Anyone who thinks that Shay did the wrong thing, raise your hands."

The hands of all of Jonathon's group went up. He scowled when he saw Marion's hand remained down.

"Hands up all those who think Shay did right."

A thicket of hands shot skyward. Many of their owners were muttering angrily in Shay's support. Dana looked at Marion.

"I declare that by the customs of our group, there is no case for Shay to answer." She looked out over them. "Things will have to change here, I know. We need leaders who are more clearly defined. We need laws written down and laid out for all. I've been leader here within the home because I was here first, those already here listened to me. But as you'll all know by now, I have heart trouble. How much time I have left I can't say. You'll all have to consider what's been said here tonight."

From the crowd Alex stood. "I'd like to say something. I think that anything done to survive or to save someone should be amnestied. I guess a lot of us did things that would have been illegal in the old days. I know I did."

He dropped back to his cushion while a woman stood.

"What about rape? What if someone who attacked one of us

earlier turns up wanting to join here?"

Jo took over. "We can refuse to let them stay if they're identified. You know if we approve someone they can stay a few days to decide if they want to stick around."

"So they leave and wait for a women to come out alone?"

Jo winced. "Look," she broke in, "we aren't going to solve every problem we may ever have in the next hundred years. We met here to sort out Marion's complaint against Shay. We can have other meetings to work on the laws we want. Right now, dinner's waiting and I'm starving."

She headed for the meal hall and others followed. Behind them Marion glared at Jonathon.

"Told you that wouldn't work. No one was going accept being punished over things they did earlier. Anyway, I never heard the whole story before. I was having a bath when it happened. Now I've heard everything, I believe Pam." She took a deep breath. "I'm not having any more to do with you and your plans. Stay away from me after this."

She turned, walking away from them towards the hall. Jonathon moved to follow, his face twisted into angry lines. Mavis seized his arm, stopping him quickly.

"No. We've got all the use out of her we can. It's taken two weeks to talk her into facing Shay. She'd be no use for anything rougher. Let her go." Her eyes gleamed wickedly in the growing dusk. "I know you'll think of something else we can try. You're so clever, Jonathon. It takes a man to plan the way you do."

She hid a smirk as he preened. *Clever!* He couldn't think of a path if it was laid out in concrete in front of him. But she could. Then with careful manipulation he ended up believing the plan was all his. Once he was leader she had plans of her own. She'd persuade him into announcing her as his second-in-command, a sort of honorary male by Divine Decree. Then Jonathon would have an accident. This settlement and everyone in it would be under her command.

She persuaded her brother back to their quarters. This try hadn't worked but there'd be other chances and other weak-willed idiots she could move like chess pieces. There always were. She knew how to bide her time until a better chance presented itself. Just so long as her stupid brother didn't ruin it all by acting too quickly or too crudely. She smiled in the growing dark. That Dana and Jo had one thing right. Women *could* rule and Mavis planned to.

But time slipped by without a chance for her to move. Mavis started to lean more heavily on her training. Being a qualified nurse had only slightly less status than being a leader. She spoke learnedly in medical terms, talked about her training. Gradually she regained the respect of many and some measure of renewed trust. She chose to make her next attempt from behind a screen of her brother and a couple of his friends. Jo and Dana were infuriated when the rumour reached them.

"Hasn't the man any sense at all? Last time he looked like an idiot." Dana growled.

Shay who was sprawled on the bed watching while her friends did paperwork, laughed. "Probably not. But why are you so bothered? None of it's true."

"You know. We know. But it's a dangerous lie. Smart too. I bet Jonathon didn't think that one up by himself. There'll always a few people willing to believe that we'd keep the best things for ourselves because they would."

"But we have records." Jo said.

"Kept by Pam, you, me, sometimes Mike or Rome, and all of us friends. Jonathon will say we'd lie to cover each other."

Shay's face hardened. "Everyone who's ever been cold or hungry here will want to half believe." She scrambled off the bed. "I'll leave you to talk about it."

She left her friends hastily. Not all of Jonathon's mob were that bad. She'd scouted with one of the women, a small blond fire-cracker named Riana, who was beginning to find that the settlement was a good place to be. Now, if Shay could find that one and talk convincingly — and if the woman was prepared to listen honestly, as Shay thought she might be...

The gathering, two evenings later, was interesting. Jonathon made his accusations in a grave quiet way, which was very convincing. It came to nothing when Riana stepped forward.

"Shay heard rumours that this was being said. She asked me to check. I was allowed in every room and cupboard. I looked through all the sheds, storerooms, everything."

Genuinely convinced of his accusations Jonathon beamed. "Then you can swear to their greed."

"I can swear to their honesty," Riana flared. "They have nothing better than any of us."

"What about that patchwork quilt Jo has. That pure-bred cat of Shay's. We've all seen them eating fruit when others of us aren't given any?"

Riana nodded. "Jo brought the quilt with her. Her mother made it. Shay's kitten was a gift to her after she almost died fighting for the settlement. The apples are a bit different."

"Ah!" The sound was triumphant. He was to be disappointed

"No. The scouts often pick fruit if they're near a place where it grows. It's allowed so long as they don't burden themselves beyond sense. Of course they share it with their friends. How far would a dozen apples go amongst all of us? They share with the children, too."

Riana's voice became edged. "There's none for some to eat because they don't risk scouting. Look at you," her hand swept out indicating Jonathon and the few who crowded with him. "You take and refuse to give. The food that's gathered in bulk is shared by everyone. None of our group have gone hungry since we got here. I think it's time we decided if we are part of the settlement or not. If we are we should do our share of the work — all of it!"

She ignored Jonathon's furious glare as she faced him. "And another thing. My mother was part-Maori. You talk a lot about the white virtues. So far all I've seen from you is selfishness, looking after your own skins and going on about how much better you all are. These people don't just talk, they think about the future and act. And before you say it, you can consider me exiled."

Jonathon spluttered, red-faced with fury. "I do. I cast you out. I name you exile, false-hearted, a liar..."

Riana's swinging blow caught him across one cheek so that he staggered. "Exile is fine. I'm no liar and you aren't going to name me one. Start that and I'll call you a few names of my own."

"You...you hit me!" His hand went to his stinging face. "You can't *do* that." Forgetting everything his voice roared up to a cracking falsetto. "You whore of Babylon. That's assault. I'll call the police and have you jailed."

Billy started it. His sudden yelp of amusement was contagious. In seconds the entire compound was rocking with laughter. The joke was repeated over and over as Jonathon stormed out. Behind him went the remaining eight of his followers. Riana stayed, as did two of his group.

The noise died slowly as Dana spoke, "If everyone is now convinced this complaint is untrue, maybe we can adjourn?"

Voices from all parts of the compound assured her they could. The people straggled out still smiling. In the sect's rooms, Jonathon was packing. As he stuffed items into the sacks he mumbled over his grievances. Riana was a liar. She was! He had scouted, so had one of his people. So had Riana if it came to that.

(A fact Riana could have testified to, however she would also have been constrained to truth. Jonathon and his toady had gone out once only. After that they'd feared the open lands too greatly. From then on they'd remained inside the walls and done only as much work as they must.)

Jonathon snarled to himself as he loaded items into the bags. Riana was a traitor and a liar. He'd lost three people from his flock over this. He fumed as he worked.

Mavis slipped in quietly. "I'm not coming with you. They blame you, Jonathon. I can stay and pass on information for you. I'll be the light in their darkness, the bitter worm in their fruit. I'll gnaw at their foundations and when they fall you can bring everyone back and take over the rule."

She waited confidently. There was no way she was going to risk herself again out there. She'd had enough cold, hunger and danger. She'd stay here. Sooner or later she'd gain power then she could let her brother back in — if she felt like it. Jonathon shook his head in renewed outrage.

"As a woman and my sister your place is with me."

"But..."

"You will pack and leave with us. That is my decision." He posed like a prophet as her own anger flared.

"I'm your sister, not your wife. I'll stay if I want to." She would have gone on to soften that. A little honey went a long way with her brother. Too late she saw his fist flick upwards.

Jonathon glared down at her. Mavis had always been the smart one. He knew that. He had no intention of losing her. They could keep her tied and gagged until they left early next morning. He would not lose another of the group. He marched out to give instructions to the remaining faithful once he'd insured Mavis would go nowhere. He gave his orders then spent the night in prayer. Mavis spent her night far less comfortably.

They'd arrived with a cart and two thin, weary horses. They were leaving with the same cart, but now the beasts were sleek and energetic. Mavis was neatly gagged and rolled in bedding. By daylight the group continually shifted about as they assembled at the gates. Eight people, the horses and cart, two bicycles and the movement made it difficult for anyone to see that Mavis was missing. Dana felt no need for ceremony. The gates were opened by Mike and Rome, Jonathon led his flock through and the gates slammed behind them.

Mavis lay miserably cramped and hot in her bonds and covering. She didn't blame herself for this. She was the victim. Oh, her brother shouldn't have kidnapped her but it wasn't really his fault either. She lay cramped and sweating, hating Jo, Dana, Shay and their friends. It was them, they'd caused all this. One day she'd be back and they'd pay. She forced herself to lie quietly. She knew she'd be freed once the group was too far away for her to return to the settlement. She relaxed to the jolting rock of the cart and laid a few plans, carefully considering the honey-tongued words with which she would sway her brother once she was free. She saved her strength. It would be needed in time to come.

Chapter Ten

Now that Jonathon and his flock were gone, Jo turned with Dana to considering law and order. It was hard to make laws that suited everyone. After weeks of discussion they were left with a greater respect for politicians than most of them had ever had before. However while it did take time, they slowly hammered out a compromise. It included customs, beliefs, the ideas of free-thinkers and plain common sense. It was seasoned with Maori laws on tapu and respecting the environment, all trimmed to fit the circumstances so far as was possible.

Jo rode out with Shay one afternoon shortly after the final structure had been written and printed out in a number of copies on Jo's printer. These copies had been pinned up in every major building as well as read out in a general meeting while other copies had been carefully preserved by laminating each page.

"Do you think they'll work?" Shay was thoughtful.

Jo smiled affectionately at her. "About as well as any laws ever do. We'll make adjustments as things occur. Maybe some of the ideas won't work. But mostly, I think they're good laws. They're what our people wanted. Anyhow, that one you suggested will help cover a lot of situations we didn't include specifically."

Shay reached over to run fingers lightly down Jo's arm. "Jonathon kept using it against us. I figured that it wasn't a bad idea."

Jo grinned back at her. "I know." She quoted Shay's law thoughtfully, "and if at any time a majority believe ill to have been done which is not covered by law, a gathering may be convened.

Firstly to determine if the deed should be judged. If a majority agree that it should be so, then judgment shall take place, before and by the gathering. The decision may be embodied as future law."

Shay laughed, "It's a lot fancier than what I did say, but yes." She glanced at Jo, suddenly serious. "I hope that won't be used by someone as lynch law in the future?"

Jo looked out over the rolling land as they rode, her face equally sober. "I hope not too. We did say it has to be a minimum of two thirds of all those permitted to vote. But any law at all can be abused. We can't cover everything, love. Just do our best. We're building for the future so we have to have some faith that the ones who follow us will have some common sense, too."

Jo's face was serious as she recalled some of the discussion. Most of the laws they'd written were logical. No food was to be gathered or hunted to the point where it could not sustain its own level. Open and closed seasons could be used to help enforce that at need. No food-bearing tree was ever to be cut down without two being planted. Water was never to be fouled if the fouling was at all avoidable. The land was to be respected as a provider. Much of that had come from the Maori customs.

Nor might beasts be killed for pure sport. Only for food, clothing, defense or some other reason which might hold good at that time. That one had arisen from Pagan belief. Already the Pagan custom of apologising to an animal as it was killed had taken hold — at least with most animals. No one apologised when they killed one of the wild dogs.

From the many beliefs of those involved had come one simple law. No one shall attempt to thrust their religious beliefs upon any other. Any belief system that respects others shall be permitted. Beliefs may be spoken of but if the one hearing indicates they have no wish to listen, the speaker must at once be silent. That had been her contribution. If they'd had that set of laws earlier it might have helped to curb Jonathon, or to expose him earlier as the danger he was.

Jo turned to look at her love. "We've done our best," she

repeated. Keeping to herself something she'd once read an SF writer had said — that commonsense, isn't (common.)

Shay nodded, heeling her pony into a run, as her challenge floated back, "Race you to the trees!"

"Hey, not fair."

A second pony's hooves made small thunder across the grass. Jo laughed as she rode. They should turn back soon, the evening meal would be ready soon and she was hungry. Ahead Shay drew rein at the line of pines and her head came up abruptly. There was an odd feeling in the air, an electricity that made her skin crawl. She shifted in the saddle rubbing her arms as she saw the hair standing on end all along her forearms. Both ponies had begun to dance.

Jo was looking puzzled, "Shay? What is it? She glanced up, "Wow... look at those clouds."

Shay followed her gaze and her mouth tightened. "Thunderstorm coming. I think it's going to be far worse than our usual ones. Ride for home, Jo, and don't stop."

The ponies raced down the old road towards the settlement. Behind them the wind was rising. Only small hot puffs at first, but rapidly growing in chill and power. It had been a warmer, drier spring, shifting slowly into a hotter drier summer. Vegetation was dried still more by the wind. There'd been more of that than usual, too, this year. Jo kept her pony to a slow gallop, scanning the land as she rode. They had good firebreaks around the settlement. But the back gullies had been extended. They helped drain the land closest to the walls but that had made some of those areas drier.

They shot through the wide-open gates and dismounted to run the sweating beasts into shelter. Shay tossed the reins to Jo.

"Rub them both down quickly. I have to see Dana fast."

"Yes, but..."

Shay was gone.

She burst into Dana's room seconds later already shouting her name. Dana would have complained but for the urgency on the girl's face. Shay wasn't an alarmist. Whatever was exciting her like this had to be serious.

"Trouble?" she asked, beginning to rise from her desk.

Shay took her arm, "Not here yet but come and take a look through the window."

Dana's small office had none. Obediently she crossed to her bedroom beyond. There, she peered out and then in response to a pointing finger, upwards. She registered the massing clouds shot with an odd livid colour at the edges. She could feel the electricity in the air and see the effects of the rising wind as it blew puffs of dust about the compound. After that Dana wasted no time, she'd lived here a long time and knew what she was seeing. Flying steps took her out of the door, her feet pounded along the passage and out into the compound. Shay raced behind.

Dana's voice went up like a trumpet call. "Fire! *Fire*! Rally to the compound. *Fire!*"

People came popping out of doors and windows like startled rabbits. Children appeared from everywhere to join in the excitement. Most people had been readying for the evening meal while children hovered hopefully. Others had been in the barns at this time, either milking or tending the beasts before nightfall. Voices rose in question, there was no fire that anyone could see. Shay didn't waste her time calling for quiet. She flipped her shotgun skywards and fired, racked it and fired again. A startled silence fell.

"Keep quiet until I've told you the danger," Dana said.

Jo trotted out of the crowd holding a box. Dana nodded her thanks, climbed up on it and began to speak.

"Everyone hear me? Good! Now, we may be in for real danger. There's a very bad electrical storm coming. I know that everyone's been working and not looking up. Many of you come from the South and will have never seen one like this. They're rare here too." Her hand chopped off the rising murmur of questions. "*Listen!* We'll get lightening strikes. We do have conductors but even so if lightening hits the buildings, we could have fire. Outside there aren't any conductors and the whole areas is dry and there's long dry grass all over. With the wind getting bad, if that catches we could lose half the settlement if we don't move fast enough when that happens. I want every bath or tub in the house filled with water. Sort out all containers we can use to carry water. Stack half a dozen by each water source."

She paused for breath. "Take the horses out into the back gully and blindfold them. It's all rock and bare earth there so without a direct hit they'll be safe. Do the same for the cows. Put the sheep between the cows and horses. We can't blindfold them but that gully's too steep for them to climb up the sides and they'll have trouble getting past the cows and horses if we pack them in."

"What about the pigs?" someone called.

"Forget the pigs. Their sties are all iron-roofed, they won't burn. There's wood sides to earth a strike from the iron, and wood is non-conducting so with luck the pigs should be fine. Take the smaller children down into the tunnels. Cats and dogs go with them. Pregnant women go too, someone needs to be with the children."

Beside her Jo hissed quietly, "What about Ngaire?"

Dana lowered her voice to reply. "Get her down the tunnels too. She's sensible. Tell her we need the children kept calm and she can do that best."

Dana returned to her louder voice, "Outside here I want all the troughs topped up. I want wet cloth ready. Old coats and jackets," she yelled in reply to another query. "Anything in heavy wool is ideal. It doesn't burn easily and it'll hold the water. If the storm isn't here by the time all that's done, fill the containers that you can't use for water with loose earth instead. That smothers a fire too." She was growing hoarse.

Now that Jo understood the danger she helped Dana down gently, stepping up to take her place. Her voice was clear and steady. The tones that said she knew what to do, and those about her listened, reassured.

"I want us split into three groups once the water and cloths are ready. No argument on this. Men and women from sixteen to forty fight the fire. Those older get any injured away to safety and take care of them. The younger ones spread out around any strike. Your job is to put out burning twigs, smouldering grass bits, anything that's carried away from the main blaze. Now, any questions, but make it fast?"

There were several, all brief and all sensible. Jo dealt with them then stepped down to join Dana and Shay.

"Ngaire?"

Shay spoke, "In the tunnels. I told Hine to go with them. She's in no condition to run about. I put the slabs back down too. That way none of the kids will be able to sneak up into the fire."

"Good. Grab a bucket and start working. We may not have a lot of time left."

There was little doubt of that. Even those from further south who'd never seen one of the huge electrical storms before could see what was heading their way now. Overhead the sky was an awful leaden colour tinged with a livid reddish hue. Clouds spun in higher and higher but appeared to have stopped moving past. They built great sky towers, broke apart, then built back higher. The wind was dry, sucking moisture from everything it passed. It slid over the toiling figures below and each person felt as if they'd been bleached bone dry by its touch.

Then the thunder began. Long low snarls that sounded as if the very sky was enraged. They deepened gradually until each sound carried a low booming vibration that was felt in the pit of the stomach. Jo paused to catch hold of Shay as she passed.

"How did you know about this?"

"There was a storm the first year I was here. It wasn't as bad as I think this one is gonna be, but it started the same way. You've never lived up here, Jo. Dana told me once that things got a bit worse around 2014 and then weather patterns changed still further about five years back in 2030 and that's when the storms got far worse." Shay glanced upwards, "With all the long dry grass around we could have a firestorm."

Jo shivered. She'd heard enough of those from the days when news came in from Australia. With the changes in climate back in the twenty-teens, much of that country had turned drier than ever. Bush fires had become a ferociously destructive part of each summer and fall. By 2030 the televid had shown the pictures often

— along with the terrifying sight of people burning alive.

Shay reached out to hug Jo roughly. "Let's get on with it. We've got water to carry."

Overhead the thunder was continuous. Lightening flared and flickered. There'd been no strike as yet, but any minute now Jo thought, as she hauled her bucket towards the nearest trough. Through the open gates she could see the line of trees she and Shay had raced to earlier. There'd been a strike there, then again, closer and closer. A long blue jagged knife ripping at the guts of the earth. The air stank of ozone as the sky bled ions.

Behind her came a crash, screams, and an odd thudding sound. Jo spun. The vegetable stores? The roof had been struck but they'd covered all the roofs with a heavy layer of earth. There was no fire but a positive fountain of turnips. Jo began to giggle. Suddenly everything seemed so foolish. Her head was splitting, they were expecting hell on earth and she was being bombarded with singed turnips.

Then it stopped being amusing. Another knife slashed downwards. It hit. Seeming to cling for long seconds to the old building below. Jo cried out. Her angry pain lost in the rolling blare of thunder. That was their own building. She ran forward, bucket swinging up to hurl water at the first flicker of flames as they showed. They died, but unseen flames bloomed deeper in the wood.

Pam ran out of the front door calling, "Jo, inside. The beams are burning."

A dozen people raced to help. A ring of older children spread out under Mike's eagle eyes and clear calm orders. Lightening snapped at the flank of a second building, taking a great bite from one wooden side. Terrible sounds came from a woman who had taken part of the strike. She reeled back, clothes flaming, one side of her face charred to the bone so that her teeth showed. Rome was there in seconds dousing the fire as he rolled her in wet blankets. But the agony continued until his fist jolted her into merciful oblivion.

Another blue slash was answered by yellow flame. Half of the settlement buildings were on fire. Cursing people scurried to and fro with buckets of water, containers of earth, shovels, or soaked cloths. Jo dragged a dirty hand across her sweating face wondering how Dana was holding up. She glanced through the gates. No grass sparked as yet. They had a fire-break all around them and thanks to Shay's insistence, it was far wider than they'd ever expected to need.

There was a respite but Jo was afraid it wouldn't last long. She stared about her, where was Shay? From above a clear voice exhorted someone to move ass. Jo smiled, looking upwards to where Shay led a group busily layering the roofs with a heavier level of damp earth. But why?

She called the question up. The reply sent her scrambling for the tower.

"Ohhh, Goddess."

Shay's teeth gleamed white through the soot and dirt on her face. "I know. The grass has caught. With this wind, it'll come at us like a bullet train the minute the direction changes. It's blowing West right now but if it veers this way..."

Jo was too busy scrambling down again to reply. She tore across the yard to where Mike and Rome stood.

"Fill every bucket you have and come with me."

The gully sides were high bare earth and rock. But if the fire swept over, the air could sear lungs, light dry wool. With a line of people carrying brimming slopping containers, she ran for the gully.

"Douse the sheep 'til they drip. Pull the blindfolds down over the animals' mouths as well and wet the cloth. If any of you want out from here, leave."

She forced a smile as heads were shaken slowly. Fred adored his four-footed changes. She'd hoped he would stay. Left unattended the beasts might well panic. If they broke out to escape the fire their deaths would only be more certain. She left him with water in a brimming paddle pool normally kept for the smallest children. They'd thrust it under the rock shelf to one side. They left buckets with Fred and his two assistants, before Jo led her people back to the settlement. Above them Shay had the roofs piled high in damped earth. Her sudden cry of warning came even as below they felt the wind change.

"It's coming!"

Jo screamed instructions. There was ordered confusion as they obeyed. At a time like this no one was stupid enough to question her. She only hoped that attitude would carry over once the fire had burned out. Small groups returned with hoses, lengths of pipe and pumps. These were connected quickly. Now was the time to use the electricity they had. From her vantage point Shay was calling information.

"Wind's still swinging. The fire may pass us. Hang on!"

They all felt the shift then as the wind increased.

"It's coming right for us now. Five minutes maybe." Her binoculars flashed as they caught the light.

"Shay, get down."

"Shut up and get the pumps started. I don't plan to burn."

She turned back to watch as Jo exhorted those below. With slow surges of power the pumps lifted shimmering curtains of spray aloft. They soaked the thick layers of earth that cloaked the roofs, water filled the guttering and rained back down onto the compound. Jo had hand pumps ready. As soon as the power was drained, they'd attach those and continue to damp the building roofs. She wondered where Dana had gone. It seemed to be quite some time since she'd seen her. Busy somewhere no doubt. At least, there'd be no shortage of water. The huge underground tanks were full. So, too, was the small earth dam where the stream neared the walls.

"Two minutes!"

The wind had picked up strength, blowing squarely into the faces of those who stood in its path. Water ran down the walls, soaked the compound into mud, and saturated the clothing of those who waited.

"It's coming!"

A scream from above as Shay catapulted from the roof edge. A torrent of directed water promptly soaked her as she landed.

She had time for one approving grin before spinning to face the inferno. Beyond the walls, driven by eager winds the monster came. Starving for fuel. Ravening destruction.

Birds flew up to safety while below feral beasts ran for their lives, many diving to haven in the dam. Grass fires burn swiftly. The flames licked at the edge of the bare ground then curved to follow the lines of dry grass. Fire reared up, leaning towards the high concrete walls. Within those walls the pumps faltered.

Jo's voice cracked out. "Pumps two and four off. Fix hand pumps. Pump teams in on two and four."

The drop in power use allowed one and three to run a few minutes longer before they, too, faltered. But by then, their teams were ready, even as the fire leaned down, four lines of water rose to meet it once more. People heaved and strained at the pump bars. But the water was there and the heart to raise it. The fire hesitated, splitting to either side of the walls. Burning pieces of grass stem spun on the wind. The roar of the flames was deafening. Still, the water poured upwards. The burning twigs landed in vain. Almost before the fire had cleared the break on the other side of the walls, Shay was back on the roof reporting.

"I can see Fred and the other two. They've waving. They're okay."

Cheers broke out below.

"The fire's going on. Even if the wind swings it back around at us there's nothing left to burn."

"Pumps off," Jo called as exhausted teams slowed. "Anything else, Shay?"

"Yes, the storm is heading away east. But there's rain cloud coming in from the west. It looks like we'll get that tonight."

Jo turned. "Mike. Rome. Check everyone. Find out who's hurt, and who was killed? Then get the tunnels emptied and everyone up here again. Billy. I want the animals and the people in from the gully and under cover. Alex, get hot food started. See to it that there's enough for everyone as they come in."

Shay dropped beside her from the lower roof edge. "I'll break out the drinks, love, one for us each. It'll help."

Jo nodded, managing to disengage herself from all those who'd like to ask questions now that the emergency seemed to be over. Once back in her room, she slumped on the bed exhausted. At least one person was horribly injured, and would almost certainly die, many would have lesser hurts. Two of the buildings would need extensive repair. She found tears were sliding down her face. She turned her face into the soft diamonds of her cherished quilt and wept. She'd had no time for that during the trip north, nor over the last year while they struggled for survival.

Now, she cried helplessly for all the times she had not had the time to grieve. She cried for the University friends she would never see again. For her mother, her father and for her home, so far away in space and time. She knew much of her reaction was shock but still she was couldn't halt the tears.

Finally there was a soft tap at the door. Jo was unable to speak but the door opened anyway. Ngaire entered, following the sounds of grief, as she drifted towards the bed. Wordlessly she enfolded Jo in her arms. She patted Jo's back, rubbed her steel-taut shoulders until they relaxed a little. At length Jo was cried out. Ngaire released her slowly.

"What's the damage out there, do you know?"

Ngaire sighed. "It was Lisa who was burned. She died. Mike thinks it was shock. Rome has a nasty burn down one arm. A lot of others have small burns, bruises and cuts. Fred's a bit scorched. The animals are mostly safe. The buildings can be fixed. Shay says that there's still enough water in the ground tanks to get us through the summer if we don't waste any."

"Then we survived."

Ngaire hugged her. "I guess we did."

Jo hugged her friend back. "I guess we did, too. What about beds for those whose rooms were hit?"

"Shay's seeing to that. With the bunkhouses finished we have plenty of spare beds. Shay says that once we're back to normal she wants to take scouts out. They need to know what farms and other places are still there."

"That's okay. She can go out when she's ready. But what about Dana?"

Ngaire cocked her head to one side. "What about her? I suppose she's all right. No one's said anything."

Jo felt a twinge of fear. "I never saw her after the first alarm. One minute she was giving orders. The next she'd handed everything over to me and vanished. Ngaire, get some of the others and look for her. Something could be wrong."

She listened to the footsteps as the blind woman hurried away. Dear Goddess, let Dana be unharmed. But deep in her heart she knew. She was dry-eyed and unsurprised when Shay came quietly into their room to break the news.

"Where was she?"

"In her room. She must have known she was having another attack. Didn't want to distract us," Shay said gently. "She was lying there as if she was sleeping." She held out an envelope with Jo's name on it. "This was on the table by the bed. Read it, love. Don't worry, Mike and Rome are in charge outside. Everything's getting done."

She watched as her friend opened the letter. Jo read it slowly, then again. Finally she looked up.

"She'd had other earlier attacks she never told us about. She had an inhaler to help but it was a particular kind."

Shay looked blank. "We could have got her more."

Jo looked down at the letter. "No. The kind Dana needed were only good for a year or so and they came from overseas. It's been over a year since the bug hit. Any we found wouldn't have been any use to her. She says her mother and grandmother both died from heart problems. They were hereditary. She knew what would happen once the inhalers stopped working. She wants me to take over as leader." She stopped, looking up miserably. "Shay, I can't."

"Seems to me you did pretty well out there today. Why can't you?"

"I'm not old enough. Damn it, I'm not quite twenty-three. Who'll listen if I give orders?"

Shay gave a feral smile. "Anyone who wants to survive."

"Love, I can't run this place on your guns."

"No, but wait until we're back to normal. It's too much of a shock otherwise. First the fire, losing Lisa, some of our people hurt and buildings damaged. Now Dana. Get her buried or whatever and people calmed down before you start anything."

It made sense. Jo nodded slowly. "Tell Mike and Rome, we'll have to work out a service for Dana and decide what to do with her."

"I will. You stay there a moment."

She slipped out to find the pair. When they returned quietly Jo was sitting, writing. She looked up. "Has the word about Dana spread yet?"

"Yes," Rome answered her softly. "What about that letter?"

Jo handed it to him. He read it with Rome reading over his shoulder. Then they looked up at Jo.

"Dana wanted you to be leader," Mike said slowly. "I agree." He grinned wearily, "I know why, too. Dana told me once that the best person to lead was often the one who didn't want to. They weren't power-hungry. You're conscientious, responsible, educated and you look ahead at what the next generations will have to work with. Really you've been de facto leader since that heart attack Dana had a couple of months ago."

"What about Shay, people listen to her?"

Shay snorted. "Sure they listen, but on an emergency basis. If I yell "duck!" everyone does. But for the long term? Dana was right."

Rome gave a grunt of agreement. "That's true. Even in an emergency they listen to you, Jo. You did one hell of a job out there today when the power faded on the pumps."

"Fine. What about Dana?" Shay looked at them.

Jo nodded at her. "Let's get on with what we can do now. Dana will wait a day or so."

Showers fell much of the night cooling the land and putting out the dangers of still smouldering hot-spots. Jo worked through part of the dark hours, before staggering exhausted to bed long after midnight. By the time she woke it was a bright and clear rain-washed morning. Shay was holding a tray and the cat was purring and pouncing at Jo's shifting feet under the quilt.

Jo sat up and stared out of the window. "Shay! How long have I slept?"

"Long enough to be rested. Now sit up and eat this before I drop it. No," as she saw Jo was about to reach for her clothes. "Sit, eat. I'll talk while you do."

She perched on the bed end listing work completed as Jo ate hungrily. "Dana and Lisa's bodies are in the coldest part of the tunnels. People are taking it in turns to sit with them. Lisa's friends want her buried in the orchard as usual but we'd all like to do something different about Dana. Something to mark her out."

"I know. We'll think of something."

They did. In the end Dana was placed in the small rock cave at the end of the gully near the settlement gates. Rocks were heaped up to close off the mouth. Finally, a flat slab of stone was fitted into the centre. On that Billy and his friend carved Dana's name and the dates. It still didn't feel quite right to Jo but the others were satisfied. The heaped flowers faded, life went back to normal and Jo was leader, Shay, Mike and Rome showing by example that they took Jo's orders. Somehow no one ever questioned it. Jo would have spoken but Mike and Rome advised her to say nothing.

"If people weren't suited, they'd say so. You know this lot, never keep anything to themselves when they don't agree."

Jo accepted the fait accompli and gradually she fitted into the role until in a few more weeks it was as if she had always led. Dana had been right in her choice.

Chapter Eleven

Almost two months after the fire, Shay went looking for her friend. With her she led two saddled ponies with a fat food sack tied to one saddle. There was no need for words, Jo swung up to join her, only too glad to have a few hours free. They traveled first at a canter, then as their mounts ran off their eagerness, at a peaceful walk.

At length Jo spoke, "What are we doing exactly?"

"Scouting locally to see where the fires went." Shay struck a pose, grinning. "You didn't think I was wasting time and resources just for us, did you?" She produced a lop-sided leer. "Or it could always be that I wanted you out here to myself."

Jo found she was giggling helplessly. Shay raised an offended eyebrow, which set Jo off even more. Finally, she leaned over her mount's neck abandoning herself and laughed until her sides ached. It felt so good to let go. Out here she didn't have anyone demanding she organise them. There were no questions. No constant invasions. At last she straightened.

"Goddess I needed that."

Shay rode close, leaning over to hug her at the end of a long arm. "I know, love. You've been looking a bit over-wound lately. I thought a day out would do you good. But this really does have to be done. I just chose to take you, and only you, okay?"

Jo sighed. "I'm glad you did."

She admired the land as they rode. It was typical country with the grass, farmhouses sprinkled about, lines of shelter-belt trees and here and there, one single tree centering a field. The secondary road they were following was showing the effects of the time without maintenance. Originally, it had been a narrow sealed strip with wider gravelled edges. Now the gravel was all grass and flowering weeds. Even the seal looked worn in places with potholes forming.

Shay halted her pony to look down at one of the larger holes. "In another couple of years, roads like this will be breaking up completely. The main highways will last though. Maybe for a long time."

"But not forever," Jo noted. "That's something to put in the records." She grinned as Shay looked puzzled. "The walls, dear, the walls. If concrete roads fall apart eventually, the walls will too. I was thinking of that a while back. I know where there's a warehouse filled with those indestructible sacks farmers used. They break down, but only if Iradiphosphide is poured over them, otherwise I seem to recall they have a life of centuries. If we collected them all to pack away, they'd be great for patching the walls when it becomes necessary."

She saw Shay was still looking baffled. "If you put one into a hole or over a broken bit of wall, then filled it with earth and tied it off, you'd have a good solid patch."

Shay's face lit up. "Hey, that isn't a half bad idea. How far *is* this warehouse?"

"Over on the edge of the forest. Rome scouted it out a few weeks back. Want to go there now?"

Shay considered. "If we went back for a truck." She visualised the roads. "Even across country and riding hard it would be too far for today." She looked a question.

Jo shook her head. "Let's leave it. I doubt anyone will steal them. We could go tomorrow, for today. I'd just like to be with you."

She was still a little shy at saying such things aloud no matter the truth of her words. But it was worth it to see Shay's answering smile. Not her usual brash grin, but a beam of love and affection that was like a soft caress. They stopped early afternoon to mark their maps for the scouts. Shay looked down at her pencil marks.

"We lost a lot of single farmhouses in that fire."

"And two townships, "Jo added. "From the look of the second one the lightning got the fuel tanks at the gas station." She smiled. "We'll run out of fuel eventually but Alex thinks he may be able to make methane and convert a lot of the vehicles. That way we may have them operational a lot longer. We should keep an eye open for things he needs when we ride out like this. I can mark anything like that on our maps."

She folded the maps carefully. It was wonderful to have them. The old Lands and Survey style showed every fold of ground, every stream, pond and gully. The maps were quite simply invaluable to the settlement. She nudged her pony after Shay who was heading for the old farmhouse ahead.

There they laid out the food and ate eagerly. Once finished, Shay vanished into the old building in search of the toilet. Jo had packed away the remnants of lunch when it dawned on her that Shay had been gone too long. A cold feeling slid down her spine. She gathered herself to charge in, then, it was as if Shay was whispering at her shoulder.

"Never bust into anything without knowing what's happening. Enemies hide behind doors for idiots who do that. Circle. Come in the way they'll least expect. Do something to confuse them. That way you have a chance they'll be off guard."

Jo caught herself back. It wouldn't help if Shay were in trouble and Jo added herself to the bag. She strolled casually over to the ponies to untie them.

As she did so she called over her shoulder, "I'll just water the ponies then I'll join you. Be about ten minutes."

Hastily, she led their mounts around the windowless corner. She could reach the stream from here but had no intention of doing so. Instead she dropped the reins. The ponies were trained to stand if the reins were left that way. She cat-footed back to consider the farmhouse. Not the sagging splintered door. That way an enemy would surely be expecting her. She padded silently past trying desperately to remember all the street tricks Shay had ever told her.

From behind the wall she heard a tiny sliding scrape. A foot moving incautiously? She froze, listening. She'd been in the old house twice while on scouting rides with Shay. She forced her mind to recall the layout. From the closeness of the sound they must be in the second bedroom. That meant she'd possibly be expected to come through the inner doorway or outer window if she'd rejected the outer door. Where would an enemy be if he wanted to cover both possibilities? The wall next to the other room would be blank as would the one bordering on the passage. But it was in that wall that the inner door opened.

Yes, of course. An ambusher would wait behind the door in the wall corner of the passage and the other blind wall. That way they could cover both door and window. If she entered from the window on the right they'd have to swing further around. Even better that was the one with two panes of glass missing — unless they'd be expecting that because of the missing panes? Oh, damn, She'd go with it. She couldn't stand here second-guessing herself all afternoon. Whoever it was would get suspicious very soon if there was no sign of her.

She crouched silently below the window staring up. A faint brush of clothing against the wall came to her ears. They were where she'd hoped. The suspense was killing her. Where was Shay? Had she been injured, killed?

Jo took a deep breath, checked her safety catch was off and stood in one smooth movement. She thrust the shotgun through the broken pane, centered it and pulled the trigger. In automatic reflex, she pumped in a second shell, firing again and again even as her enemy was falling. It wasn't until the gun was empty she was able to lower the weapon.

She still couldn't see her friend. In a complete panic by now Jo raced around the house, and burst through the doorway to scan the room. A muffled thumping drew her attention to the dust-covered twin beds. On the floor between them a long bundle thudded its heel against the floor. It was Shay, blood smudging her forehead, her eyes furious. Jo pounced, dropping her gun on the nearest bed.

"Shay, oh Goddess! Are you all right?" In return she received a glare and a frantic mumble through the tightened gag. "Sorry." She ripped it free. "Is that better?"

Shay worked her mouth for a minute. Once she could speak she did so, tersely and to the point. "Load your gun, check there's no one else you can see. Jam your knife into the floorboards. I'll get these ropes off while you check."

Jo thrust the knife into the boards before stumbling to the window to stare through. The horses weren't in sight. Was that good or bad? Her vision was graying in and out. That grew worse as her gaze fell on the body lying behind the door. She sat abruptly on the bed, coughing as dust flew. Shay had freed herself. Gently she took the gun from Jo's shaking hands, loaded it and returned it to her friend.

"Don't shoot me by mistake. I'm just going to take a look around out there." She was back in minutes. "No sign of anyone else." She led Jo to the other bedroom before gathering Jo's shaking form into her arms.

"You did very well, love. He had plans for both of us I'd rather not have featured in." She hugged and held until Jo was calm again. Then her caresses changed from soothing to exciting.

"It'd be a shame to waste all this adrenaline."

Gently she undressed Jo. Hands, mouth all loving, reassuring. Jo found it was true. Perhaps it was the adrenaline but she co-operated with an abandonment that was foreign to her usual self. Shay left her for a few minutes at last. She returned with the man's pack that she emptied on the bed. Both women blinked down.

"Maro!" said Shay flatly. "He was completely maro."

They studied the heap of glittering jewellery. Shay stooped to run her hands through it. Jade pendants and earrings mixed with sterling silver bracelets inlaid with iridescent shell panels. Carved whalebone curved around flashing diamonds. Here and there, gold coins sprinkled the heap. Apart from that, there were only a box of shells and a can opener.

"Maro!" Shay said again. "He's better off dead." She took Jo's hand to lead her away."Let him keep it. I've got the gun and shells."

Jo followed in silence. She was going to have nightmares about this, she knew it, but better nightmares than the reality that this could have been. For the first time she fully understood what Shay had been saying during their time together. It *was* better to kill than be killed if that was the only choice. She couldn't find pleasure in it. Couldn't enjoy the stalk and the hunt. But at least she no longer felt guilty. Saving Shay made up for a lot. She rode quietly home with her love beside her. Not happy but content. She'd done the right thing.

She had a quiet few days after that, if one didn't count the rebuilding, stock work, Rome wanting to know if he and Mike should bring back a truckload of the sacks, Ngaire asking about more wool for spinning, and everyone else asking questions and expecting answers Jo often didn't have. That unexciting if overworked period was ended with the death of Hine. She had borne a son but after that she faded almost unnoticeably until Pam found her asleep with a quiet smile on her face. The sleep was a permanent one. They buried her after their customs, each who had known her recounting some small event. It seemed as if Fred had held to life only to be with her. He came to speak with Ngaire as she sat spinning one afternoon the week after Hine's death.

"I may not be around much longer."

Ngaire looked surprised. "That's a bit abrupt. Are you planning to leave us?"

A soft chuckle came to her ears, "No, my dear, no. But you know Hine and I were very ill when the bug hit. I was worse off but she was determined to have the child. She said she wanted to leave a legacy for the future. Someone so that our names and blood wouldn't be lost. It killed her but she expected that. Now my own health is catching up with me as I expected it would. I can feel it."

"How?"

"I'm a bit weaker every morning, it's more of an effort to get up, more of an effort to do anything at all in fact. I eat less, too. My appetite is going. There's no real pain, just a twinge or two. But with Hine gone, there's nothing to hang on for and I won't allow myself to be a burden on the rest of you. I just want to be sure the boy will be cared for."

The blind woman nodded slowly. "Jo will see to that and the rest of us, too. I'll make certain of it. I'll promise if you wish?"

"Thank you very much, my dear."

She heard the slow footsteps fade just as lighter ones came towards her. They were familiar and she turned to smile at the doorway.

"Jo. Fred's just been here. He seems to think he's dying."

"He is. We've known it for weeks now."

Ngaire said nothing but the tilt of her head was invitation to explain.

Jo did so. "The kids started calling him 'Ol' Fred.' Some of us found we were doing the same and took a second look at him. It was true. Neither of he nor Mary were out of their thirties but they looked twice that age. We think the bug may have damaged their hearts. We don't really know but Mavis Gallan thought so and she was an experienced nurse. Fred was really ill at the time the bug struck. Billy says they all thought he'd die. Hine was up in couple of weeks but Fred was ill almost to the time we found them."

"He thinks that Hine died because of the baby?"

"It's possible. Mavis claimed that Hine being pregnant would run her health down. And, well truthfully, I don't think she wanted to live in the world she'd been left with any longer. Fred's looked worse ever since she died. He's tired all the time now and I'm sure he's getting chest pains. We've all seen him stop and hold his fist into his chest."

"Are you going to try to stop him doing whatever he plans?"

"No, love. We can't force him to live if he doesn't want to. We'd only make his last days miserable."

As Jo and Ngaire talked Fred had found Shay. She was up to her eyebrows in oil as she, Bob and Billy stripped down one of the scout bikes. Her hair was tied back and she was completely happy.

"I need to talk to you."

"Okay. Just let me finish here." She gave instructions to the tall boy beside her as she wiped her hands on a rag. Fred stood watching them both. It was almost a year and a half since he'd met her. She hadn't changed much but the boys had shot up in that time. They looked tanned, competent and content with their lives.

Shay glanced at him, "We can go over to the pumpkin shed. There'll be no one over there at the moment."

They reached the shed and Shay stood waiting to hear. Fred studied her. In many ways she was an enigma to most of those in the settlement. Proud, amoral, self-educated, and ferociously loyal to those she loved or cared about. Jo was her lover and no one ever doubted that the love between them was genuine — or that Shay would kill, or if need be, die for her friend. Shay had her own way of looking at life. This time he was hoping that would be to his advantage.

He started with a quick clear recounting of the facts ending with his own belief. "I won't last another year even if I take to my bed. The boy will be older by then though. He'll miss me. If I die now, he's too young to notice I'm gone or to grieve. Ngaire's promised he'll be cared for. Hine's gone. Let me follow her."

"What do you want me to do?"

"I have to say it? All right then, you kill people."

He saw the sudden wicked look in her eyes and spoke quickly. "I've never said anything to anyone. But it was Johnny's woman. The one who chose to leave while we were in Palmerston North. She hated us all, you in particular. She'd have found someone to tell out of spite and she knew too much. I couldn't sleep. I saw you go out after her and come back again. I guessed. That was right. For all of us to be safe."

"So I do as you want or you talk?"

Fred shook his head. "No," he told her gently. "Someone has to make the really hard decisions. Jo's a good, kind, person and she's level-headed. She tempers justice with mercy. She's the right person to lead here. But she needs you for the hard choices. The settlement needs you. But, Shay, if it's right to get rid of enemies,

160

isn't it also right to help a friend?"

Fred paused. "Help me for the good of everyone. What good is it if they have to nurse me for months? If I can't work and I'm just another mouth to feed?" He straightened proudly. "I want to go. I'm asking you to help me do that. Help me find Hine again."

He stood, holding himself to attention, as once he would have faced an officer. He saw Shay consider. Then slowly, very slowly, she nodded.

"When?"

"Give me two days to say good-bye to my son and my friends. I need to say who gets my gear. Then you bring a drink to my room the second evening. I'll wash out the glass. No evidence to embarrass you." He glanced sideways at her. "You know Mike and Rome have guessed. I heard them talking once. Not a lot but enough to know what they meant because I already knew."

"I thought they might. They're realists."

"And Jo isn't." It was half statement, half question.

"Jo is Jo. She believes in democracy, romance, education, and she cries at sad endings in books. As you said, she's a good leader but she needs someone for the hard decisions. The ones she could never accept still less carry out."

He nodded as she looked at him. Shay eased her shoulders, "All right. Not tonight but tomorrow night. I'll bring you a glass of the good whiskey."

Fred took her hands in his and held them briefly. "Thank you."

He marched away across the compound as Shay looked after him thinking of all they had said. It was true. Jo was a leader but she believed strongly in the rights of those she led. Most of the time that was fine, but occasionally it was dangerous. It was then that Shay moved in secret to hold the balance.

She didn't always like what she had to do. Shay blew out making her lips flutter. It was the times that made it so. She hated killing children although so far that had happened only once. No child having found a haven like the settlement would be keen to leave again. Not if they were honest. But better the occasional child than the whole settlement. Jo accepted any child who appeared. She also allowed them the right to leave if they wanted. That first time Shay had trailed the boy. She'd found him meeting a hard-faced dangerous-looking man who interrogated the lad as of right. Shay had listened.

It was quickly clear that the boy was not only older than he appeared, he had been sent in to learn the settlement secrets and defenses. Now he was listing them one by one. Shay hadn't hesitated once she was sure of their plans. She shot, both barrels catching the pair. The man survived briefly. Just as long as it took Shay to lay down her gun and bring out a blade.

She made other decisions as well. After that, she had her own system. She arranged that those who chose to leave were given a farewell, a package of their favourite food and drink to take with them. Under Shay's hands that package became death. Shay followed each departure, waiting until the end then stripping the body for the dogs.

Sometimes where she had quite liked the person she was sorry. But that was no deterrent. Her over-riding concerns were Jo and her friends in the settlement. She was protecting them, that was all that counted. She acted with care, knowing that if her lover ever found out what Shay was doing their love, and even their friendship, would be over. She shrugged. Many of those who'd died were not deliberate traitors.

But there were others out there who'd tear knowledge from them anyway. Shay had tried for months to convince Jo they should get rid of these other ragtag mobs. She'd failed thus far. But she'd keep trying. In time the big city to their south would be a permanent barrier. But it wasn't as yet. And too many came seeking a place that seemed to have become a new El Dorado in post-collapse myth.

Her eyes gazed out over the compound as she stood there thinking. The children who'd survived the bug were growing up. Jo had started a school at the beginning of the year. It was her intention that every child should be able to read, write and do simple arithmetic. Those with ability would be taken further. Marriages, too, were beginning again. Alex had married the owner of the Siamese. Billy and Bob now both seventeen were starting to look at girls and even without weddings there were pregnancies.

At last count, they were over two hundred people and Jo was becoming expert at finding what a child or incomer was best able to do. During the days many left to rework the nearby farms, or tend the vegetable gardens and berry bushes. The nearby veggie gardens had all been established along the stream with irrigation trenches leading through the neat rows. Piping led the settlement's waste water to the gardens nearest as well. It wasn't a bad life. Everyone worked hard yet they still had time for evening songfests or listening to Jo read from one of the many books of fiction they held here. Jo. Shay smiled, that reminded her, she had something that she wanted to talk over with her partner. She went in search of her.

"Shay?" Jo jumped as she was tapped on the shoulder. "I thought you were fixing that bike?"

"All done. The boys are taking it out for a test run. I thought we could take a ride. I found a farm out by the harbour that's still self-sowing some items. There's potatoes,"

"We could use those, what else?"

"Pumpkins, silverbeet, rhubarb and quite a lot of fruit. We should start sending a work party over there. They had red current and raspberry bushes in fenced enclosures so the birds couldn't get at them. Those're loaded."

Jo moaned. "My weakness. There's nothing urgent at the moment. I could take the day off if you really want me to. What say we go alone?"

She draped an arm about Shay, receiving a hug in return. This she'd been given, Jo thought. Not only love but also the ability to show it. Her family had always been a loving one but never demonstrative about that affection. Shay was a warm and tactile lover. As time passed Jo had learned to respond without embarrassment. She detached herself to trot into the shed, returning at the wheel of a small carrier. Shay had her bike waiting.

She struck a dramatic pose as Jo began to smile. "Follow me!"

The bike engine roared as Shay accelerated. Giggling, Jo followed with the carrier. The berry bushes were richly loaded as Shay had said. They picked contentedly, filling basket after basket until Shay leaned over.

She made a face, "Ah-ha me proud beauty, I had an ulterior motive for luring you out here alone." Jo saw with surprise that Shay was nervous under the joking. She waited. This must be quite something. She reached out to touch the slender hard-muscled arm.

"Whatever it is I'll listen."

Shay sucked in a deep breath and let it out speaking fast. "I want us to have a family." She waited.

"So do I, love. I suppose you're thinking of Mike and Rome," Jo said.

For a moment Shay stared, incredulous. Then she whooped, seizing her lover around the neck. She pushed Jo back onto the sun-warned grass as she nuzzled her throat. "You miserable so-an-so. You've been thinking about this too."

Jo squirmed, laughing a little. "Yes. Why not? I talked to Hine before she died. She knew how we could do it. Even in the last century women could manage the procedures without actual sex. Mike and Rome talked to me more than once. I think they were hinting that they'd like children. You know how good they are with the kids. We can talk to them when we get back." She eyed Shay thoughtfully. "That isn't all on your mind, is it. What's the rest while we're alone."

"That's okay. The other stuff isn't personal, it'll wait." Shay rolled over to look up at the clear blue of the sky. "Talking of kids, have you heard what they've been calling the settlement lately?"

"Yes. It's an odd variation. I wondered where it came from."

Shay grinned, "From some of the little ones. They were calling the place Dana's Pa. You know, the Maori word for a fortified settlement. But they sort of slurred it."

"So it wound up as Danapa. I see. And you think we should make it legal? I think that's a great idea, Shay. It was her place. If she hadn't shared it with us, we wouldn't be here today." She stroked Shay's hand. "I can stand up tonight and ask for a vote on it?"

Shay grunted, "That's something to think about too. We've gone along with everyone having a voice. But one day it's going to come up that we can't reach an agreement but we have to act. Then we vote and accept the majority verdict. But who has the right to vote? Adults? How old is an "adult"? Why not the kids? If they're old enough to work and fight, don't they deserve a voice?"

Jo groaned. "Your first problems were the easiest. Babies are fine. A settlement name is fine. But who has the right to vote could get awkward."

"You'll manage."

"Oh, it's 'you'll manage', is it? What about you?"

Shay laughed. "I think up the questions. That's my half done."

Jo pounced, tickling. "Done, is it? People who ask that sort of question should be punished." Shay squirmed as tickling fingers dug into her flanks.

"Ah! I'm sorry. I'm sorry."

She rolled frantically, clutched in turn. A quick flip and it was Jo who was underneath. They tussled, enjoying the sun and the warmth between them, the scent of the grass and berry juice. Slowly the game merged into loving until they broke apart to sprawl happily. Jo leaned over, tickling Shay's nostrils with a grass stem.

"I'm so glad you found me. I know I don't say that sort of thing much. But I love you. I'd die if anything happened to you. That's why I want our children. They'll be a part of us that never dies."

Arms reached over to embrace her. "That's why I want them too." Shay heaved herself onto one elbow glancing up at the sun. "Look at the time. We'd better start back before they send out search parties."

They strolled back to the loaded carrier. Jo set it in motion heading for the road as Shay's bike rumbled in pursuit. Atop the carrier seat, Jo was thinking. She knew Mike and Rome would agree. They'd talked to her several times on the subject. She'd guessed then that they were hoping she'd come to a decision that would involve them. It was this voting business which was likely to cause problems. Her mind turned to the difficulties of sorting out who could vote — and even harder — who couldn't.

The suggestion of the name won unanimous applause when Jo spoke that evening. Those who'd known Dana approved strongly. Several stood to say so and why. When they voted there were no dissenting voices. The settlement was now and forever Danapa. The more private decision was also easy once Jo and Shay had found their friends.

Mike looked steadily at both women. "I always wanted children. So does Rome. But we don't want to be shut out."

Jo nodded. "Say as a base decision Shay and I each have two children. that being one from each of you. We bring the children up as a quartet. It's better if they have four parents. That way if anything happens to one of us or if one of us is away a while, there's still three adults to keep the group stable"

"We get on well," Rome said. "I think it would work. We can set up a suite with double bedrooms on either side of the kids' room. Okay?" He collected three nods. "Then let's go over the place and see how we can do that best and where." He reddened a little as he turned to look at Jo. "You let us know when's the best time." His voice, "I...it's a wonderful thing, I'd like..."

His arms came halfway up, fell back. It was Shay who understood. She took one light step towards him, her hands encircling as she pulled him into a quick hard hug. Then they were all hugging, laughing, sniffing a little. One decision remained to bother Jo as leader. Their home had a name, and she would soon be part of a family. But the 'right to vote' question remained.

That dragged on once it had been raised. Some of the adults strenuously resisted the idea that children should be able to vote. Eventually, after a series of votes in which only adults took part it was decided. Children should be regarded as adult at fourteen so long as they were of normal intelligence. However if a younger child contributed to Danapa in such a way that they were found worthy in full assembly, then they might vote from that age, no matter what it was.

The latter suggestion had been Shay's. To her the right to vote was a privilege. Younger children should be given an incentive to strive towards it. That night, she made love with fervour. Teasing and touching until both were too tired to continue. Then she lay a while watching her love sleep.

They'd weathered almost two years together. She hoped there would be many more years together. Long enough to see their children grow up. Years in which they'd see Danapa prosper and the laws that they were making now grow into a way of life for the settlement. But just in case she'd talk to a few close friends. Make contingency plans. She smiled as she slipped into sleep. All would be well. She was certain of it.

Chapter Twelve

It had been a pleasant delusion, Jo thought wryly, four months later. Both she and Shay had become pregnant easily but where Jo was carrying without problems, Shay was not. She had begun to bleed, just enough to worry them all. Jo made cheerful noises but looking at her friend, she was beginning to fear. Shay didn't look right. Her fine-boned face was puffy and her skin unhealthy-looking. She was sick, not just in the mornings, but any time she ate.

Shay knew she wasn't well. Her own body was losing weight. She'd weighed herself when they began this and she was as she had always been. Just on one hundred and twenty pounds. It was a see-saw. The baby growing, while she lost. She hated not having the energy. She loathed vomiting all the time. The mood swings drove her crazy.

Lately, she'd taken to vanishing to be by herself. It was the best alternative to savaging friends verbally. Or even worse, fighting back the desire to physically attack someone. She knew Jo worried about her, but it didn't help. In fact, being fussed over constantly was making her feel smothered. Shay found she was blaming Jo for the awful way she felt. Today, she had taken the carrier out to one of the farms where there was a small orchard with late apples. The peaceful rhythm of the picking, the silence of the day, soothed her. She gradually relaxed, her mind beginning to drift to new plans.

She turned over an idea she'd been considering lately. It would be something to take Jo's mind off Shay's health. She trundled slowly home to meet reproaches with an abrupt announcement.

"I've been thinking about an annual celebration."

Jo looked interested. "Oh? What?"

"One day, our guns won't be repairable. We'll run out of shells and fuel for the vehicles. But we'll still have dog packs and human dangers. We'll still need scouts and hunters. If we start an annual games using different types of weapon, we can encourage the children to learn them."

"What sort of weapons? Bows, I suppose. Spears?"

"Slings, boomerangs..."

"Boomerangs?" Jo was startled.

"Why not? They work. We could break the games into sections. One competition for any throwing weapon. One for propelled missiles and so on."

"I see." Jo found the idea good. "You'll have all the children becoming experts with that sort of thing before we run out of guns and shells. It's a wonderful idea. We can add to it, too. The arts are just as valuable. What if this celebration runs longer. We can have sections in singing, dancing, poetry..."

"Weaving, spinning, dying," Shay took up the list. "And what about carving, painting and stuff like that?"

Jo smiled. "Ngaire would like the spinning and weaving section. I bet some of the others would want cooking and jam making added too."

Shay laughed feeling light-hearted for the first time in weeks. "I can see this celebration stretching out for at least a week. Do we have running, jumping and following a trail, too?"

"As you said earlier, why not? We could add horseback riding as well. The idea is to encourage everyone to be good at some of the skills we're going to need to make a self-sufficient life here. As for when we have it," she considered, "I'd say the best time was the end of January. By then we'll have the hay in, the lambing and calving over and a lot of the fruit and vegetable harvests put away. We're usually in the middle of a long fine spell, too."

"No," Shay interrupted. "I've got an even better idea. Listen, love — we split things and have two celebrations. One for all of the outdoor stuff and one of all the indoor. We have the outdoors section when you say. The other section goes on for a week and ends with a mid-winter feast."

Jo stared. "That's perfect. We make it the last day of January and celebrate the New Year. Then have the feast after the other items, and on the last day of July to celebrate the end of Winter because by then it'll be showing that winter's ending. They aren't the original dates, but they're closer to reality." She hugged Shay gently. "Lets get some sleep. Are you going to school in the morning still?"

Shay nodded. She'd started lessons as soon as the school was set up. At first, she received some funny looks from the children. But once they'd seen she was serious they found new interest in the work themselves. Shay was the War-Leader for Danapa. She had mana with many of the smaller children admiring her almost to worship. Shay's appearance in the tiny school had real impact. So, too, did the casual comments Shay dropped from time to time. All emphasised how foolish anyone would be who didn't take advantage of learning while it was there.

Of course with other work, Shay was unable to attend every morning. But she did make an effort to be there at least two or three mornings a week. It was as well she would be part of a four-parent family rather than only two of them. With her scouting, hunting, and schooling she was busy enough as it was. Adding a baby or two would require extra hours in the day.

That was, if the babies arrived. Jo stayed healthy but any pleasure in that was cancelled by her fears over Shay. Her friend continued to be ill with the weight slipping unobtrusively away until she looked as if she were merely skin over the long fine bones. Finally Shay became dizzy when she stood quickly. The first anyone knew of that was when she jumped to her feet and fainted in the seventh month of her pregnancy. Ngaire reached her first, listening to Shay's breathing then straightening with a sigh.

"I think she's all right but she really is going to have to rest. I think she should be put to bed and kept there."

Shay was. That is, she was put to bed. Keeping her in it was something else again. Jo coaxed, cajoled and finally lost her temper.

"Do you want this baby or not?" she yelled

"I want it," Shay snarled back at her. "But does that mean I can't have a life too?"

Jo looked at her. The flare of rage disappeared in her concern and affection. Shay hated being kept anywhere.

"No, love. You can have a life, but not for the next twelve weeks. Ngaire and Pam did more medical reading and ran your blood sample. They don't know a lot but the books and medical machinery we bought up with us say you're toxaemic and malnourished. We know a lot of the drugs still around are useless but Ngaire remembers an idea that may help. Ani's very upset about you, too. She's away with Billy right now looking for some plant she thinks will help."

Shay muttered. The words weren't clear but the tone was resigned. Jo hugged her carefully before pushing a stack of science fiction books closer. Then she left quietly to find Mike and Rome.

"How is she?"

Jo allowed the worry to show. "I'm scared." She said frankly.

Mike's head jerked up as he stared at her, "She's *that* bad?"

"She isn't good. If we can get her through this we can't risk her again. I know we said two babies each but..."

Rome's voice over-rode her. "That doesn't matter. We won't risk losing Shay. I'd rather she lost this baby than we lost her."

Mike was nodding vigorous agreement.

Jo found she was crying, "You're both great."

Rome put his hands on her shoulders. No, we aren't. Listen, Jo. We all want children, but not at anyone's expense. Let alone at the expense of either of you. We'll get through this and then that's it for Shay." He studied her, "How about you, any problems?"

Jo snorted, "I'm as healthy as a horse." She swore savagely to their surprise. It was unlike Jo to use that sort of language. "If only we knew more. You know, we've been lucky up until now. I forgot just how much medical knowledge we've lost since the bug."

"We all forget, until we need it," Mike said quietly. "How often did you stand around thinking medical science was wonderful before the bug hit? It isn't your fault, Jo. It's just going to be one more thing that we'll have to re-learn as far as we can."

Jo left it at that. There was work to do and Shay to care for. Reclaiming medicine would have to wait its turn.

Later, she complained about it to Ngaire who smiled, "Jo, listen to yourself. We lost a whole civilisation out there. We lost ninety-nine per cent of the population if not more. I doubt a single doctor survived. They were the second bunch to die after they'd rushed to help the first cases. Some medical personnel survived the bug, sure. But you didn't hear all the stories I've been collecting. Even where a doctor did make it through the bug they were either killed by some group so someone else wouldn't have them or killed by someone who'd gone crazy over losing their family and everyone they knew.

A lot of people turned on medical staff and any known scientists as if they'd deliberately allowed this to happen and the same for a lot of nurses. Mavis was an exception and she survived because only her own people knew what she was. Of course, it may not have happened everywhere. There may be groups in the South Island that have doctors and scientists surviving. I wouldn't take any bets on it though. Mike is right. We have to re-learn all that but I don't think it'll ever be the same."

"Why not?"

"Because a lot of what we knew was scientists working across from country to country. How long do you think it'll take before that happens again? That's if it ever does," her gentle sightless eyes turned towards Jo. "And are we sure we want it to happen. Think, love. No one knows for sure but I heard a broadcast just before everything went off the air. The people talking blamed modern medicine for the bug. They said it had mutated in response to some of the things done to cure earlier versions."

Jo threw up her hands, "I don't know. We can't just stop trying."

"No, we can't. But maybe we should let those who can't live without more than basic medicine, die." Her voice was suddenly very bitter. "Did you know, Jo, that I'm blind because my parents insisted on having me? They both had a similar hereditary problem.

They were told that there was a more than seventy per cent chance that any child they had would be blind. They ignored that and went ahead. I won't have children. I wouldn't do that to them."

She turned away, making it clear Jo should leave. Jo did so thinking as she walked. So that was why Ngaire had always refused to be more than a friend to any man. Despite her blindness she was an attractive and intelligent woman and an asset to Danapa. In the world before the bug they could have done gene scans on any man who wished to marry her. Nowadays, they had no idea of who carried what. Ngaire wouldn't risk that and Jo understood.

It was fortunate that both Mike and Rome had had special scans only six months before the collapse. They'd planned on approaching a surrogate agency but wanted to be able to prove good health and a clear genetic inheritance first. The medical clearance papers had been some of the small prized possessions they had retained when they joined the trek north. They'd shown them to Jo once. It had helped her decide on them as co-parents. In the world they had now, there must be very few men who knew and could prove their genetic suitability.

She smiled to herself. She'd have picked Mike and Rome even if they'd had no certificates. But it had certainly made her happier to know they did. Shay shouldn't risk having more than the child she now carried. Perhaps Jo would have more than the two originally promised. After all, she seemed to be having no trouble with this one. She looked in on a sleeping Shay before returning to her paperwork. Danapa made no rules about marriage although many still chose a ceremony of sorts. But there was always a record made for babies. With the small gene-pool remaining they dare not risk inbreeding in succeeding generations.

She finished the latest certificate and sat back. They must consider names for the babies she and Shay would have very shortly. Shay had suggested names that were a mixture of their own in some combination. She sat playing with that idea for some time before being interrupted by Pam.

"I've brought your lunch and Shay's. Shall I take both trays through, so you can eat with her?"

Jo nodded. "Is Ani back yet?"

"She's having lunch, then she has to do something with the stuff she brought back. She said to tell you she'll see you both this evening."

Jo nodded. Hopefully Ani could do something. The child was devoted to Shay. Jo remembered the slight ten-year-old that she'd first seen three years ago. Ani had grown considerably, both in size and in abilities. She had impressed some of her people's customs firmly on Danapa as well. When Hari had been killed by the dogs, it was Ani who had insisted on a proper tangi. Now, somewhat modified by time, that was standard for all those who died. The body was kept only twelve hours, not three days. But the waiata, the chants of mourning were sung. Those who attended the tangi mourned openly, allowing their grief to flow out and healing to begin. It had proved a valuable custom for everyone.

She was an idiot, Jo thought suddenly. She knew that Ani sometimes produced medicines made from native plants. The child had said once that her grandmother had known all their uses and had been training Ani in these before the bug. There would be books, tapes, vids of such things. She should have someone search them all out. They'd had their own medical sources all along but she'd been too stupid to see. She'd talk to Ani when the girl came that evening.

Shay awoke when Jo entered. "Hi, love. Is that lunch?"

"No," Jo said, gently sarcastic, "It's poison, I always carry some around in soup bowls."

Shay grinned. "In that case I'll still take it. I couldn't feel much worse," she said wryly. She spooned up the soup slowly. To Jo's delight it stayed down.

"That's an improvement."

"That's Ngaire's binder." Shay contradicted. "She read somewhere that they used to use one a couple of generations ago to stop this kind of problem. You bind the stomach flat and sometimes it helps to control the nausea. The other thing was to eat very small amounts more often and much more slowly. Sort of allowing the stomach time to accept each mouthful before you dump the next on it."

"Makes sense to me."

"Me too. It isn't working every time but I am keeping more down than I was." She spooned up another mouthful of the soup. "I haven't just been lying here either. Bob was in earlier talking about the grass."

Jo looked blank.

"The grass, love. Stuff the cows and horses eat?"

"Oh, yes?"

"It's more looking ahead to what we'll need to do." She settled back against the pillows. "As we grow we need more horses and more sheep and cattle. If we graze them all around Danapa we'll run out of grass pretty fast. With horses it isn't as if we'll only need the mounts we ride. We have to breed them, that means mares, stallions, foals and young stock growing up. But we don't need all of them right here."

Jo understood now. "No, and there's the cattle. We need milk cows here, but not the bulls and the beef animals. With sheep we only need the ones we plan to kill kept close in. So what do we do with them?"

"We send them out to graze in a big circle around the area. We bring the horses in once a year to pick out the ones to break for riding or work. The sheep and cattle go out to graze the same way. Once the milk cows have dried off before they calve again they join them. That way we save the grass by Danapa for the horses we're using at the time, sheep we're planning on eating in the next couple of months, and the cows in milk."

Jo saw a problem, "But what about..." she paused and Shay grinned as she filled in the word Jo didn't want to say.

"Rustlers?" Yeah, well. That's what I've been saying all along. For Danapa to survive we have to draw a line. We need to hold all this area."

She leaned forward earnestly. "We're growing, Jo, in time we could even be too big a group for us to all live in Danapa. I know we've built the place up. Mike estimates that we could house around four hundred now. Once I'm back on my feet we plan to do more. We reckon we could expand the buildings again to house another two or three hundred. But that's about it and do you want people living overcrowded in a new slum?

"People are still coming in, Jo. Oh, not many. Not at once. But it's a steady trickle so that we're just over three hundred on last count. Babies are being born. We've been lucky so far, I've been the only one with real problems. But just you look at the age of most of us. We took in so many kids who were between eight and fifteen or thereabouts. In another few years, all of them will be producing kids of their own and we'll have a population blowout."

That was true, Jo thought. Of the three hundred people in Danapa, more than half were under twenty still. There was also a strong imbalance towards women in the older range. The children were mostly equally divided between male and female. But the adults had arrived in a ratio of some five women to two men. There'd been two reasons for that. More women had survived. With closer contact with their children more women had picked up an infection that had helped to immunise them. Then too, as word spread of a place where women were safe and welcomed, more had managed to find Danapa.

Shay was continuing, "Any time a bunch with mostly men has moved in around here they've been trouble. They take one look at what we've done and what we have, and they want it for themselves. If we hold the whole area down to Auckland they'd have to come through the city."

"So?"

"So in another generation that'll be hard to do as the place falls down. And if we draw a line and make it clear, less people will be keen to risk it. Oh, I know your argument. We'll be isolated. But we don't have to be. We have boats. We fish the Kaipara harbour regularly. In summer, we can sail right down past the city along the coast. Once other groups have stabilised — and I think they will — we can visit, trade with them. But until then I say we draw our line and hold it. Better to fight our battles a long way short of Danapa."

She sank back against her pillows again and Jo changed the subject. Shay allowed it. With every attack against their home, more of its people swung to her way of thinking. In the three years since they'd come north, Danapa had beaten off several serious attempts to take over their settlement. There'd been other minor tries, ranging from attempts to divide and rule internally as Jonathon and his sister had, to attacks on two or three of Danapa's inhabitants when they were outside the walls. That included skirmishes as small bands of would be looters and rapists appeared in the area.

Jo left but Shay continued to remember. Every time one of the people lost a friend, they came further around to Shay's belief. She had only to be patient. She recalled Sue's funeral a few months ago. The woman had been killed by two wandering men who'd been killed in turn by others from Danapa. They'd bought Sue's body back, tangied her on a bier of green branches and Sue's friends had sat up all night singing, recalling events in their friend's life. Together all had laughed, wept and remembered. The body had been dressed in her finest clothing, decked in bright jewellery.

They had laid the dead woman in a trench lined with grass and flowers. In her left hand they had placed a roughly carved gun to show she had died fighting. But in her right she had borne a far more beautifully carved model of a sheep. Sue had been a shepherd who loved her beasts. The gun was donated by a friend, but Sue herself had carved the sheep. The custom was growing up that once a member of Danapa knew what they wished to do with their life, they would carve a life symbol of that. This would go to their grave with them.

Jo, Shay and Ngaire had stepped forward to speak before the grave was filled in.

"Our friend is gone," Jo said. "We have remembered her deeds. We have mourned her passing. We have filled her spirit with our love. Let her pass on in peace. As symbol of our tears we give her water." Leaning down she had sprinkled water gently across Sue's breast.

Ngaire had taken Jo's place then. "Our friend is gone. We give her earth that she may remember our Mother. Let her spirit return to Her." She sprinkled a handful of dry earth and retired to be replaced by Shay.

"Our friend is gone. Let her spirit be warmed by our love and the spirit of fire where ever it may travel." She dropped lightly into the trench placing a lit candle end at the head of the body. At the feet she placed a tiny sealed clay container.

"And let the air of this time and place be yours forever, sister. Know that we love you." With a quick spring she'd rejoined Ngaire and Jo, who moved forward again.

"Earth, Air, Fire, and Water. Let this our sister, Sue Candace, depart in peace. She was. She is. She has gone ahead."

She stepped back as those bearing sheaves of dried grass and flowers flung them down to cover the body. After that more earth had been added until it mounded high. Later, once the earth settled, a fruit tree would be planted at the head of the grave. Danapa's cemetery was becoming an orchard. This was of threefold benefit. The pragmatic — that the trees grew wonderfully. The mystic — that in the fruiting the dead lived on. And the superstitious — that anyone stealing fruit or damaging a tree would bring vast bad luck down upon themselves.

Shay nodded to herself. Many of Sue's friends had sought her out later. They had spoken vaguely, but clearly enough for her to understand. They were agreeing that Danapa should hold all of the land right down to the city. Ani would say that the land held the people. Either way intruders needed to have it made plain. She drifted into a light sleep to be awakened by Ani as the girl entered.

Shay eyed the glass she carried, "What's that?"

"Karamu bark." Shay's eyebrows went up as Ani giggled. "No, really, Shay. It works. I boiled the inner bark. My Kuia — my grandmother — taught me that it helps stop someone being sick all the time."

Shay sighed in resignation. "I'll try just about anything. Give me that glass." She drank it slowly, grimacing at the taste. "It should work. Anything that tastes that horrible has to be good for you."

To the surprise of most of her friends the Karamu did work. Shay was able to keep food down, although she retained her binder and continued to eat carefully. Jo wasn't one to waste a resource.

She found Ani working in the vegetable storage shed and drew her aside.

"Is anything wrong with Shay?" The girl was anxious.

"No. She seems to be much better. It's you I want to talk to. Just how much did you learn about Maori medicine from your grandmother?"

Ani looked up, "A lot. I was the only one interested. My mum was her youngest daughter so Gran was very old. She taught me as long as I can remember. Some of it I didn't understand but she made me memorise it anyway. She always said one day I'd be grateful that I knew about it." Ani's voice softened, "I guess she was wise."

"She certainly was. Ani, are any of your friends interested?"

"Billy took me up into the mountains to find the Karamu. Pam was interested when I told her I thought I could help Shay. Why?"

"I want you to write down everything you can remember being told. After that, start looking for books that deal with native plants." Jo eyed the girl. Ani was thirteen, old enough to see the possibilities. "In time you may be — well, not our doctor perhaps — but our healer, our tohunga. We need someone in Danapa who can do that. If you don't want to do the work, you can share what your grandmother taught you with someone who does." She grinned down at Ani. "Maybe you can be our pharmacist instead. You can make the drugs, then someone else uses them. What do you think?"

"Pam 'n Billy would help." The girl spoke soberly. "I think Pam wanted to be a doctor when she was old enough. Billy would like finding the plants. It'd mean having to scout all over up in the mountains and down towards the city. He loves doing that. I could make the medicines. An" if we all knew about everything none of it would be lost. Gran used to say that was the danger if only one person knew." She considered. "I'd get Billy to find me Koromiko for a start."

"What does that do?"

"You soak the young unopened leaf tips in water. I can give it to Shay when the baby starts coming. It helps the pain." She chuckled,

"I'd have him find Paretu roots as well. That's for babies teething."

Jo laughed, "Yes, I suppose we will need all those things soon. Go and talk to your friends. If they're willing then the three of you can begin. I'll explain to Mike that you have other duties so he won't expect you here. And since that Karamu is working so well you'd better prepare more of it. I just wish you knew something to keep Shay in bed now that she's feeling a lot better."

They parted still smiling at the idea. At least, Jo thought, her love was improving. Shay had only two months to go. If the baby did arrive early, there was a good chance it would still survive. The baby did arrive early, but only by a week.

Shay went into labour early one morning. She was still a little weak from her long illness but the child was small. A day later she lay, grinning down at the squalling scrap, pride and amusement vying in her face.

"Future leader of the choir by the sound of that."

Her three co-parents laughed as the baby stopped yelling to latch on to food. The small mouth worked at Shay's nipple energetically.

"Have you and Jo decided on a name?" Rome asked.

"Joya."

Mike blinked, "How'd you come up with that? I like it but I've never heard it before."

Jo glanced across. "It's simple. It's the first two letters of my name with Shay's last two reversed. J O and Y A."

Mike suddenly roared with laughter. The others turned to look at him. "Have you thought what happens if you do that the other way? Jo's baby will end up as Shoj. Sounds like a Serbian takeout." He started to laugh again as the other three joined in.

Jo stopped giggling to protest. "My baby will not sound like a takeout. If it's a girl we're going to give her a Goddess name. If it's a boy you two can name him. Maybe mixing names the way we did. Miro would be nice. The Miro tree is beautiful and it's the same mix of your names as well."

Mike stopped laughing. "Yes. Yes, I like that."

They admired Joya a while longer before Shay and the baby

fell asleep. Then they tiptoed out. There'd been a long discussion earlier while Shay was still awake. Joya would be the first and last of her children. Even with Ani's remedies, Shay had been dangerously ill. Nor had the birth been quick or easy. Next time a pregnancy might be disaster for Shay. No one was prepared to risk that.

In contrast two months later, Jo gave birth without fuss. Her son was a healthy bouncing boy promptly named Miro. Jo went back to sorting out Danapa's problems with a baby on one arm.

A couple of months later, Shay led a team of scouts southward. There had been a number of increasingly odd scouting reports from that direction. Now that she had much of her strength back, she planned to see for herself what was going on out there.

Chapter Thirteen

Back at Danapa, Mike and Rome were guiding a pair of the huge old fabrication machines. Fuel had been scraped up from every place nearby that still held some fuel. In almost all townships now the power was gone. Yet if one had hand pumps and the fuel was uncontaminated it could still be raised for use. This was probably the last effort to fortify the settlement while at the same time providing still more homes within the sheltering walls. The machines hummed busily, one adding a further five feet height to the outer walls as well as extra thickness at the base. The second machine was laying foundations for another row of store sheds.

Once they were finished, all supplies would be shifted out of odd corners in the houses. That would leave them free for the people. The two bunkhouses had been gutted and re-built within as real bedrooms. The machines would add three bunkhouses, longer and wider to replace them. This would expand Danapa to where it would house six hundred people in comfort and safety, seven hundred in safety and slightly less comfort. There would also be ample places to store the required food and gear.

Not that this was to be the end of their work. Once it was done, the machines would be driven towards the north along the old main highway. Billy had located fuel supplies in a township on a secondary road. With the horse and cattle herds now mostly semi-nomadic, it would be useful to have safe havens where they could be held. The machines would refuel and split off, one to the east, the other west. At the chosen sites, they would each raise two large circular corrals attached to resident farmhouses.

In time of danger, these corrals could act as holding pens for the animals, shelters or forts for those who moved with them. In addition, the machines would coat the old wooden walls with a thick layer of concrete. Only windows facing onto the corrals would be retained and they'd be fitted with inside steel-shutters made from stripped car doors. Secret caches of food and weapons would be hidden in the houses. Shay had commented wryly that they had only to ensure no enemy ever reached the corrals first.

If fuel could still be found for building, Shay wanted one small settlement on the east coast and further north to be also fortified as a miniature Danapa. Paparore was tiny, but it was on the inner sheltered side of the huge harbour there. Nor was it on the road that ran to the very end of the land. It would be harder to find and less likely to be stumbled across by wandering marauders. It would be a place to go if Danapa was ever over-run or if a new settlement was needed in the generations to come. They had studied the township. If another wall with a wide outside overhang was raised around a small clump of the houses, it would shelter some one hundred and fifty people plus their stores.

As Jo watched the walls rise higher she considered the idea. The machine's computers could calculate. It was possible to lay in a plan of the building you wanted and add the amount of fuel available together with a list of materials. The machine could then say if the work could be completed. If not the building could be scaled down until the machine agreed it had sufficient fuel and supplies. With this system, it was impossible to be caught with partly finished work.

At present, they had enough to complete the buildings here and the corrals for the stock. After that there would be fuel for the long trip north-east. The township Billy had found, which still had fuel, was closer to Paparore. Yes, the idea was good. She'd suggest it to a full meeting in a few weeks once the planned work was done. Jo stretched. It was hot. She wondered what Shay was doing. Her love had taken a small group of scouts to the south to check the disappearance of one of their number. Although knowing Shay, that was half an excuse to get out into the open once more.

They'd talked last night about Jo having a second baby very soon. Miro was four months and Joya was six months old. Shay had teased her, asking if her lover wanted a boy or a girl. Jo didn't care. A healthy baby would be sufficient, but it would be nice to have a girl. If it happened she wanted to name her Shayna. It had come to her as a name once, she'd liked it, writing it down on a scrap of paper she'd tucked away. Jo glanced at her watch and then up at the sun. Shay would be back soon. It was close to sunset. She had settled to watch again when the alarm went up.

In the watch-tower Pam was hauling on the bell, then leaning over to scream, "Rider incoming with wounded!"

Jo ran for the gate as a white-faced girl spun her bike through the entrance and into a skidding half-circle of whirling dust.

"Quick. Dogs got Suze."

Billy and Alex were undoing the ties as Jo raced up. She made no move to interfere. Those who were helping knew their job. She gave no sign of her thoughts but underneath fear and anger raged. Beneath that her mind wept. There would be no new baby now, not if this were as they feared. She turned to listen to the gabbling of the scout.

"Dogs got her. We stopped to watch a couple of them, Acting real odd too. We were gonna circle. Her waiting there. Me coming up behind. Dogs moved first just as I got around them. They went straight for her one at each side, so she couldn't dodge. Then they had her on the ground."

She shuddered as she remembered the screams. The savage snarls as the dogs ripped at the body of her friend.

"I had my shotguns an' I got them both before they knew I was there. Then I got her back here fast. Bloody dogs..."

Jo laid a hand on the quivering arm. "We'll do everything we can for Suzy. Listen, Ceto. Tell us about the dogs?"

She concentrated as Ceto talked. From the watch-tower came another call. One Jo was relieved to hear.

"Scouts incoming."

Thanks be. That would be Shay and the others. She halted Ceto's narrative to run for her friend. Reaching Shay, Jo explained quickly. Her friend said nothing but fell in with Jo as they returned. Once there she nodded to the shivering scout.

"From the beginning." She listened in silence. It had to be enemies. That behaviour wasn't like dogs. Not the ordinary wild packs. This sounded like attack-trained animals. It could also explain the disappearance of the scout they'd been out to find. She passed Ceto to Jo before trotting through the crowd to haul Billy and a couple of his friends away.

"How many spare operational bikes?"

"Three."

"How many pairs of scouts still out?" That question was aimed at Bob who kept the scout roster.

"Five. All of them on ponies. Ceto and Lisa had the only bike because they were going furthest. I know where everyone is."

"Good," Shay spoke swiftly. Once they understood she added. "Find them all. Warn them about this. No one is to take chances but they stay out on scout. It sounds as if this could be another group trying to take over. I'll take my bike and move south. In four nights as many scout pairs as we can put on bikes meet me at the gorge. Take food and sleeping bags. Load up with weapons and shells. If I'm not there, wait one night. Two at most. After that, back-track me but be very careful. Same with the scouts you're warning. Any injured come back here, the rest of you shift up to pair off again and head for the gorge. Okay?"

Mike had joined her as she finished. She looked at him. His head shook slightly. Shay bit back her rage, now was not the time. She waved Billy and the others to leave while she stood with Mike watching bike after bike wake twin thunder in the hills. The scouts weren't wasting time. She glanced at Mike.

"I'm sorry. She died just after they got her inside. Blood loss and shock we think. The dogs ripped her open in too many places for Ceto to stop all the bleeding." He paused. "It's probably just as well. They'd torn out most of her leg and arm muscles bringing her down. If she'd lived she'd have been pretty much paraplegic. Ceto's tearing herself up about it. Jo wants her to stop scouting."

Shay snorted. "She was heart-sisters with Suzy. What Ceto

wants is vengeance. Not pampering. I'll be surprised if she isn't with the other scouts in four days. Tell Jo to let her go if she wants." She patted Mike's shoulder. "You all look after Joya while I look after Danapa. See you in a few days."

She headed purposefully for her own bike. Scout pairs operating close to the settlement. mostly used the ponies, some even preferred them. But there were sufficient bikes and fuel when required. Shay judged this a suitable time. It took minutes to load the carrier, and then she was swinging the bike off down the narrow track to the main road with murder in her heart.

While he lived, old Fred had taught her as much of tactics as he'd learned from army lore and peace-keeper experience. Since then she'd read widely. She'd absorbed all the tricks and traps written about a dozen guerrilla wars, adding the information to her own years of gang and streetwise experience. She was faster and more dangerous than she'd ever been.

In the past few years, her simple loyalties had not changed. Jo, Joya and Miro came first, and her friends, then the settlement as a whole. Apart from that, she cared nothing for anyone. Shay's upbringing had convinced her early that this was the order of life. Others might talk about caring for those they did not know. She'd never seen much sign of it. Her foster parents had come from an assortment of faiths. All meaningless to Shay as she watched them commit all the sins there were while paying bare lip-service to their religions.

At one time she'd lived with an all-female street gang and learned that to survive one must be quick and savage. There could be no holding back. When you fought you had to go in to kill. It might not be necessary, but just that willingness was often enough to scare the opposition into retreat. Shay loved Jo in part for what she saw as her love's weakness. For Jo's inability to hate. It would have amused her to know Jo loved her for opposite reasons. For Shay's boldness, lack of fear, and ferocious readiness to fight. With Shay nearby Jo felt safe, not only loved, but protected. They were two halves of a whole and it bound them strongly. The characters of each balancing the other's attitudes.

To Shay a diffuse compassion for the world was meaningless. She reserved her caring for her loves. But for those she would fight to the death. It was on that point she sometimes clashed with Jo, who'd been raised to give charity and to care for the less fortunate. Shay worried about holding all of their land. She believed Danapa would be in danger of unexpected attack until they did. Jo was wary of what she saw as pointless aggression.

As Shay rode she wondered. Would this change her lover's mind? She watched as she moved. There were no signs that anyone had passed, no obvious camp sites. The roads were falling to pieces along some of the secondary routes now. The main highway survived. She used all the side-tracks she knew as she scouted the area. There was nothing yet she still had the feeling of danger. On the fourth afternoon, she reached the gorge and waited. Her scouts joined her near dark.

In Danapa, Jo kept contact with events. They had buried Suzy while a weeping Ceto stood by. The girl had slept all night aided by the drink Ani had provided. Later the next morning, she had taken her bike and vanished. Jo could guess where she'd gone. She sympathised with the girl's grief but she feared for her — for all of them. Shay had warned her that there would always be someone to covet Danapa. Jo could almost agree they should draw a line to hold. Only her stubborn fear that aggression bred further aggression still held her back.

She had been brought up to believe that war bred war as well. That once a war began it acted as a whirlpool dragging other countries into the devastation. It had been that way in the conflicts of the nineteen-nineties, and again in the African wars of the twenty-twenties. Jo feared that Shay's drawing of boundaries would provoke men who until then had been undecided.

Yet, by now, she had seen from her own experience what could happen to those who weren't prepared or able to protect themselves. Pam and Billy had paid. As had Ngaire. Jo would have suffered herself, had Shay not come in time. Recent experiences fought against long-time teachings. Jo was still undecided but as her own knowledge weighed more heavily on the scales, her mind was beginning to change. Perhaps, after all, Shay was right. Jo would wait and see what came out of this most recent trouble. It might be necessary to allow Shay free rein after all was settled. She hugged Miro to her. It was the children who suffered most in conflicts.

Mike and Rome had ridden out to the gorge. Jo sat playing with Joya and Miro while ordering Danapa's defenses into place. She gently removed a wooden block from Joya's mouth while she prayed that all her loves would be safe. She sighed, looking up at the walls. It was fortunate that those and the other work had been completed before her friends left. It gave her people remaining in the settlement work to take their minds off the dangers that might be closing in on them.

Right now, they had a host of smaller and larger items to shift into the new storage sheds. People who'd had no room of their own before now were able to choose one in the altered bunkhouses. There was a continuing bustle of people carrying personal possession alternating with those moving stores. Danapa was busy but Shay and her scouts were probably no less occupied, Jo thought. In that she was correct.

During the day, the scouts moved, fanning out into long lines to sweep their land. To the east there was nothing unusual. To the west, it was Rome who discovered tracks.

"Someone was through there. They moved on that old road."

"How many?"

Rome shook his head. "I couldn't tell. Someone's quite bright. Whoever was last along there was dragging leafy branches from the marks. It's brushed out all the tracks. I followed far enough to find last night's camp though. I'd guess only a few people but more than a dozen dogs. There are two paw-print sizes. Some medium. Some really big."

"How big?" Shay's interest flared.

"*Bloody* big! Come and take a look. Mike's better at this than I am but I'd have said around a hundred pounds or more each."

"Mastiffs maybe," Mike noted. "We used to see some in show classes. The medium ones could be Dobermans from Ceto's description. It makes sense, they'd have one type to run down game...or people and the other for heavy fighting. Dobermans are fast, really fast. Not much apart from a bike would get away from them."

Rome grunted agreement. "We were at a friend's place years back. Just for fun he ran his Doberman girl behind the open truck. She was keeping up at fifty kays. Then when he called her, she just speeded up and jumped aboard."

"Yikes!"

"In other words," Mike said, "forget feet, forget horses. Even with a bike you'd have to move fast. If we run into any of these dogs I'm taking no chances. I'll shoot first."

Shay chopped off the muttering with a quick flick of one hand. "We all do that. We aren't out here scouting to make friends. Keep both eyes open for any dogs. Dodge them or shoot but don't get caught."

Over the next few days, the scouts came in and out of the group, reporting to Shay as they found her. Two other pairs met dogs. In one case, both escaped safely. In the other, one partner had been bitten but not badly. Her friend had arrived in time to shoot the attacker. The second dog had been left behind. They had seen no people and none of the larger dogs. Then Ceto rode in late one day. She brought messages, information and notes from friends. She also brought bad news.

"Tam and Jessie left before me. Why aren't they here yet?"

Shay stared. "When did they leave?"

"The day before. They said they'd be here that night."

Mike glanced up at the darkening sky. "Too late to start looking now. By tomorrow, they'll be two days late. Something's happened." He touched Ceto's arm to draw her attention back. "Do you know which road they were taking?"

"The secondary one down the middle of the land."

Rome swore bitterly. "That's the one where I found the camp site.

"I want everyone out in pairs at first light," Shay spoke decisively. "Keep in touch. No one is to get too far away from the group. We'll spread out and hunt down the road line from where Rome found the site. Don't fire shots if you find Tam or Jessie. I don't want any enemy alerted. Ride down the line to call us in by voice. Now get bedded down. Guard out on night duty."

They obeyed in silence. It was mid-morning, with four hours of searching behind them, before the missing scouts were found. Bob led them to where birds had alerted him that something had been hidden in the brush.

"There was a small bunch of wild dogs here already." His hand came up to brush a tear away. He and Jess had been friends. "I chased them away but look, Shay." His hand waved at the tumbled bodies. "They may have been killed by dogs but dogs don't strip the bodies. There'd still have been all their gear and some clothing. What's more, where have their bikes gone?"

Everyone stared at the tell-tale signs. "They have to be idiots," Mike said blankly.

Shay shook her head. "Not that daft. They probably expected the bodies to be cleaned up by dogs before we started looking. In which case we might never have found anything. Apart from that, I think they've jumped to conclusions." Her smile was dangerous as her look swept the gathered scouts. Mike's gaze followed hers.

"What do you...Oh! Yes. I see. The scouts are almost all — ah — younger." Billy grinned at him. Mike smiled back before turning to Shay again. "You think the enemy thinks we're short on adults. That most of our group are children?"

"Yes. I also think," her words came slowly as she thought it out. "That the small group we know about are scouts too. Somewhere there's a larger bunch. I also see that their scouts, if that's what they are, took Tam and Jessie's bikes. So don't assume that's a friend riding towards you. They may hope to fool you with the bikes and clothing while they get in close."

She looked down at the bodies, pain and anger in her eyes. "Rome, we have body bags with us in case. They're back in camp. If you and Mike take care of that, we can take Tam and Jess back with us to Danapa once we're done out here. The rest of you, start hunting. Spread out further but keep in touch. Make as little noise and be as unobtrusive as you can. Go on foot up hills to watch down-slope. Climb trees and look out over lower ground." Her voice was harsh then, "I want this lot found!"

The bikes dropped down a long slope moving slowly but still in high gear. With the slope's downward momentum the engines were quieter. Far ahead, they could see the trio of dogs and the man they had scouted the night before. The bikes swung out into a huge circle then slowly the ring closed in. The man paused before running for the trees ahead. Two bikes shot out to cut him off from shelter so that he halted, doubling back. The dogs ran barking beside him. Part-way down the slope, Mike and Rome sat their bikes beside Shay. All had binoculars fixed on their prey.

Mike hissed softly. "He's one of them all right. See, then when he turned to us and stopped. He's wearing that pendant Tam always wore."

Rome was studying the dogs. "Dobermans. He'll try using them to hold the scouts off him."

Shay nodded. "I'm always sorry about the animals. They only do as they're told." She glanced down to where the man was waiting motionless, growling dogs flanking him. "Let's go and talk to our catch. There's a few questions I'd like answered."

The bikes circled, tightening the noose. The man stood at bay, back to a rock outcrop. The dogs bounced, waiting in stiff-legged enthusiasm for the fight. They'd attack any minute. From the slope Mike whistled, a loud clear sound cutting through other noises. Obediently the bikes wheeled, every second scout whipping out in a widening spiral to check for other invaders. The whistles had been Pam's idea. As a small child, she'd seen sheepdogs herding sheep in contests. Now the scouts had their own language and system of whistles. A second signal and those remaining halted to watch with engines just ticking over. Three bikes rolled down hill to join them, then past the scout ring, closing to speaking range.

"Who are you?"

There was no reply.

"Why are you killing our people?"

Silence.

"How many of you are there?" Mike called. "You aren't going anywhere. You may as well talk."

The reply to that was moderately imaginative but definitely coarse. The dogs snarled a counterpoint. She nodded. He whistled. Scout guns came up menacingly.

"One last time," Shay said. "Who are you? Why did your people attack ours?" To Mike she spoke softly, "Be ready."

This time the enemy reply was longer and more vicious. It ended with a few comments on what the speaker could do for the women amongst them. The tone was enough to set off the dogs. They jumped forward, racing low over the ground towards the scouts. Mike shrugged and whistled. Guns cracked out almost before his signal died away. The dogs howled, kicked and died. A complicated series of whistles came then. Ceto drifted her bike off to one side as the man turned to face nearer scouts. She dismounted to run silently forward as his head turned watching others. With a flick of her hand, the slung stone took him across the back of the head, dropping him in a stunned heap.

Ceto reached him, cords already in her hands. Expertly she and others tied the lax limbs, gagged the slack mouth. Then they sat back. One by one, the outer ring returned. Two other sets of 'one man/three dogs' had been sighted. One was several miles east, the other to the west. It seemed the enemy also scouted in lines. Shay smiled grimly as she gave orders. The dogs were hidden. Since people rarely look up, the bodies were hauled high into the forks of nearby trees. They'd be unlikely to be accidentally discovered.

The prisoner was tied to a bike carrier as the group headed back to an abandoned farm they knew. It was over an hour's ride. The enemy would be less likely to be looking for a missing man that far away. The prisoner was awake again when they arrived. Rome looked him over. A brutish type, he might have courage or not, but they had to know about his people as soon as possible. If that meant trampling over rights and decency — well, it was this one's people who had attacked without cause.

Shay ordered the prisoner stripped, his hands tied above his head to a sturdy roof beam. Then she ordered all scouts out on wide patrol. All but Mike, Rome and Ceto.

She addressed the prisoner. "We know you're one of those who killed our people." Shay's hand darted into the opening of his jacket. "That's the pendant one of our scouts always wore."

"Lots of those around."

Shay revolved the jade slowly. "Not with that name engraved on the gold band." She held it up so the prisoner could see something he'd failed to notice before. A series of tiny letters running around the band that provided a loop for the chain. With it that close he could even read the name — Tamara.

"Tam was named after her grandmother and she inherited the pendant from her. She valued it. The only way you'd have it is if you took it off her body."

Implacable, her eyes met those of the prisoner. "I want to know who you are. Why you're here. Why you're killing our people?"

He spat at her. "Bitch! I'm saying nothin' an' you can't make me."

Shay looked at him in silence for a moment, then her voice came very softly. "You're threatening everything I love. I really wouldn't swear to that if I was you."

Chapter Fourteen

The prisoner talked. Filtered from the threats, the obscenities, the screams of pain, it boiled down to an intended take-over. His group was mostly adult men with a sprinkling of women and mostly male children. One of their original number had been a soldier, he'd pushed domination of the group too far and been killed. Another had been a dog trainer, a man who taught attack training for the larger breeds. Originally the group had laired in a large city to the south of Auckland. Both he and his interrogators puzzled why the group had moved.

Shay left the man cursing them between gasps of pain as she led her friends and the scout outside.

"It wasn't an accident they ended up here. They came straight through the city towards us. I don't think they know just where Danapa is but they know the general direction." She glanced at them, "Any ideas?"

Mike nodded slowly, "One of the lot we cleared out of Auckland a year or two back?" Shay and Rome nodded in turn. "We know there were a lot of them that escaped. We killed their leader and most of his best men, but plenty of the others got away."

"Such as Terry Morgan," Shay spat. Mike and Rome's heads snapped around as they stared.

"Yes. Who'd have a better motive for starting another war against us?" Mike agreed in a tight voice.

Rome swore, "That's right. That's too true. That animal says his lot was down in Hamilton. Whoever persuaded them to trek all the way up here would have to be convincing."

"You heard him. They have thirty or so men but only half a dozen women and maybe a dozen boys. They live off the places they pass, travel light except for weapons." Shay's face twisted in disgust. "Want to bet on the abuse the women and kids are suffering?"

"No. So, do we stay out here, kill off a few more of their scouts or go back to warn Danapa?"

"Both." Shay turned to look at Ceto. "If you want revenge for Suzy, now's your chance. We don't need that one any more." Her chin jerked to indicate the door. Ceto slid her knife from the sheath.

"Thank you." She opened the door, sliding silently inside. A voice was raised in query before they heard a startled cry, then a long gasping moan dying in a choked gurgle. Ceto returned wiping her knife, her eyes a little sick.

Shay draped an arm about her, "Good job. Now, we don't want his friends to know he talked. One look at that body and they'll guess so we give them nothing to see," She dug in the bike pack, then tossed Ceto a box of matches. "Set the place on fire. Shut the doors and windows. By the time it really gets going we'll be somewhere else."

She turned back to Mike and Rome. "We'll send a pair of the scouts back to warn Jo. Rest of us will drift around and see who else we can net. Stay in pairs but keep in touch. Some of their scouts may try for a scout pair again if they think that's it. Play bait if possible. Draw them to a good place for ambush then have a second pair take the humans alive if possible. I'd like a double check on what that one said."

Ceto rejoined them. Shay smiled at her. "You can stay with me. Billy, sort out who you want to send back."

The boy rattled off brief orders. Two bike were started reluctantly. The others listened to engine-hum fading up the road. Billy dusted off his hands.

"Now what?"

"Now we hunt!" Shay's face was hard.

They split into pairs, trailing their presence during the next two days. Twice, they made a kill but each time it was impossible to take a live prisoner. Still they remained busy. Then, they found a double treasure as two of the enemy came together. Ceto and Shay chose to be bait — temptingly trailed. With the enemy so short of adult women the two of them should provide a treasure hard to resist.

They zoomed casually over the crest of the small rise. Saw the enemy and swung their bikes in apparent panic. Both fell. Shay's engine — judiciously assisted — stalled. She broke, leaving the bike, to run frantically for the hilltop and her partner. Ceto had swung back, caught the bike's wheel and fallen. Shay reached her and both women hauled the single bike upright, trying to restart the engine while glancing back at the men and dogs. The engine roared and stalled out..

Face averted, Shay gave the whistle trill that meant "be ready". Then taking Ceto's hand, she raced with her over the rise and out of view. Shay gave one swift glance back as they dropped over the crest. It was working. Behind them the dogs ran their track, heads up, snarling. The two men panted along in their wake. Reaching the tree chosen Shay and Ceto went up it hastily. The dogs sat at the base to await their masters. The men panted over the brow of the hill, dived towards the tree — and the trap was sprung.

Mike stood up from the patch of nearby brush. His shotgun began to boom, from another patch of cover, Rome began to shoot as did the rest of Shay's scouts. The dogs fell. It wasn't possible to take the beasts alive. Dogs do not surrender to a pointed weapon and a threat. But men do. Mike gestured to their guns. He said nothing but the half-circle of hard faces and lifted weaponry backed the order. The enemy dropped their guns, hastily raising their hands.

One of the men ran to his dogs. His fingers stroked their heads before he stood to stare back. His eyes glared hatred, a rage out of control. He poised. Shay lifted her gun shooting him dead beside his dogs. Mike looked at the scouts.

"Get anything we can use. Dump the bodies." He took the second man by the throat. "How near are your friends?"

"Near enough. They'll get you, you..."

Mike's hand closed so that the words choked off. "I asked how close they were? Next time I have to ask a question you'll beg to tell us."

He released the man's throat a little allowing him air. The captive's eyes had gone from rage to fear as his face fell into sullen lines.

"Well?" Mike's voice was dangerous.

"Yeah, yeah. All right. Us two were the only ones over this way. The rest of them have headed for the harbour. Our Boss was told you were near a big harbour."

His listeners exchanged looks. Shay's guess that it might be an old enemy behind this was looking better. That had been the lie told to Morgan. Danapa wasn't that close to the inlet. Nor was the harbour that this group were near, the right one. But it seemed someone in their lot knew too much. They tied their captive carefully, before beginning to question him more thoroughly. A man like that has no loyalties. Once it was clear to him he'd hurt if he kept silent, he talked busily.

"Yeah, we get the odd one coming in to join up. Men mostly." He snickered in uneasy bravado. "Of course, women get found sometimes. We give them a real welcome." Shay flicked her knife out of the belt-sheath. She leaned forward smiling. Something in that savage grin made the man scrabble backwards. Her hand shot out to take a grip on the crotch of his jeans.

"We could give you a real welcome too." Her voice was incongruously low and sweet as she explained just how that could be done. Her knife hovered as he sweated in terror. "You're here to answer Mike's questions. Not to explain your employee package. Talk the wrong way again and you're mine. No one will stop me. You aren't flavour of the month."

Mike and Rome hid smiles, waiting until the prisoner's shivering lessened. Then Rome took over the questions.

"You do get new people coming in. Who came in lately?"

"Gee, I can't..." Shay allowed the knife blade to catch the sun. "Uh, yeah sure. I remember. Some skinny little bloke. Seems to spend a lot of time talking to the Boss. Where'd he come from?

Geeze, I dunno. We were in Hamilton when he turned up. That's all I know. Yeah, it was after he came that the rumour went round. Suddenly everybody's talking about some place where there's all the women a man could want. Good food. Good weather. Even booze, maybe, and some kind'a fort where we can be safe."

Mike added another question.

"Well, the guy's kind'a skinny. Ordinary, nothing much I can say." He cringed back from Shay. "Look, hang on. I remember somethin' I saw his neck once. He's got a mark partway around it. Like some kind'a burn. An' his eyes. They're a pale gray, like old washed out jeans. Okay? That what you wanted to know?"

Mike whistled softly, a command. "What you doing? What...!" He slumped as Shay slid the knife out again.

Rome stared down absently at the body. "It's that weasel Morgan most likely but I don't remember any scars around his neck?"

Shay spoke thoughtfully. "I do. When we tapa'd them I had the scope on them all first. The Boss was going to hang our weasel, remember?" They did. "I had a good look at him. I think they'd half hung him for fun beforehand. He already had a line of blood partway around his neck. Look at what this one said." Her foot nudged the body contemptuously. "The new man is skinny, medium hair, size, weight, but with a neck scar and pale gray eyes. It could be someone who just looks like that but if it isn't our traitor, what persuaded this lot to come up here and who else knew about us and's likely to talk?"

Billy cut in, "It'd take a lot to move a bunch settled in that well. So what's the main thing they were short of?" He met their eyes, nodding. "Yeah. More people. Women mostly. The weasel could have told him where he reckoned there were dozens. He was with us a night or two. He'd only have to list the ones he saw. Say how many others he thought we collected later. Sounds as if he talked us up, too. Food, booze, all they'd want in one package."

Shay rose and stretched. "It's likely to have been him then. Anyhow, it's safer to act as if it is and be wrong than to say it isn't and take the risk. Dump this body, too. Check there's nothing we can use."

The body was hauled away as the bikes lined up. Shay had no intention of leaving the area just yet. One of the scout pairs sent to Danapa was due back with the latest news. Her group would go to meet them. Shay wanted to be sure Jo had the warning and to hear back what her friend planned. As she rode she reflected. The Danapa scouts must have died in silence. Otherwise this pack of brutes wouldn't be wandering around the wrong harbour still. Unless — she grinned viciously — the scouts had deliberately misdirected the enemy.

The Danapa bodies found hadn't seemed to be tortured. Apart from the rapes and casual brutalities that was. Possibly because they'd acted terrified and talked first. She made a mental note to find out about that from any of this lot they took who might know. If she were right, she'd have Jo write an acknowledgement into the records. That set her mind off on a new track. She missed Jo on these trips but her love would never be able to handle the things that sometimes had to be done.

In three years, Jo had hardened by necessity. She'd begun to understand that in this new world you couldn't always be kind and gentle. The survival of one's friends and family could require the non-survival of others. With a child of her own to protect, Jo was becoming more realistic lately. Once this business was over, Shay would discuss drawing a line again. Danapa should hold all land to Auckland. It would be safer.

They met the returning scouts.

"Danapa's ready. Jo wants to know if you need any more help out here? She's sent watchers out in a screen with binoculars and those army radios. If they see anyone, they're to sit tight, signal back. They let them go past. If Danapa's attacked we'll have a force with high-powered scoped rifles right on their backs. We can get in and out through the escape tunnels. Jo says good luck and don't worry about home. It'll still be there when you get back."

Shay found she was smiling. Damn, but it sounded as if her love was learning sense at last. She wrinkled her face as she sorted out what orders to give.

"I want you to ride back. Tell Jo we need all the bikes out here.

Two riders to each bike. Food, water bottles, weapons, and a *lot* of ammunition. Tell her we'll pick the enemy off one by one as long as they're spread out and don't realise we're out here. Once they group we'll hit them hard. I don't want them to get close enough to Danapa to know too much. Just in case any of them escape."

She watched as they ate and drank hastily. "Ceto, I want you to ride back with them. Take Jo aside and tell her everything we know or suspect. You can come back to us if you want to but I'd prefer you stayed there. You know as much as any of us about the enemy." She patted the girl's arm. "You've done a great job."

She noted the waiting scouts had finished and spoke to them. "Ride wary. You did well to find us that quickly. Now get back even faster."

Mike moved to stand beside her as the scouts, Ceto with them, departed. With him, Billy was counting busily. "We should get another dozen bikes. I've got spares and gas stashed for emergencies. Pam knows where. She'll speak up once the message comes in. I just hope Jo knows who to chose as riders."

Shay's voice was dry. "She'll know. I made a list before I left, just in case. I picked all the best riders and fighters but dropped some of the bigger ones off it for weight. Do all the spare bikes have those hidden guns?"

Billy beamed. "They sure do. We did extra sets of the special fairings that carry them. Pam will make sure they're fitted before the bikes leave."

Shay nodded. Fred had told her a lot of stories from the army. Her favourites had been tricks used against an unsuspecting enemy. She'd gone over their equipment with him before he'd died and they'd come up with several ideas of their own as a result. One had been to dig caves into the hillsides around the settlement. These were then camouflaged. It was in these that the hidden watchers now waited in ambush. A second idea had been wholly Shay's.

With the new varieties of plastic it was easy to make a pair of moulds, one for the right side of a motorbike, the other for the left side. These were then fitted as fairings on the bikes, ostentatiously to protect the legs of a rider. Actually each concealed a loaded,

200

sawn-off shotgun held securely in brackets. The shaping made the fairings look thinner than they were, and both front and back openings had sealed covers. These didn't just slide. There was a knack to their removal — a twist required which made it unlikely they'd be easily found. The dog men might well be using the scout bikes they'd stolen, but it was likely they hadn't found *all* their secrets.

The Danapa group found the enemy a day later. But not before they had picked off two more of the scout trios of man and dogs. They scouted their enemy carefully at a distance. The Dobermans were there in plenty and it would not be wise or safe to attract their attention. Shay with Mike and Rome with Billy lay on a ridge near the enemy camp. The wind blew firmly towards them.

"Mike? He said there were over thirty men, didn't he?"

"So he said." Mike was sarcastic.

"Humph. I count twenty-four."

Beside her Rome stirred. "Don't forget we've cut them down a bit." He pointed. "They do have mastiffs, too. Look."

His friends looked. Below, seven of the huge fawn dogs lazed around the periphery of the camp.

"I wonder what they're for?" Shay muttered.

"Maybe the trainer bred them before the bug. Didn't want to let them go. You have to admit they're impressive and they'd make anyone have second thoughts about an attack." Rome kept his voice low in reply.

Shay was studying the camp. "I suspect they might be used to keep the women and kids in line. See how the Dobermans roam all over but the mastiffs stay in a circle around the people. We need to lure all the damn dogs away before we attack. If they're there, we have triple the enemies and they'll give the alarm too early when we close in."

Billy gave a small chuckle. "I heard about something once that drives animals crazy. Some stuff called aniseed."

Rome jumped on that. "Yes. He's right, Shay. We could lay an aniseed trail. If someone dragged a bag of wool scented with aniseed behind a bike the dogs would follow for miles. Once whoever does it gets a long way away they can tree. Have a bag of meat scraps wiped with aniseed already waiting in the tree. All they have to do is toss the dogs a scrap every so often and they'll stay."

"What if they've been trained not to take food from someone else?" Mike was thoughtful.

"We can check that. Drop a single scrap just off the line of their march. A piece a dog can swallow in one gulp so a fight doesn't get started."

"Makes sense to me," Shay said. There was a mutter of agreement. "All right. That's our plan for the moment. Where do we find aniseed?"

Billy grinned cheerfully. "That's why I thought of it, I guess. There's a factory that made candy 'n stuff not that far away. I..."

He paused as Shay smiled at him. "Yes, okay. I got a load of candy to take back for Pam and the others. Most of it's crystalised but it still tastes okay. They had aniseed as well, I saw whole labeled drums of the stuff. Do you want me to go back and get a bottleful?

"Yes, and bring back something nice for us all too." Rome was smiling. "I don't see why the dogs should be the only ones to enjoy themselves."

They scouted quietly for several days, watching the way the enemy moved and its direction. It was obvious there was no mechanic in the group. The trucks used were new but ground slowly over the rougher terrain. Once, as they watched, several men went off to return with a new truck from a nearby town. The older slower vehicle appeared to have been left behind there. None of the enemy drivers looked to be bothering about maintenance either. It was Rome's belief the trucks were suffering from lack of care, but the enemy may have felt that there was no need. Trucks were available in the hundreds to any who went looking. Why work when you didn't have to?

On the third day, Billy moved ahead to drop the scented meat. He did so without ever setting his feet on the ground. The dogs would not react so strongly if there was no human scent. To ensure that, he had doused the bike wheels in oil. It must have worked as the dog that found the meat gulped it in eager silence.

Shay had all the scouts working hard, hunting a suitable place to make their attack. They found it two days further on. So far, the enemy had continued to hunt along the inlet's coastline. If they did so for another two days, they would be reach an ideal killing ground. Almost ten miles ahead of it there was a line of trees. Not the standard pines but big oaks. In the upper branches, Billy cached a large bag of meat scraps, gloves, cloth and a bottle of aniseed. To that he added an extra item from Shay.

She had made a detour to a township, returning with several tubes of cyanide paste. The paste had been regularly used to kill off wild possums in the bush areas and Shay had found a case of the tubes at the local Pest Destruction Board offices. Add that to the scented meat and the dogs would not return from their hunt. The enemy allowed the dogs to have free rein once the camp was set up. And one of the Danapa scouts laid a trail at a distance. If fortune held, the dogs wouldn't find that until after the camp was set up and everything in position.

"They're a lazy lot. They camp early, break up to go late." Mike was contemptuous.

"Thanks be that they do. It makes everything easier for us. Tomorrow they arrive where the trail's laid. Cross everything that this works."

Shay sat back. There was no fire tonight. She'd allow nothing which might be spotted. Nothing to start any alarm. Tomorrow afternoon would be busy.

"Everyone who isn't on guard, get some sleep. I want us fresh."

Despite the growing light they dozed quietly. Scouts and guards watched in shifts, one to cover the enemy, the other to watch over their drowsing friends. But everyone was up and alert by early afternoon. Ceto who had returned, readied bikes with the aid of another scout. Passengers mounted behind riders. They looped wide around the moving enemy until they were ahead of the line of their march. There they waited, engines ticking over silently, motionless in the thick patches of brush. Shay and her three friends watched the enemy, binoculars focused on every move.

"They're slowing." Billy was jubilant.

To the west, the four could see the line of trucks slow and stop. Women and children dropped from them and began to collect firewood. Two fires were started and cooking pots were placed over flames. The men lolled to one side, allowing the released dogs to roam outwards. A dog struck the aniseed trail. It began to sniff silently along the track nose working eagerly. Another joined it. Then a third, until all the Dobermans were vanishing quietly away to the north-east. A mastiff rose lazily to inspect the ground. The sudden delighted howl brought all its friends.

Before surprised owners could halt the exodus the dogs had gone. Loping enthusiastically along the trail of the best scent they had smelled in years. Bewildered men ran about screaming for the animals to return. As they bawled in exasperation, milling about by their fires, Shay signaled. From the patches of brush bikes leaped out to swing in line, charging down on the confused camp, passengers leaning over a little to shoot clear. For a moment as the bikes reached the camp, they halted. A volley of shot smashed into the panicked dog men. Before they could reach weapons, the bikes were in motion again.

Wisely, the women and children had gone flat when the bikes appeared. Men joined them, writhing and howling or lying limply. The unexpected attack had killed or badly injured at least a third of enemy numbers. But they were experienced even if the experience was mostly in being the attackers. For their lives they rallied, turning to face the bikes, as they started to shoot back.

Mike whistled a shrill command. From behind the enemy camp a second line of bikes had rolled silently into position. They lined up, covers were twisted off the hidden guns as from behind the enemy, Shay gave the order to fire at will. She slammed her bike forward as carnage exploded. On her shoulder a shotgun on a wide strap hung by her hand. There was a gap in the enemy ranks where men had fallen. Shay whipped her bike through that, sliding to a temporary halt amongst the women.

"Make your choice!" She tossed her spare gun to a bruised-faced woman, gunned her bike and was gone again.

The woman stood a moment holding the weapon, stunned as she stared after the flying figure. A woman rode freely with their attackers, a woman with guns? She stared at the circling bikes and realised that with them there were many women, all of them free to ride and shoot. An expression of triumphant hate exploded across her face. In one movement, she swung the shotgun, pumping the action and firing into the men of her group. She was screaming although none of Shay's people could make out the words.

But they could see the results as woman after woman seized the weapons dropped by men. After that it was a massacre as men tried to run but were cut down, either by the camp women or by Shay and Rome's encircling troops. At length, the noises of battle and vengeance ceased. Shay left her bike to walk forward and look at the women as her friends covered her.

"You're free to stay or go. We don't want anything you have."

"What if we'd be interested in joining you?" The spokeswoman was the big woman who caught Shay's gun.

"Then we'd be interested in having you. Talk it over. No one has to make any decisions tonight." Shay lowered her voice eyeing the woman meaningfully. "You may want to clean house completely first. None of our business if you haven't joined us yet."

She received a long slow stare. "Yeah. Well. Let us alone tonight then. In the morning we can talk." The woman took a step forward holding out both hands. "My name's Illeana. We're all grateful to you whatever choice we make. We owe you."

"No, you owed yourselves. Good to see you got paid. Let us know if there's anything we can do to help tonight. Apart from that we won't bother you." She moved to rejoin her friends.

"Hang on a minute. Can I ask a question?"

Shay nodded.

"Well, then. You're a woman, are you their boss?"

"No. I suppose you could say I'm their war leader. But if you mean, do women have an equal say where we are then the answer's yes. Our group is Pagan. Inside the settlement Jo leads. She's a woman too. Our men are all decent, the ones who weren't got run out or left. If you join us and decide to stay you have voting rights. No pressure to take a man. But you have to do your share of the work. Sound okay?"

"It sounds like heaven," the woman told her frankly. "We'll talk to you in the morning but I'd say everyone will be keen to join up with your people."

Shay trotted back to join her friends and relay the conversation. Behind her a short commotion indicated the events she'd expected. She'd noticed a woman amongst the survivors. Too well-fed, without bruises, and too well-dressed to have been anything but their boss's woman. She swept her group back when they might have intervened. No one was much better off in a group like that without it being at her fellow's expense. It was the business of those freed.

The sounds hit a crescendo and chopped off, dying into a groan. Shay turned to watch as a body was hauled away, dumped into the thicket nearby. From the clothes that had been the woman Shay noticed. Good enough. It looked as if this lot could clean their own house if they had the opportunity given them.

Shay had already sent Ceto back to tell Jo all was well. Two days followed from the next morning, in which the Danapa and the freed group mingled, learning about each other and talking. By that time all of the woman had voted to go with Shay. The children, too, seemed keen to find refuge in a place where abuse was absent. Mike took the older boys aside. He knew just how they'd been abused. Knew too that it was common for the abused one to turn abuser, now he made it clear that while he understood, such things were forbidden.

If a boy found the need to abuse was there, he was to seek out Mike or Rome. It was acceptable to want revenge, but not on the innocent. He saw they understood what he was saying. A plea that it had been done to them would not be acceptable as it had all too often been in the pre-bug court. Mike could only hope no problems would arise from these brutalised children that he or his friends couldn't handle.

With the scout screen wide-spread the merged group began the trek back to Danapa. There was no hurry. Jo had sent Ceto back with a message. Let the trip take a few days so all were more comfortable with each other. Danapa people could learn the histories and abilities of those saved. That way they could be slotted into the right places when they arrived. In the settlement everyone worked, the trick was to find work at which they were happy, or at the least, content. After five days, the Danapa gates were in sight.

The woman who had accepted Shay's gun had become leader of her group of survivors. Illeana slowed as she saw the waiting crowd at the gates ahead. From their midst Jo stepped out, pausing to look lovingly at Shay as she stood waiting.

Then she spoke to Illeana, "Enter in the Name of the Goddess and be welcome." She folded the suddenly weeping woman in gentle arms. "Be very welcome, my sister. Here are strong walls and a refuge for all of you."

Chapter Fifteen

Jo lay sprawled on the bed late one evening beside Shay. In their cradles in the next room, Miro and Joya napped peacefully. Their parents were not so serene.

"For the Goddess's sake, Jo," Shay was becoming irritated. "I thought you'd come around to seeing sense."

That annoyed her lover. "Sense. We've just finished with something close to a war and you want to start another one! We lost people. Or do you enjoy seeing friends die?"

Shay sat up, eyes flaming with anger. "No, I don't and well you know it. But I won't see Danapa wiped out just because you're as nervous as an old woman about it." Her mouth curved into a sneer. "Or is it being pregnant again that makes you so dumb?"

In turn Jo too lost her temper. "At least I can give Danapa children. All you give is death." Too late she remembered how close to dying Shay had come in her efforts to bear Joya. "Shay, I didn't mean it! Shay..."

The younger woman looked at her with eyes gone cold. "You meant it. What you mean now is that you didn't intend to say it." She rolled off the bed, thrusting her feet into light boots. "I've got people to kill. See you later."

Jo sat on the bed, tears running down her face, as the footsteps pattered away down the passage. How could she have said that? It wasn't really true. She'd just been infuriated by Shay's air of righteousness. Jo had been changing her mind. But the smug attitude of her friend, the "I told you so" of her hints had angered Jo into striking out at her. This pregnancy was only three months into its span but she wasn't finding it as easy as the first one had been.

In a way, she wished she'd waited. But at the time, she'd felt that having a second child had already been delayed by the dog-men. She wasn't prepared to wait any longer. Mike had been willing so that now she carried his child. Yet, it was less than four months after the battle. Perhaps she should have held off. Been less openly happy about it. She sighed, wiping her eyes and blowing her nose hard. She would apologise to Shay as soon as her friend came back.

Shay didn't. Instead Jo woke to a louder than usual bustle in the compound. She crawled out of her bed in answer to the indignant bellows from both wakened babies. With one on each arm she peered out of the window just as Pam and Ani tapped on her door. Jo laid the now soothed babies back and called a welcome. The girls came in, clearly bursting with news.

"Jo, Shay says she's leaving. Can we go with her?"

Horror-struck, Jo made to speak before common sense warned her to think first. Shay wouldn't be leaving for good. Not if Pam and Ani were asking to go with her. She found she was holding her breath. Her silence encouraged both girls to continue.

"Shay's taking some of us down past the city in boats. She says now is a good time to hunt for other small groups who might want to join us."

Jo breathed again, Shay was getting away from the situation for a while and until they both cooled off. "I'll consider it when I know how far Shay's going. Has she said how long she thinks she could be away?"

"Months," Ani told her gleefully. "You'll miss her, won't you?"

Yes, Jo thought, she would and she couldn't let her love leave her for months without an apology. What if anything happened to either of them? She listened to the excited pair as they chattered. Her hands went up to her face, she'd said an unforgivable thing to Shay. If her lover was killed on this trip, Jo wouldn't be able to live with the belief Shay had died still angry at her.

Another memory crept into her mind. Shay saying how great

such a trip would be if they went together. Was that part of it? Jo had arranged this pregnancy without recalling the trip. Did Shay feel that what Jo wanted had over-ridden Shay's own wishes? She remembered how Shay had saved her, backed everything Jo wanted to do. It was too much. Jo was four years older, it was for her to be mature about this and she'd failed. Feeling as if she was the meanest, most inconsiderate lover anyone had ever had Jo dissolved in tears again.

In the compound Shay had grabbed Ani. "Where's Jo? Did you ask?"

"She was getting ready to come out. She said we could go once she knew how far we were going." Ani eyed her suspiciously. "Did you and Jo have a fight? She'd been crying. I could tell."

"Just a disagreement. Run along and help pack." She watched as the girl dived into the confusion. Jo had been crying? Shay's heart melted. She remembered her love standing in the window firing again and again at the man who held Shay captive. She recalled Jo shivering afterwards, unable to even re-load the shotgun. Jo, who hated violence, had still found enough strength to kill a man for Shay.

Maybe she'd been pushing too hard about the land. She'd been pretty smug about how the dog-men had shown the wisdom of a border. Jo was pregnant after all and Shay knew from experience how you seemed to be short a couple of layers of skin at that time. Almost anything made you snappy. She'd goaded Jo into snarling then stamped out and abandoned her. Oh, hell! It was half Shay's fault. Best she found Jo and said she was sorry. It would be terrible if anything happened while they were apart. She ran into Jo as the older woman left their room. They clutched at each other.

"I'm sorry. It's my fault. I was horrible," Jo was crying again.

"My fault too," Shay muttered, "I kept pushing you. Don't cry, love."

"But you're going away." Jo's voice broke in a wail.

Shay found she was giggling hysterically. "Love, we planned this trip ages back. Half of this was because I was mad I'd have to go without you. Look, I'm sorry I was nasty."

Jo threw her arms around her, "I'm so sorry I said those things. If you want to take Pam and Ani they can go. When are you leaving?"

"I thought we'd go in a couple of hours." Shay hugged Jo back gently. "But I can hold off until tomorrow. We can go to bed early and talk."

"Just talk?" Jo teased.

Shay laughed, "Well...now come and see how I've planned." She took her lover's arm, leading her outside to where Mike and Rome worked.

Behind a half-open door further down, Ani grinned at Pam, eyes sparkling. "Told you they couldn't stay mad at each other. Not once we'd told Shay, Jo was crying." Pam grinned back giving her friend a shove.

" So you were right. Want a medal for it?" They scurried out to join in the work. All was right with their world once again.

That evening, Shay gathered plates of cold food and joined Jo in their bedroom. Mike and Rome had baby duty so the night would be quiet.

"What do you plan on doing?" Jo was curious.

Shay swallowed a mouthful of the cold chicken and reached for a map. "We'll take boats from a harbour just before central Auckland. Once we pass the city we can run down the coast to one of the big inlets. There'll be vehicles we can use there somewhere. We hide the boats and take to the road from then on." She hesitated, "I plan to go all the way down to Wellington, Jo. I'm taking real numbers and firepower with me. I want to send a couple of our people back with any small lot of people we find."

"Just how many are you expecting to find?"

Shay shrugged. "Dunno. It's been almost four years since the bug. Other groups have probably organised by now. I'd like to check that out. See if there's any threat to us. Pick up stray people to build our numbers if they're suitable. We'll be back before the baby's due. Don't worry. But forewarned is forearmed."

Jo said nothing to that. The original idea for the trip had been hers. Not so much as a reconnaissance but in an effort to find more lost children. She knew Shay would do that, too. She smiled at her friend.

"Yes. Now eat your chicken before I have it all."

Shay grinned, hastily snatching another piece of the cold meat. "Know any good after-dinner games?"

"I know one. It's perfect for people who won't see each other for ages." She waited until Shay had finished her mouthful, then she reached up, fingers tickling sensitive spots as her lover squirmed and yelped. The tray went one way, the remaining chicken the other but neither noticed. This night would have to last for months. They weren't going to waste a minute of it.

Shay left with a trail of scout bikes and trucks the next morning. For a few days, Jo missed her badly but soon other problems required her attention. The summer was fine so many from Danapa chose to ride across to the harbour. Plump shellfish were available there, and cool water to swim in. Jo had no objections to this and gradually over the unusually hot summer more of the settlements people made the trip. It was Ani and Riana who awoke her to trouble.

"We need a law about it." Riana was adamant.

Jo rolled over lazily to stare upwards at the drifting clouds. She was halfway through her pregnancy and feeling disinclined to be energetic.

"A law about what?"

Riana was irritated, "Haven't you been listening? We need a law about the beaches here in the inlet and harbour."

"A law to stop everything being taken until it's all gone," Ani added.

Jo sat up looking blank. "Look, what is all this? Taking all what everything? Driftwood? That's going to come in on every storm. Fish? There aren't any trawlers out there any more," her wave encompassed the entire ocean. "We already have laws on stripping a resource. What is being taken?"

"Shellfish," Riana said flatly. "Jo, there's more than four hundred of us in Danapa." Right now with all the animals done producing and the hay and most of the harvest in, we all have time to come over here." She too gestured at the scene. "And all of us have. Try counting the number of people digging shellfish each day. Try counting the shellfish. And don't tell me that there are so many it doesn't matter. That's how we ended up with none in most places before the bug. With four years to come back they've recovered to some extent. But they'll all be gone again if everyone's allowed to take them all right down to the baby ones."

Ani nodded firmly. "It's true, Jo. The beach needs a tapu."

"A tapu?"

"A tapu!" Riana told her. "Ani's right. It was custom amongst our people to put a tapu on any place that should be left alone a while. If it was done here, the shellfish would be able to recover. There should be a tapu on taking the small ones as well."

This was making sense to Jo as she studied the busy scene. There must be fifty people hunting the shellfish right this moment. It was true that the harbour was large but so far there had probably been this many people down here every day for several weeks. Riana and Ani were right. At this rate there soon wouldn't be any of the shellfish left, not if they were taking even the smallest ones as well.

She stood. "I'll l call an assembly tomorrow night. That way everyone will have had time to hear." Gathering up her towel she marched over to the carrier. She'd go home and think about this. She returned to a different crisis. Pam met her at the gates looking desperate.

"I was hoping you'd be back soon. We've got a problem."

Jo groaned, "What happened?"

"You know the last lot Shay sent back with Billy and Marion?"

Jo did. They'd been a group of half-starved children with one older girl named Lois. However, it had been one of the slightly younger children who had made cautious contact with Shay when she halted on her way south. Lois was the oldest at fourteen and used to ordering the younger children around. The adults had gone out one day and never returned. It was unknown why. Lois hadn't wanted them to come north but under Shay's eyes democracy had ruled. The other children, ranging from twelve to eight, had without exception, wanted Danapa. They had settled in here happily. Lois had not.

"What about them?"

Pam threw up her hands in mingled anger and despair. "Lois is saying that on their way north, Bob attacked her."

Jo stared at her, "*Bob*?"

"Yes. I know he's my brother's friend but he wouldn't do something like that, Jo. Lois has been trouble since she arrived. I think this is just another try at getting her own way."

"In what?" Jo asked sharply.

Pam looked surprised. "She still wants to leave here and for the kids to come with her. She'd like it to be just her and them."

"Do they want to go?"

"Not likely. One of them told me they do a lot less work here."

Jo realised they were still standing out in the sun. She was tired, thirsty and hungry. "Give me time to think and can you please go get something for me to eat."

Back in her rooms, she dug into her files while Pam vanished to find food. Jo found the letter she was hunting just as Pam returned. She accepted the tray with absent-minded thanks, eating while she read. Finally she looked up.

"This accusation of Lois's is something we have to face. We were bound to hear an accusation from someone sooner or later." She looked gently at Pam. "I don't want to rake up old memories, dear. But both you and Billy had bad things happen to you. Well, so did most of the people who arrived here I suspect."

Pam stared, "You too, Jo?"

"I wasn't raped," Jo told her, "But I was caught by two men. So was Ani. They would have raped us but Shay came looking for Ani and killed them both before anything happened. Things like that can make you strange."

"How?"

"Well, Lois could have been raped earlier. Now she's putting the event onto Bob for her own reasons. Then, too, Bob might be reacting against something that happened to him earlier. Sometimes someone who's been hurt wants to hurt other people back."

Pam opened her mouth looking indignant.

"I didn't say that's what happened, Pam. I just said it could be." Jo finished her food and nodded. "I'll call Ngaire in on this. She was training in this type of problem. See if you can find her. Don't tell her about this. Just say I'd like to speak to her urgently."

Pam shut the door on her way out so that Jo sat alone waiting. She picked up Shay's letter to read it again. This might tell Ngaire something useful. It certainly said a lot to Jo. Hmm. Before Lois was confronted it would also be wise to talk to the children that had come in with her. Ngaire tapped on the door while with her was Riana who'd returned from the beach. Jo beamed at her.

"Riana, just the person I wanted. Will you please go and find all the children who came in with Lois. You know Lois?"

"I do!"

Her voice was tart and Jo made a mental note that here was another one who disliked the girl.

"I want all those children sorted out and kept away from her. She isn't to see or speak to them from now on. She's made a serious accusation and I don't want her persuading the kids to say things to back her up if it isn't true."

"Right."

Riana went, while Ngaire found her way to a chair and sat. Pam stood at the door.

"Do you want me to stay, Jo?"

"Yes. You do a lot of the records these days and I may need you to be a runner for me. Sit down at the back of the room and don't speak. I don't want accusations later that you influenced us. But don't worry too much."

She turned to Ngaire explaining the accusation Lois had made before she picked up the letter. "Shay saw the group over a couple of days. She wrote me about them. Mike and Rome have added notes. The envelope was sealed so there's no way Bob could have tampered with or even read it."

From the corner of her eye she saw Pam jerk in indignation then subside.

Ngaire leaned forward, "What does it say?"

215

"I'll summarise. I can read it in full later if you want the actual words. But briefly it says that Lois never wanted to come to Danapa. She had a nice little dictatorship where they found her. The other children are all at last two years younger and she had them doing the work. She's a big strong girl for fourteen and she apparently didn't hesitate to use force to make them obey. Most of the other children had bruises. One told Shay that Lois had beaten them if they didn't work hard enough."

"Shay is pretty shrewd," Ngaire said slowly. "She believed them?"

"Yes. Mike and Rome have added notes to the letter. Mike says that in his opinion the girl will be a problem. He thinks she came from a violent and manipulative environment before the bug. Once she was on her own she has simply followed the pattern. Rome says that all the children said they wanted to stay where they were found and with Lois — while she was present. Once they were separated they all wanted to get away."

"Wow." Ngaire blinked. "Sounds like a real little charmer. But I suppose we couldn't expect every incomer to be perfect. The question is, are her accusations true? Can we prove it either way and do we keep her if we prove she's a liar?"

"That's it. Let's have her in now and see what she says."

Lois arrived looking distressed. Jo spoke kindly.

"Lois, I have to ask. Tell us how Bob attacked you?" Where were you when it happened?"

"I don't want to talk about it. Okay?"

"No, I'm afraid it isn't. If you're accusing him we have to know exactly what accusation you're making."

"I don't want to say."

Jo glanced across at Ngaire and cleared her throat quietly. Ngaire heard the agreed signal and took over the questioning smoothly.

"Lois, listen to me. If someone comes to us and says you stole from them, we'd ask them the same questions. What happened, when and where. We wouldn't allow them to walk around making the claim without investigation. If they couldn't prove it to our satisfaction then we would ask them to keep quiet."

It wasn't that simple both Jo and Ngaire thought as they waited for a reply but Lois would understand the reasoning enough to persuade her to talk — they hoped. "We don't like to do this but we have to insist. Either you answer questions, tell us what happened, or we must tell you to say no more about it," Ngaire added.

Lois stood there looking into Ngaire's sightless eyes. Her voice as she answered had developed the very faint note of contempt.

"Okay, if those're the rules. You wanna know what happened, I'll tell you. Your precious Bob raped me, that's what. He came around after dark. Held a knife at my throat and said if I screamed he'd kill me. I kept quiet."

"This was more than once? What time at night?"

"Late, after everyone else was asleep. An' yeah. He did it four times."

"Did you say anything to anyone afterwards?"

"Nah. What was the use. Anyway, I didn't wanna make trouble here." Her face screwed up as if she was crying. She rubbed tears from her face ostentatiously but Jo noticed that there seemed to be none showing in the calculating eyes which watched her over the masking hand. "Seeing him every day I got scared he'd come after me again. I talked to a couple 'a the others to see what they'd say. Guess they talked to you."

Jo nodded, catching the girl's gaze. "They did. Run along, Lois. We'll want to talk to you again later so expect to come back here in a couple of hours. We'll look into this quietly. If Bob did what you say, he will be punished." Lois smirked at them then left. Jo signed turning to Ngaire.

"What do you think?"

Ngaire looked doubtful. "I think she really was raped — but not by Bob. Most likely by one of the adults she and the others ended up with before they deserted them or were killed and we found Lois and the children. She may have suffered incest before the bug." Her brow wrinkled, "That isn't the problem. It's going to be hard to prove she's lying. It's the sort of accusation that some people always want to believe and it's almost impossible to prove a negative. She may be only fourteen but she looks closer to sixteen or seventeen and she isn't unattractive."

"So what now?"

"Now we listen to all the other children. I want to hear what they have to say, both about Lois as leader and about the trip back. Be clever, Jo. Ask them about everyone, not just Bob."

They listened to stories of horror as one by one the children talked of the days after the bug. Jo choked back bitterness. Children shouldn't have these kinds of memories. They must be careful that none of these little ones became abusers in turn. She steered the talk to later, when the adults had vanished and it was Lois who led. The stories were less of sex after that but almost as much of violence. Ngaire finished with the last child and sent her away gently. Then she sat thinking for several moments.

At last she spoke, "I believe that Lois was badly abused. Many of her actions and the things she said to the children reflect adult abuse. She is simply passing it on, often by handling a situation in the only way she knows. But that makes her a danger in Danapa where we don't want that kind of legacy."

"What about Bob?"

"The children have made that fairly clear too. Lois thought that bringing the children back here was his decision. She lost all her authority through that decision and she blames him. I suspect, too, that there may have been some interaction between them."

Pam made a small furious sound and Ngaire turned her head smiling at the girl. "No, not what you think I mean. It's my belief that Lois tried to seduce Bob and he refused her as kindly as he could. It's often a pattern for an abused girl. She's learnt to buy what she wants with sex. She may have hoped to persuade him to drop them all off in some town along the way. I think we get Bob in now and ask him. You'll have to leave for that, Pam. But you could call him for us now."

She heard the girl leave shutting the door rather firmly behind her.

Jo spoke quietly then, "Do you really think that?"

"Yes, I do. Not the least because I've heard Lois talking over the past few weeks. She isn't as careful around me. It's as if she thinks that because I'm blind that I'm deaf too. She's very good at not quite saying something but making people believe she did. She asks questions in such a way her listeners think the way she wants them to. I hate to say it about a child, Jo, but we may have to get rid of her. In a small community we can't afford someone like that if they won't change."

"And you think she won't?"

"She'll say that she will. I think she'll do he best to manipulate you into believing it. But once this dies down she'll merely be more subtle about her scheming. But the choice in the end will be hers first and then yours. My advice is that you get rid of her."

Jo gaped, "I couldn't do that!" Her voice was horrified.

"No," Ngaire agreed. "You probably couldn't bring yourself to do it. I could though. I'm telling you, Jo. Danapa would be much better off without her. In the meantime, that's Bob I can hear." She fell silent as the door opened.

The talk that followed was enlightening for Jo. With quiet questions Ngaire drew out the whole story. How Lois had first suggested that if Bob left her group where they were if she'd provide sexual services. Refused, she'd threatened that he'd be sorry. Over the trip home, she'd attempted to seduce him any time they were alone. He'd countered that by telling Marion and pleading with her to stick around. Bob's face twisted in embarrassment. At barely nineteen he found the story a difficult one to tell but he was adamant.

"Marion can swear I never touched Lois. Honestly, Ngaire. I can't stand the kid. She's a nasty little piece of work. You should hear some of the things that the other kids with her told me."

Ngaire lifted blind eyes to where Bob stood. "We have heard. Personally, I believe you. But now we need to prove nothing happened. As I've said to Jo, proving a negative isn't easy." She stood up and went to the door where Pam waited outside. "Pam, find Lois and bring her in here again. Bob, you go. Find Marion and ask her to come into the room behind this one. I want her to listen at the connecting door."

Ngaire's voice went hard. "Tell Marion that she is not under any circumstances to let Lois know that she's there. I don't care what Lois says or how bad her accusations may be. Marion stays where she is and keeps quiet. Do you understand?"

"Yes. I'll tell Marion."

Five minutes later Lois slipped into the room to stand looking innocently helpless in front of them, or as helpless as a girl who is tall and well-built can look. Ngaire began in a gentle voice. Once the rhythm of question and answer was established she spoke more quickly. Lois snapped back the answers with an underlying hint of smugness to her voice. It was nothing you could point to but both women got the impression of a performance. and that Lois was well satisfied with the way she played it.

"All right, Lois. That's all for the moment. Please go to your room and stay there." Ngaire's voice stayed level.

Jo ushered the girl out before turning to open the inner door. Marion came in first, followed by Bob — his expression a mixture of disgust, horror, and embarrassment. Jo waved him to silence at once.

"It's Marion we want to hear from."

And hear they did. The thirty-year-old woman was spluttering with rage as she started. Once into her narrative she calmed but it was still obvious her opinion of Lois was low, to say the least. She ended with a few comments on the girl's veracity, character, and personal habits which made all of them smile briefly.

"Look, I know I'm no saint. I was a fool with Mavis and Jonathon and I took up with Johnny before that. But I've worked here. I've put a lot of time an" sweat into the place and I don't want to see it ruined by that little — " she choked back further invective. "I'm telling you. She's a liar." Marion finished flatly.

Jo sighed, "I believe you, but there still isn't absolute proof. Someone could say we're refusing to believe this because we like Bob and we don't like Lois."

Marion smiled, a slow unpleasant look, which signaled one final revelation. "Um, Bob? I can say what I want to now?"

He nodded, none noticing the faint puzzlement in his eyes.

"All right then. I know Bob wasn't in Lois's bed the way she's claiming." She paused, "Because he was always in my bed on the trip back. Lois says that Bob came and spent several hours with her threatening her to silence on four separate occasions. Each time she reckons that was after we'd put all the children to bed, except that he came straight to me each time after that so her story's totally impossible."

Jo would have liked to ask why this hadn't been said earlier. One look at Bob and Marion and she realised. The boy was nineteen and Marion was more than ten years older. Both had feared comment from some of their friends. She doubted it was love. Just enjoyment on both sides but neither had wanted to flaunt the affair. She hid a grin. Shay had said once that something similar was likely. Danapa had a large number of adult women and a growing number of teenage males. But the news did deal with one half of this problem.

"Pam!" Jo tapped the gaping girl on the arm. "Go and get Lois."

Ngaire spoke quietly, "Pam? Just say we've come to a decision and she needs to be here." Her face was sad. "Jo? Will you send the girl away? I think you should."

Jo was anguished, "I can't possibly. She's only a child for all the trouble she's made. I'm sure she didn't understand how serious her claim was. And if she goes, how will she manage? What's to prevent someone finding her who'll abuse or even kill her?"

She would have said more but for Lois' entrance. The girl glanced about those waiting. Her face went blank but her eyes despised them all.

Jo didn't waste time. "Lois, you claimed Bob attacked you on the trip back. You said he threatened you with his knife to make you keep quiet. We know this is all untrue." Her voice broke a little, "Why would you tell lies like that?"

Lois stared at her in silence before shrugging. "So I lied. What are you going to do to me?" she said at last.

"Nothing," Ngaire told her. "Go back to what you were doing. There'll have to be an assembly tonight. Since you've seen fit to tell your lies to half of the people in this place, we'll have to tell everyone that we've investigated and we can prove that they were lies. That will be your punishment. That we'll all know your word can't be trusted. You're to be in front of the assembly before evening meal."

The girl gave her a look of pure hatred before leaving the room. The others left in silence, leaving Jo alone to worry. Maybe it was too harsh making the girl face everyone. But then it was right that Bob should be exonerated. She bent to the records, adding a short summary of the day's occurrences. She dreaded having to drag Lois before the people. She was sure the girl wouldn't go willingly.

In the event, neither she nor any one else had to do that. When assembly was called and Lois sought, the girl had already fled. With her had gone weapons, a good bike, and an assortment of small valuable items from the store-rooms. Jo was afraid that they'd never see the child again. Out there anything could happen.

It was Marion who had the last word on that. "The little cow is trouble. I'd like to think it'll be someone else's now. But she's like a fake fifty dollar bill, damn thing is always likely to come back to haunt you when you least want it."

Chapter Sixteen

"So what do you tell the assembly in a few minutes?" Pam asked.

"Go and find Riana and Ani," was Jo's answer. "We'll discuss the tapu. I want this whole business with Lois kept quiet. I'll just say that she was proved a liar and fled rather than face them."

Everyone in Danapa was gathering in the compound for assembly as rumours flew. Jo took her place on the dais in front of the store sheds. At the back of her mind, she was amused by it. Shay had found the little platform in some church. It was ideal for raising a speaker a couple of feet higher than the crowd. She missed Shay with a sudden pang but now was not the time.

"All right. This meeting was originally called because there were serious charges against one of us. I'm happy to say that the accusations were proved untrue."

She waited for the muttering to die away. "We asked that the accuser face you and acknowledge this but she preferred to leave. This being so, the meeting has no need to discuss her claims and we can consider another problem. Riana, perhaps you'd like to speak now.'"

Riana marched through the crowd to the dais. For almost ten minutes, she explained the system of tapu, ending with, "Tapu isn't another word for forbidden. It's the Maori system of — well — I guess it would translate best as sacred relationship. It's the balance between humans and the land, the natural world. The relationship says we should never destroy a species by taking too many or the young. It's one of the reasons the Pagan beliefs meshed here in

Danapa in our early days. Pagans also respect the land and the beasts of the land. But within Maori there is the other side of tapu. To break it is to break relationship with your own spirit. This can open you to evil. A tapu must be respected."

While Riana spoke, Jo scanned the people listening. Most there seemed to understand and agree. Some however were looking sour. Jo marked them. She recognised at least two or three who'd been taking the young immature shellfish. Clearly they saw no reason why they should not continue.

Ani spoke after that. Jo admired the child's clear words, recalling the ten-year-old Ani she had first seen. This girl was four years older, wiser and more confident. She and Pam had been friends from the beginning, despite the three-year age gap. They were a lot of help to Jo, and acknowledged leaders for many of the children. The assembly considered the laws of tapu and the debate heated up.

"It's stupid. The shellfish are there. Are you saying we should starve?" asked a young man with thin lips.

"No!" Riana was adamant. "No one is saying we should starve. Who thinks if we don't have a few dozen shellfish all of Danapa would starve?"

There was a ripple of quiet laughter. Someone called out. "That's crazy. A few dozen shellfish wouldn't even be one each."

"No. So what we're saying is that one person might not have something they like. And just for one season while we allow the shellfish beds to recover. Which of you is so selfish they can't forgo a treat for one season so we can all continue to enjoy the food later on?"

The original complainer shut his mouth. "Not me. I was only asking."

Another stood, an elderly woman with a scar down one side of her face.

"I say we agree with Riana's system. We've seen too many species die out over the past hundred and fifty years or fall to almost unsustainable numbers. Now that there's fewer people some of those last lot are coming back. I saw wood pigeons in the trees last week."

"I heard tuis and a bellbird," another woman chimed in.

Jo smiled at that. "The tuis have come for the flax bushes. Shay wanted us to plant a line of them all along the stream when we first came here. Now they're flowering so well this year the tuis are coming back. They love flowering flax."

The man who'd first protested tapu nodded. "I love to hear tuis. I had a pair in the reserve next door to where I lived. Oh well. I suppose I can live without shellfish for a few months. But as soon as they pick up we have a day gathering them?"

"A day gathering and a barbeque on the beach," Jo said with a smile. He grinned back and nodded.

"That'll do me."

Other voices agreed. The law would hold. It was for Jo to state when and where a tapu was placed in consultation with Riana, Ani, and an elderly Maori male, Hemi Paratai. But sufficient objectors could call an assembly to challenge that if they disagreed.

Jo stepped up to her small dais, "Then I declare a tapu placed on all shellfish around the beaches of the inlet and harbour. I also declare tapu on all small shellfish anywhere. None shall be taken that are not clearly adult."

She stepped down as the gathering began to disperse. That should do what Riana and Ani had wanted. She returned to her rooms to pick up Miro as he woke and yawned. He was so delightful, so warm and sweet. He nestled into her arms in a way that made her heart melt.

Joya moved and Jo scooped her up as well to sit cradling both. Shay had been gone six weeks and might be gone another six. They'd found a small settlement on the east coast. Shay's letter hadn't been approving. The people seemed to believe that no lifestyle but their own was acceptable. They were regimented, with children repressed and women second-class citizens. In some ways it was an exaggerated form of the Danapa settlement where the demand was that any who joined tolerate Maori and Pagan beliefs and that no one was less that equal under the law. But in the East Coast group that toleration had gone. You followed their beliefs or were cast out. Nor was there equality for women or children. Shay had left.

Jo rocked the babies. Not that they were really babies now. Joya had already walked. Miro crawled with speed and enthusiasm. Tonight, he still had a bruise on his forehead where he'd crawled into a chair. Then too, Pam was spending a lot of time with her brother's friend, Bob. Jo hoped it would last. She hoped Shay would come home safely. For Jo, Danapa wasn't the same without her.

The weeks trickled past. Another small group came back, composed of various people Shay had found in the towns of the central country. There had been a few there who survived in ones and twos. Most were happy to join an established settlement. Shay and her friends had weeded out those they considered unsuitable. Jo smiled at the letter she received. Rome and Mike were up to their tricks again. She could remember how they'd done the same to her. It had been weeks before she found out that Shay had known both men for some time.

For this trip it had been Shay's idea to use Mike and Rome to sort out others. Those who were horrified by the sight of two men in makeup, false eyelashes and chattering in high-pitched affected voices were unsuitable for a tolerant settlement.

After that, there were weeks without word coming back to Danapa. Shay was combing Wellington, finding the city was mostly deserted and falling to ruin in places. The tower blocks, the office blocks, the Government buildings in the city's heart still stood. It would take centuries to bring those down. But the suburbs had mostly built in wood and had had more green areas to start with. Those suburbs were falling into ruin and enveloped in vegetation, some had burned out in great patches and a quake two years after Jo and Shay had gone north had done other damage. It had not been large, about six point seven. The older buildings would not survive long.

Here and there, people scratched a bleak living on the remains of the city's carcass. They sneered at the very idea of work. They told her, 'Don't we have all they needed there in the ruins?' Shay realized their ilk would be worthless to Danapa.

Out of curiosity, she visited the house where Jo had grown up.

Much of the street had burned but the fire had stopped with Jo's home only half-razed. Undamaged within a mildly scorched case under the remnants of a bed, she found a stored dress. It had been carefully packed away with moth- and insect-proofing and it was beautiful. Jo would want this. She didn't have to know the house was gone. Later, in a shop she discovered a case for the dress as well as additional items. After a few more days, Shay, Mike and Rome were sure there was nothing here for Danapa. They gave orders and started on the long drive back.

The welcome they received was wild. It wasn't until two days later that Shay was able to talk to her lover in peace. Her face was so serious that Jo eyed her with suspicion. She knew most of Shay's looks by now. Something was being planned. Shay talked for a few minutes about the need for stability. Jo stared. What was all this? Shay moved on to partnership, the need to set standards and be examples. By now Jo was completely baffled. Shay ended with a particularly fancy sentence before glancing at her lover's bewildered face. She was hard put to it not howl with laughter. Best put Jo out of her misery. She took her friend's hands.

"What I'm saying, love, is why don't we make a commitment before everyone once you've had the baby? We could make it a double celebration. Name the baby and..." she waited.

"Marry?" Jo said at last, her voice squeaking upwards.

Shay did laugh, a soft chuckle. "We can work out a special ceremony for us. Besides, I brought something back in case you said yes."

"I do. I do. What did you bring?" She hugged her love.

Shay produced the case. Jo opened it smiling. It was the kind of container used for wedding dresses with all their trimmings. On top was a veil, an airy concoction of fine lace and tiny pearls. Next were slippers, a spray of artificial flowers to carry and matching pearl and silver jewellery. Jo gasped before lifting the dress underneath.

"Shay! Where did you find this? It's my mother's wedding dress."

"I stopped off at your old house, love. I found this and since I planned to ask you, I thought you'd like it." She struck an attitude, "If you reject me, if you break my heart, one of our children may want to wear it."

Jo understood. Shay tended to clown where she felt the most deeply. Folding the dress again she placed it on the bed. Then she reached out to her friend.

"No children are wearing before me." Her voice wavered. "I love you. You're the only one I want for always." She was unable to continue as she choked. Shay hugged her hard.

"Well, good. Because that's how it is for me too. Now, we'd better sit down and work out what we're going to say and how many of our friends can do something at the ceremonies. No one will want to be left out and what's more, it's only another two months before you have this baby."

"Don't remind me."

"Has it been that rough?" Shay was surprised.

Jo moaned. "You haven't heard the half of it. I'll tell you about the new law first. After that you can hear all about Lois."

She talked while Shay listened. Later, after Jo had fallen asleep Shay lay, thinking. The tapu law was good, but Lois could be a danger. She'd only been in Danapa a few weeks, but she'd been the prying, listen at doors type. Once Jo had her baby and the twin ceremonies had been carried out, Shay might just take a long ride. If she happened to run across Lois during that it would be too bad for Lois. She slept then, curled beside Jo, her face smoothed out into the gentleness she rarely showed awake.

Waking first, Jo looked down tenderly. Shay looked so young lying there. She'd had her twenty-second birthday while she was gone, but asleep she looked even younger than the not quite eighteen she'd been when they met. Jo rose quietly to get them breakfast. They ate and whispered until they emptied their plates.

Jo went to check records. With the new people, these had to be up to date. A middle-aged couple, Joan and Morgan McCormack had taken over the records work. It freed Jo for other administration and she was heartily grateful. Still, it was part of her job to check and while she was there she could enjoy a chat with acquaintances, many of whom were rapidly growing into friends.

Shay went in search of Mike and Rome. Once they were found she swept them outside away from the men who had been helping re-roof the old pigsties. It would be wise to have no eavesdroppers to this conversation. Since she'd helped Fred's passing, she'd known her friends had guessed something of what Shay did to keep Jo and Danapa safe. Now she slipped obliquely into that, talking until she was sure. Finally Mike nodded.

"We do know what you've been doing. What you want to know now is whether we'll take over doing it if anything ever happens to you."

"Yes." She kept her face from showing anything.

Mike consulted his partner with a quick glance. "We've talked about this between ourselves. We guessed that if you came to anyone about this, it would be us. We decided we'd agree." He looked at her, "We think it's important that sometimes there's a way to keep us safe even if it isn't always within the laws or agreed in assembly."

"Rome?" Shay asked him.

"I'm with Mike on this. I'll tell you something too, Shay. In another ten years, you could let Ani in it as next in line. She thinks the way you do. Make a special oath to do it for the good of Danapa and only where there's a clear danger. No more than four of us knowing about it. It could be a destructive thing to do for personal reasons."

"I know. I killed Jessie. I'd never directly killed in cold blood before but she was a danger to all of us." She shrugged. "There's a cleansing ceremony I read about once. I used that as soon as I could get away alone for a few hours. After that I felt better. You two could sort out something similar."

Both men nodded.

Shay was relaxed now, having done her best. She went in search of her love and listened to the records as they were read to her and had no disagreements. Shay prompted Jo to talk more about the trouble while she had been absent. Then hiding a smile

229

she went to find Marion where she worked in the midst of a group of workers tending the vegetable garden. She drew the woman aside speaking quietly.

"You're almost as good a liar as Lois."

Marion froze, then nodded. "But you aren't going to say anything? Yes, I lied. You met Lois. I knew she was lying right from the start. But there was no way to prove it and she'd have ruined Bob's life here. Just to get back at him for not doing what she wanted. I lied so she'd have to admit her own lies. She did." The woman laughed quietly. "It isn't a lie now though. Bob and I got close after that."

"I'm glad." Shay said.

"Me too." Marion looked up, "It sort of makes up for Johnny and for listening to that idiot Jonathon. I saved Bob and he's worth more than both of them together."

Shay patted her shoulder, "Yes, he is. Jo's thinking of giving him an official position. Don't tell her I told you. She'll probably raise it with him next month. Well, that's it. I just wanted to know." She strolled away leaving Marion smiling after her.

Jo's baby was born seven weeks later. She was small but healthy with blue eyes that would stay blue and fine wisps of dark hair. They called her Shayna in a double ceremony six weeks after the birth, which first named the baby then joined Jo and Shay in a life-commitment. Jo wore her mother's wedding gown, remembering that it had been her grandmother's gown before that. Afterwards, she laid it away in the moth-proof case, together with the other items Shay had added. One day Joya or Shayna might wear it if they wished.

Shay felt restless again. Her scouts reported that they found traces of camps. Not close-by, but further to the southeast. She decided to say nothing to Jo about it. That would only begin the old argument. Whoever this lot was, they shouldn't be dangerous. There never seemed to be more than a handful of them and no scout had laid eyes on more than their passing traces.

Shay decided to take Billy and another young man named Martin and tour up towards the end of the land along the east coast. After that, she would return down through the west. It would allow her to see how the grass was doing, visit the horse and cattle herds. In many ways she'd liked Danapa more when there was less of it. There were smaller places where people who felt the same way could eventually settle. Paparore might be inhabited in another generation.

Jo pounced on her friend two nights before Shay was to leave. "There's been some discussion you should hear. It's about Dana."

"*What* about her?" Shay looked surprised. "We buried her. There's a stone for her. What else do they want?"

"We bury ordinary women. We give men to the birds in sky-burial and bury the bones once they're mostly clean. That's our way. But her friends would like Dana to have a special remembrance. I snow we did that with a cave and the stone but they want something else. They'd like her bones taken out and burned. Then the ashes could be scattered around the outer walls. They think her spirit would like that. She'd be a part of Danapa forever."

Shay considered the idea. After several minutes, she spoke decisively. "I'm for it but why not do it up really fancy? There's a factory that made tombstones north of here. We could get a big one and set it up by the main gates. Then we'll bring the bones out and burn them. Scatter the ashes with a full procession around the walls.

"That's perfect. How soon could you get the stone here?"

"Tomorrow or the next day with help from some of our friends. You sort out the procession stuff while I'm gone. I won't be away long this time. Just a couple of weeks."

The stone arrived two days after that. As Shay had said, they'd made it big, a head-high, body-length wide slab of black artificial stone. Shay lingered, over-seeing the stone's placement into a concrete base set beside the main gates. With that done she sought out Bob, noting with interest how responsibility and Marion seemed to have settled him into adulthood. He looked older than the almost twenty she knew him to be. She handed him a heavy case of tools.

"These are for carving Dana's name and dates. There's some that will run off electricity and another set for doing it by hand. Put her name at the top and add, "FOUNDER OF DANAPA in capitals'." She grinned, "That's a lot easier than putting, 'founder of the commune which became Danapa.'"

"Since I'm carving it, I couldn't agree more," Bob told her. "I'll do a good job. How many scouts are going with you on this new scouting trip?"

"Billy and Martin, maybe a third. We'll check out the herds and Paparore, then come back from the west coast inland along the inlet. One more thing, Bob. Some of the scout pairs have found camp-sites south-west of here. Make sure they continue to keep their eyes open."

"I'll tell them."

Shay headed off to finish sorting her gear. There was still fuel to be had but she was in no hurry. They'd take ponies and a pack horse. Make a slow peaceful ride of it. She led her tiny group out of the gates early next morning. She looked back once to wave to where Jo stood with Miro and Joya beside her, baby Shayna in her arms. There'd been almost half a year of peace now. It looked as if that might last.

Jo had no time to miss Shay. She was caught up with complaints that two of the children had fought and that the noise of Bob's carving was upsetting the ponies. She was able to settle the latter problem by ignoring it. The carving would take only a day or two and the ponies would get over it. She called Bob in. Now would be a good time to give him the responsibility she'd intended.

"Have you heard about Marli and Kev?"

Bob snorted. "Everyone's heard about Marli and Kev."

"Good." Bob looked surprised. "What do you think we should do about them?"

He considered briefly then looked at her. "Send them out to scout together. They've done a bit but never without older scouts. Together with just the two of them they'll stick together. They'll be too busy jumping at every stick-crack to fight each other. Scouts learn to work together fast or they don't survive and they do know that."

"Then call them in and tell them what to do. I'll be leaving it to you from now on to run the junior scouts and their roster. Pick the kids you think will train up to that. You'll be deputy under Shay. Is that okay with you?"

"Does Shay know?"

"Yes, she approves." His face lit with quick pleasure. "Go on, call that pair in. I'll leave it to you. Right now I have other things to worry about rather than two kids who can't stop arguing and upsetting too many people." She departed leaving it to the new deputy to give the children their orders. He took advantage of that to fulfill the promise he'd made to Shay.

"Go south. Scouts have found small camp sites which aren't ours in the south-west. Be very careful but see if you can find anyone there. Watch them if you do. Don't take chances but we want to know as much as possible." He saw them leave, satisfied he'd done everything he could.

Messages came back from or about Shay and her scouts. There was always someone riding to and fro from the herds. They could tell Jo that her friend had reached the cattle herd, then the horse herd, she'd stayed a night before riding on and yes, Shay was well. Jo was happy to hear any word, but her days and nights seemed so busy she hardly missed her friend lately. Miro and Joya were at the stage of getting into everything and Jo spent as much time as possible with them. Shay's cat too demanded notice. Then there were Pam, Marion, Billy and Alex all working on a ceremony for Dana.

Four weeks after Shay had left, Jo was talking to Mike. "So if you can look after our two, the baby should sleep most of the afternoon."

Mike laughed, "No trouble. Rome's planning to take a carrier out to one of the old farmhouses where there's some self-sown potatoes. We'll take Miro and Joya with us. We should be back this evening."

Jo watched the carrier rumble out of the gates. After that, she worked with Pam a while before realising that Shayna would be awake. Shay should be home soon, it would be good to have her lover home again. Jo listened as she strolled towards her rooms. No sound. It was a miracle the baby wasn't howling her head off. Maybe one of the others had gone in to comfort her. She reached the cradle and peered in. Shayna was gone but whoever had her had left a note. It would be Ani most likely.

Jo picked it up glancing down casually. Then she stiffened. Her terrified eyes stared at the words.

Come to the old farmhouse beyond the stream. If you want your baby in one piece come alone. Don't tell anyone. We'll be watching. If anyone else comes with you you'll get the baby back after we've — Jo read the vicious graphic threats which followed. Dear Goddess. Terror for her baby overwhelmed her. Without thinking she dropped the note, running from the room.

Outside she forced herself to calm down. She was riding through the gates as Billy entered. He had a glimpse of her face and stared. Something was very wrong there, where was Pam? He found his sister and together they headed towards Jo's room. The note was found on the floor and read before they stared at each other.

"Where are Mike and Rome?"

"Out gathering vegetables," Billy said slowly. "It'd take hours to find them and get them back. We need to do something at once."

"What about Shay? Jo thought she'd be back any day now and Bob knows which way she's coming home."

Bob was in the stables when brother and sister found him. They gabbled an explanation, gave him seconds to read the note, and then demanded immediate action. Not that he had any hesitation in complying with their plea.

Chapter Seventeen

Shay was riding towards Danapa at a peaceful walk as Bob came galloping towards her. She listened in silence before kicking her pony into a controlled gallop. Behind her rode her scouts. They entered the track from the main road to Danapa even as two young riders arrived, faces hot with excitement. They swung their ponies towards Bob, both over-running each other's words as they made him listen.

Bob called ahead to Shay as he understood what they were trying to tell him. "Shay! *Shay*! Wait! This is Kev and Marli. They were fighting so I sent them out to scout the south-west. They've found something. It could tie in with what's happened to Jo."

Shay spun her beast so quickly that it staggered, she dropped lightly from the sweating pony. The children came at her signal, each trying to out-talk the other. They'd found another group. Lois was with them.

"Lois? Are you sure?"

Both were. There'd been a woman, the leader. She'd looked familiar as well. There were men with guns. They had ponies and a couple of trucks."

"How many people did you see?" Shay kept her voice quiet.

"Gee, maybe forty," The boy said. The girl nodded agreement.

Shay was adding up possibilities. It was unlikely that there was a second unknown group in the area. With both Jo and Shayna, the enemy had hostages they probably hoped to use to buy a way into Danapa. It could have been Lois who took the baby, probably using the escape tunnels to enter and leave again.

"How did they get into the main part of the place? We keep the Danapa ends of the tunnels locked."

Bob glanced at her. "Pry-bar, by the looks of it. Door lock was wrenched right out. Lois wouldn't have been strong enough if it was her that got the baby. I'd say she had a man with her, maybe more than one. They'd have been there to cover her retreat if anyone saw her. Damned if I know how she knew about the tunnels either. She did snoop a lot though, and you know what kids are, one may have found out and told her without meaning harm."

"Seems likely."

Fucking Lois. If Shay'd been home when that mess blew up she'd have made sure Lois didn't go further than her grave or a dog-pack's belly. Shay considered as she rode. Lois could have made the enemy group believe Shay would open the gates to buy Jo and the baby's lives. Not that it would but they might believe she'd take the risk. There were other risks she'd prefer. She saw her friends listening, understanding the choice. Shay was first through the gates, dropping briefly from her tired mount.

"Saddle Dusty and Rumpus for me. Bring them here now." She turned to Bob. "Go ahead and get the fastest ponies saddled. Thanks to these two we know where the enemy's main camp is. From what you say about the note, Jo had to ride miles so they could check she was alone. Then they have to take her to their camp and they'll probably circle a bit going there too. If they're seen by a scout they'll hope to mislead us. I can go straight there."

Her hand chopped off the sound of protest. "No! One can sneak in. Maybe get Jo and the baby out. If I get Jo free we'll ride for Danapa. Have someone go to our rooms. I want an army case that's there. Don't open it, just bring it quickly. You'll find it under a stack of clothes on the bottom shelf."

Bob was already giving quick low-voiced orders. Scouts sped for the items demanded.

Shay continued, "Gather everyone who'll fight. I want odds of two to one at minimum. Hold them back until you can ride in force. Don't start until midnight when the moon's giving really good light. Ride careful. Keep scouts well ahead. If you don't meet us before you reach them hit them with everything you have."

"And what do we do if you're all hostages" Billy asked harshly.

"You hit them with everything you have," Shay said, her voice even harsher. "I may be able to protect Jo and the baby long enough for you to get to us. The one thing you do *not* do is listen to them. In the end, everyone in Danapa is more important. Do you understand me?"

He nodded as a scout returned leading a lean dun horse with a short ragged tail and a nondescript bay. Shay held Bob with her gaze as she mounted Rumpus, the bay. "Don't let them open the gates to save us because it won't. Tell Mike and Rome that, say it was my order."

She kicked her mount into a gallop, Dusty following on his lead-rein. They rounded the bend and were gone just as the two men arrived. They'd been with the cattle on the far side of the settlement and had heard only the sounds of hard-running hooves.

"What's going on?"

Only Pam paused to tell them. Two hours later, as Danapa organised for war, Bob passed on her words to his friends. They looked at him in silence. Both understood something the boy had not. At the last, Shay had finally taken a wider view. The lives of those she loved were still less than Danapa. One was her future. The other was the future of all of them.

They took over some of the organising making swift order out of chaos. There was moonlight. Vehicles with off-road ability and the bikes would leave at dawn. Those on ponies could leave now, keeping to a steady pace. They would head for where the side road crossed a bridge to the southwest. The enemy camp was several hours over the other side of the river. But if Shay could get Jo and the baby away, then that was the way they would run.

In the enemy camp, Jo was realising how stupid she'd been. These people were led by Mavis with no sign of her brother. Jo had tried to talk, only facing the truth as she was casually slapped to the ground. The woman was insane. Mavis saw herself as Moses leading her people to the Promised Land. She was charismatic enough to have swayed them with alternate ranting about the wicked, who must perish, and tales of how well off they should be once they owned the settlement and had the wicked as their slaves.

Jo wondered if the promised loot, slaves, and the comforts of Danapa weren't swaying Mavis's followers as much, if not more, than her lurid descriptions of Danapa's "wickedness." Beside her, Lois encouraged this, talking of the tasty and ample fresh food supplies, the solar powered lights, the clean running water cold — and hot. Mavis had taken the girl as her chosen daughter speaking of her as Heir.

At least Shayna had been given back to her, Jo thought, clutching her baby as she stared around her prison. The group had taken over a old country store with a large house attached and a number of outbuildings. Jo and Shayna had been shut in what had once been the woodshed. A few logs and a small stack of kindling remained. Mavis had made Jo and her child's future chillingly clear before the door was shut and they were left in the dark. If the Danapa gates were not opened, Shayna would be crucified before them. If the gates remained shut, it would be Jo's turn.

If Danapa did not allow Mavis in after that, they would be assailed, as Mavis put it. She appeared to be expecting the walls to fall down at that point. Once Jo had realised the extent of the woman's madness and of how the others followed both the intent and the mania, she had kept silence. She did wonder what had happened to Jonathon. Yet she dared not ask. If Mavis had succeeded him by force and Jo mentioned his name it might identify her still further as one of the wicked. Jo rocked her baby, comforting and feeding the child even as she bit back her fear.

No one knew where she'd gone. They might find the note once they noticed that she'd been gone longer than usual, then look around for her, but her captors had taken her in a different direction from what they'd read. The first they'd know for certain would be her appearance before Danapa's gates as Mavis's key. A key that would fail, but she wouldn't think of that. Shay wouldn't open the gates and see Miro and Joya killed as well. Shay was a warrior, she wouldn't allow the settlement to be taken. Jo wiped tears from her face with the back of one hand. Yet if Shay watched the baby and her lover slaughtered and did nothing, it would break her inside. Beyond the shed it had become dark and she could hear Mavis preaching.

Shay could hear also, out on the camp fringe. She'd ridden the horses almost to exhaustion directly across country to the bridge. They had stumbled several times but Shay had driven them onwards. None of that mattered. She had to find Jo and the baby and get them out. She left the animals standing, tied, weary heads down in the shadows. It would take time to find Jo and get her free. They could rest for a while. She slipped around the house, spied the shed and a bored-looking guard standing against the door.

It took time. She must not hurry or be careless. The shed was to one side and slightly to the rear of the house. The door looked solid. Likely that was why Mavis had thought only one guard was needed. Thanks be for Mavis's revival meeting or whatever the woman was yelling about. Even the guard was now straining to hear as Mavis's voice soared up. Shay reached the back of the shed unseen, unsheathed her knife and began to whittle quietly at a pine-knot on the edge of one board. It would make a good start, if she had to break off and hide, and they found the hole it would simply look as if the knot had fallen out at some time.

Inside the shed Jo was too afraid to sit or relax. Instead, she walked, pacing the small shed by the light of the candle stub she always carried in a pocket along with matches. When she heard a tiny sound at the back of the shed she leaped nervously. There was a scratching then a soft thump as a knot fell from a plank, landing on the floor. Jo was almost afraid to believe but the quick whisper came in Shay's voice.

"Are you both okay?"

"Yes. Who's with you?"

"I'm alone. I had a better chance of getting to you that way. I can't get a bike or one of their trucks. They aren't as dumb as I thought and they've got all those immobilised. But I brought a spare horse for you in case they'd been that smart. Just sit tight and I should have you out soon. Don't panic. It might take me a bit of time. I have to see to the guard and I don't dare give him a chance to make any noise."

Jo sat nursing Shayna and waiting. The seconds stretched until she was panicking, convinced that somewhere out in the dark, Shay too must have been taken prisoner. Then the door swung half-open and Shay hissed at her. Jo padded out to join her, almost tripping over the guard's body as she passed the door.

She found herself thanking the Goddess that it wasn't Miro she carried. He cried at the slightest thing. Shayna was far more placid. Shay led them in a half-circle into the night. Two ponies stood tied to a branch just off the road.

Jo paused to size up the situation. "If you lead my horse I'll carry Shayna. Which horse should I take?"

"Dusty. He's the fastest and the surest-footed. We'll walk them a ways until I'm sure we're out of earshot."

Behind her a small figure shifted silently, closing in. The knife slid home in Shay's back. Shay felt only the blow and turned. Close as her attacker was even in the trees' half-shadow Shay could see Lois's surprised face. If you stick a knife in someone they're supposed to die, not turn to glare at you.

Jo was saying something, but Shay ignored that. Drawing her own knife with flickering speed she struck backhanded with the hilt against a temple before Lois could step back. The girl went to the ground, her temple crushed in, the surprised look still on her face. Shay reached down, felt for Lois's throat and, making sure, she slashed again, bone-deep. Shay's Law. This was one dead enemy who'd lay no second ambush.

In the twisting shadows Jo could make out nothing but oddly confused movement.

Then, Shay was speaking again. "That was Lois, I've killed her but they'll come looking for her sometime, maybe any minute. Hand me the baby and get up quickly. We have to get out of here."

We sure do, Shay thought as Jo obeyed. Any minute now, that maniac is going to start yelling for Lois. Once they find the body, she'll have the whole camp straight down the road after us. We can't go across country either. Not even in moonlight. She handed the baby up to Jo, moving to her own mount. She bit back a cry as she dragged herself into the saddle.

She could feel blood from the wound trickling down inside her clothing. Jo was more important. She had to get Jo and the baby to safety. They couldn't make the bridge before the hunt would be up, but if she could send Jo on...if she could delay Mavis and her followers long enough for Jo to reach the Danapa people who would racing to join them by now... She hustled the ponies along the road. Jo clung to Shayna, crooning softly. The baby mustn't cry, sound carried a long way on a quiet night like this.

Jo's pony tripped on a rock and halted, holding up a foreleg as the baby yelled in fright. Shay slipped from her mount to run gentle fingers down Dusty's injured leg.

In the camp behind them, Mavis fell silent, sucking in her breath. She looked around for her claimed daughter and ground her teeth. She'd survived Jonathon's mad abduction of her. Gradually he'd fallen back into the old habit of listening to her, his older sister. He'd allowed her to be second-in-command again. She begun to build her own power base then, knowing she might not have a second chance. She'd always been the better speaker, the one with the ideas. He ruled only because he stole her cleverness for his own.

Mavis had waited for the right time, which came when they met another group. She'd persuaded Jonathon these others planned to take over his people. He must attack them first. He'd done so and in the fighting he'd been killed. Mavis smiled briefly, a strange lop-sided leer of satisfaction. It had felt so good to kill her brother. She'd always hated him. He was the one who got everything. Attention, love, the better education. He was the boy. She was just a girl. Now Danapa would see what a woman could do. She rid it of the whores, the stupid women who opposed her. Rid it of children who spoke up as if they were equals. As for the filthy queers.... She had lurid deaths planned.

She had an heir too. Her mind snapped back to the cry of a

baby she'd heard as she howled her creed. It hadn't come from her people. That bitch from Danapa?

"Someone check the whore and her brat, Tom, you, *now!*"

Running footsteps returned. "She's gone. The guard's dead. His throat's slashed wide open."

"Find them. Find Lois, where is she?" Obedient to her howled demands, her people spread out to search. They quickly found the heir's body.

On the road, Shay slipped down from her mount. "Get up on this one, Jo. I've got a better chance on foot than you have. Our people are on the way. Stay on the main road." She spoke over the yells from Shayna who was now thoroughly upset.

"But..."

"*Jo!* Listen to me! One pony can't carry the two of us and Shayna. You have to get her clear, our people will be coming, go that way!" She pointed, as her hands writhed and twisted busily in the semi-dark. "I can hide from them where you can't with Shayna yelling. They won't get here for a while, that'll give me time to get clear." She clung to Jo's hand a moment. "Now you see why I wanted to have all this land cleared, just ours. I love you. Now get out of here!"

Her hand slapped the horse's rump so that he set off at a rocking canter. Jo clung to the howling baby, feeling for the reins where they were looped over the pommel. The pony cantered onwards, staying on the smoother road.

Shay slumped to the ground. With the reins twisted like that, it would be miles before Jo could stop that animal without dropping Shayna. By then, she was sure Jo would see sense and ride on. Their friends might already be near enough to meet Jo. After more than four years riding all over this land Shay knew it well. Up ahead, the road narrowed between a sheer-sided hill and a steep drop on the other side as it followed the river towards the bridge. There was an old building by the road. It may have been an electrical sub-station once although it was empty of machinery now, but the walls were heavy duty concrete. If she held out there for a short time, Jo would make the bridge and by that time their friends should have arrived for sure.

Ahead the hoof-beats faded, Shay started to plod down the road. It wasn't far to the hut. She reached it and slipped inside the door. Behind her, she could hear engines approaching. Shay smiled viciously. Let them come. If she couldn't escape, she had something saved for this moment.

The first of the two enemy trucks rounded the bend, Shay reached into her shoulder case to flick a missile under the front wheels. There was a roar as the grenade exploded. The truck skewed to block the road. Its engine caught fire and any minute now, Shay thought, it would...the fuel from the ruptured tank went up in a gout of flames. They wouldn't pass that lot in a hurry.

Shay felt her body sliding to the floor of the hut. It hadn't been a bad life all in all, and the last four and a half years had been great. She'd had Jo, Joya, friends and a home. She'd never have believed it when she was younger, but she was leaving something permanent behind. Land she'd helped hold, a fortress she'd helped create, and her bloodline that lived there. She hoped Jo and their children would remember her.

Voices screamed in the background. With the last of her strength she slipped the other grenades beneath her, pulling the pins and waiting very briefly before letting her body lie on them. Her body would hold the levers down. The grenades were of the type that leaped upwards as they exploded. At chest height that many would be death's own scythe in an enclosed area. She'd have blood for her going. With fading sight she saw her enemies enter
— *Jo, my love, goodbye...*

Shrieking with fury, Mavis pounced. She rolled Shay over and dragged her head back, ready to finish her hated opponent. As the body moved Mavis saw the trap, she screamed, dropping Shay she jerked upright to escape — too late. Final blackness claimed Shay in that flickering second of triumph, as Mavis's upright body took half the blast, while those crowding behind her took the remainder. Below the main blast Shay's body lay with those of her enemies, her face serene.

In counterpoint to the agony of those writhing by the hut's

doorway came the roar of engines, the thunder of racing hooves. Along the road poured Shay's avengers, Jo in the lead. Shayna left with Pam and Marion who had ridden with Danapa's army for that purpose. Jo was first into the hut with Mike and Rome at her heels. She had heard the blast as she rode and knew what it meant. She fell to her knees in the blood that spattered everywhere, dragging Shay's still-warm body to her to cradle in her arms.

"She kept them from following me. She died to make sure they couldn't follow me and Shayna." She hugged the body. "They murdered her!"

She looked up, shaking in white-faced fury and grief as Ani shook her arm, "Jo? Jo? Do we fight?"

"Fight? Yes!" Her face twisted into madness. "Hunt them down, all of them. Shay was right all along. We have to sweep the land clean. We have to hold the land to be safe." She stared out of the doorway, not seeing the girl. "Kill them! Every single one, every living thing with them!"

She was disobeyed in as much as the babies and toddlers lived, still everyone else from Mavis's band died; men, women, older children. Even those who hadn't loved Shay were caught up in the frenzy of vengeance and the need to feel safe again. Jo remained cradling her love, her usually gentle face like stone until it was done. Mike and Rome oversaw the massacre outside. Like Shay they believed in not leaving enemies behind. From now on they would make that choice for Danapa. Later, they led Jo out to the litter they had made for Shay. Then they carried their sister home.

For a day and a night, they couldn't part Jo from the body. She crouched blank-eyed beside the bed, holding Shay's cold hand. Remembering how they'd met, recalling her first sight of her love — of Shay standing there, shotgun in hand, enemies dead at her feet. Shay who would kill almost casually but also rescue a child because she could not bear to see Ani wandering with no one, alone and afraid. Jo remembered how she'd found that she loved Shay, recalled her jealousy of Neith and her fear she would lose Shay to the other woman. She found she was smiling through her grief as she remembered the day she'd found that Shay loved her too.

How could she go on alone? She knew she had to, she could not abandon the children, hers, Shay's daughter. Yet she couldn't face life without Shay — her other side, her dark lover who had fought, killed, and in the end died that those she loved might live. Jo moaned in anguish. Shay, she needed her love. Goddess, bring her back or take me too. She sank into pain and could not climb from the pit of her sorrow.

Tai, Shay's beloved cat, worked some healing in the end. A Siamese is hard to ignore on any occasion. Now his howls rasped Jo's nerves until she looked up to see him crouched at the end of the litter, staring at his adored human who did not get up to hold him, stroke and feed him. His human smelled of death and his loud mourning broke Jo's stony composure. Scooping him up she cried, soothing him, loving him as they comforted each other. At last her tears gave way to calm. Shay was gone but she would not let her love lie in the ground. Dana had gone to the fire. So, too, would Shay.

They gathered a pyre just outside the Danapa walls. On it, Jo placed her treasured patchwork quilt. Beside Shay they laid a rifle and a knife, her life symbols. They wrapped the quilt about the body, while at her head, they placed the unlit candle, the fire would light it. At Shay's feet, Ani laid the sealed clay pot that symbolized air. Fire and Air, then a sprinkling of water and earth, while over the quilt-wrapped body they heaped dried grass laced with flowers. Then Jo spoke.

"She is gone. A tree in the Forest has fallen. Yet sunlight comes where she was, because of that we shall grow taller and stronger. She shed her life's blood to buy our lives and the safety of Danapa. She was the willing sacrifice, and be sure that the Goddess shall know her own, as we do."

She said more. Later she would not recall what she had said. She only knew that she had wept again — as had almost everyone there. Without Shay, Jo wouldn't have survived. Nor would many of those others who stood by the pyre. They would not have made the trek north or known where to find refuge. Shay had known, Shay had led, and by these things she had given them a chance at the future.

Jo flung the flaming torch into the pyre before walking back through the gates and into her rooms. The door clicked shut. By the pyre other stayed, feeding the flames as they would for twelve hours until everything was consumed. Later, when the fire had been allowed to die, they would scatter the remaining ashes in procession about the great encircling walls of Danapa. Shay would hold it safe for them forever.

In her rooms Jo mourned, holding Tai who had come to her for comfort again. Her love was gone. She must live with that. She knew it, as she listened from her window to the sound of the flames. They roared and leapt, but they were no longer dying embers, now they were the symbol of a blazing, triumphant dawn. Danapa and its people would live, they would grow and prosper, and so long as they did, they would remember Shay.

Epilogue

Two young girls, heart-sisters and second-cousins, trotted out of the Danapa gates. Each, as she passed the great black stone set at an angle to them, slowed her pony and leaned over to brush the stone's crest with the first two fingers of one hand in an established invocation of good fortune. They did not pause to read the deeply incised lettering. They had known what it said since long before they were old enough to read the carving. The words started halfway up the left-hand side, arching across the top of the slab and part way down the other side. They said —

These hold our Land, their ashes hold our Honour.

Beneath was a list of names, those deemed sufficiently wise and great to be given to the flames where others were given burial in earth or by sky. The list began with Dana, revered founder of the settlement. Then came two names together. Shay and Jo. With the names were dates from the founding of Danapa along with the dates of birth and death. Each young girl performed her tiny rite of acknowledgement with care. Both were descended from the now semi-divine couple and owed them the courtesy twice over. There were other names by this time, but everyone knew it was the first three names that were the most important.

After more than two centuries, their fore-mothers blood and the stone remained to remind them of events. Those, and the fireside sagas, telling of lovers who had fought against a devouring evil set loose by those of long ago, a malevolence that might have destroyed the world. The stories were oft-told tales of lovers who had been forever faithful to each other. Great sweeping epics of two women who had led the long trek north to find a place where they and their friends could live in freedom.

And there were special songs, too, the most significant pair written by Shayanna, one of the duo's grand-daughters. One was a war song about Shay's death at the hands of the enemy who would have razed their home and slaughtered the people, and how instead she had risen up to destroy the enemy even as she died. The other song told of Jo's love and the fifty years she lived on alone, no one else ever taking Shay's place in her heart. Both ballads were sung at the year-end and mid-winter festivals and the people competed to contribute the best singer.

The girls raced each other, laughing, across their land once they had cleared the gates of Danapa. Nomadic horse, sheep, and cattle camps would be at the far side of the harbour this season. They could drop in on the tribe's coastal salt-pans as well and spend time with their friends who worked there. The young riders blended with the brown lands of summer that they crossed. Both were brown of hair and eyes. Even their young skin was of a pale warm brown, weathered darker by the sun. In them, the blood of many survivors had merged into a harmonious whole. Jo would have watched them smiling, arms about her love.

They were the creation of twenty generations thus far. So often, over the first years Shay, Jo and their friends had wondered what the future would be. They had worked for it, prayed for it, many had shed blood for it, Jo's love had died for it, and, they had succeeded. They called themselves the Danapa, although by now they had other prospering settlements besides that of the founding site.

From the sprawling, ancient, ruined city far to the south, to the eastern and western seas and the rough, rock-strewn earth of the northern land's-end where souls took flight, the people of Danapa held their realm. Male and female, they lived and rode equal, free and proud. Out of the coals and ash of a dying civilization, the vestiges of flames had been stirred back to life. Goddess willing, the fire's light would never die again.

About the Author

Lyn Mcconchie began writing professionally in 1990 after a crippling motorcycle accident forced her to retire from Government service. Since then she has had over 30 of her books published and almost three hundred short stories. She owns a small farm in New Zealand's North island where she breeds colored sheep and has free-range hens and geese. She shares her 19th century farmhouse with her Ocicat Thunder and 7,469 books by other authors. Lyn plans to continue writing so long as her brain and eyesight hold up.

CPSIA information can be obtained
at www.ICGtesting.com
Printed in the USA
FSOW01n0518200116
15803FS